PORTRAITS OF THE DEAD

JOHN NICHOLL

Chapter 1

2:20 A.M. Saturday, 2 May 1998

Emma didn't know how long he hid, silent and unmoving, in the large Victorian wardrobe to the side of her single bed. She didn't know how long he peered, salivating and drooling, between the two heavy dark oak doors and watched, mesmerised, as she slowly drifted into fitful sleep. She didn't know what time he pushed the doors open and crept towards her in the drab grey darkness of the night. But he did. She knew that he did.

Emma woke with a start, tense, alert, and opened her bleary eyes, telling herself insistently that the dark silhouette slowly approaching her was the nightmare construct of her subconscious mind. But initial anxiety became blind panic as the inky shadow took on an obvious human form that suddenly gained pace and loomed over her. And then a hand, a large hot clammy hand, pulled the bedclothes over her head, clamped her mouth tight shut and silenced her scream before it materialised.

A myriad unwelcome thoughts invaded her troubled mind as he pinned her head to the pillow and raised his free arm high above his head, before closing his fingers tightly, forming his hand into a formidable weapon and bringing it crashing down, again and again and again, with all the force he could muster, rendering her unconscious and bleeding.

She didn't know how long she remained senseless, or what he did to her while she slept. She didn't know what time he lifted her from her bed and carried her from her student bedroom, down the creaking wooden staircase and out into the Welsh city street. But he did. She knew that he did.

When she first awoke from her enforced slumber, Emma thought for one glorious, but all too fleeting moment, that the events of the previous night were just a nightmare. But the invasive throbbing pain seemingly erupting from every inch of her face and the congealed blood around her nose and mouth brought reality into sharp unrelenting focus, as she realised that one swollen eye wouldn't open and reluctantly recalled events prior to the assault. Oh, God, it was real. It was all too real! Life had taken a dark and unexpected turn.

Emma fought to control her bodily functions as her apprehension escalated more and more rapidly and threatened to overwhelm her completely. The bed was too soft, the quilt too heavy, the room too warm, the total absence of light alien to her experience and terrifying, totally terrifying. There was no denying it, however tempting it was to try. She wasn't in her familiar surroundings. Her memories were real.

Where was she? Oh, God, where on earth was she? What should she do? Should she shout out? Should she scream? Should she yell for help and continue shouting, louder,

4

louder and louder, until someone finally responded to her plight? Surely she should call for help? But, no, hold on a second… What if he was there somewhere and hidden by the darkness? What if he was listening intently with eager ears and ready to feed on her fear like a rabid dog? What if he was poised, ready to attack and silence her as soon as she uttered the slightest sound? Come on, Emma, do something. Don't just lie still, girl. You have to do something.

She ran her hands over her body and realised that she was naked, as she slowly eased back the quilt, sat upright, and climbed off the unusually high king-size bed, inch by cautious inch, with both her hands held out in front of her. Keep me safe, God. I'll be a good girl, a really good girl. Please keep me safe.

Emma cried warm, silent, salty tears as she took her first tentative unseen step forwards in the gloom, then another, then another, then another, willing herself onwards, four steps, five steps, six steps, seven, until her probing fingers found a solid wall only seconds later. That's it, Emma, that's it, find a switch, you can do it, girl, find a switch. There had to be a light switch somewhere.

She sucked repeated gulps of warm, stale air deep into her lungs in a forlorn and increasingly despairing attempt to calm her pounding heart, as she urgently ran the palms of both hands over every inch of the wall, in every conceivable direction. But she didn't find anything of note, not a thing, nothing. Don't give up, Emma. You've got all your life to live. You can do it, girl. Please don't give up. It was much too soon for that.

She leant heavily against the wall, supporting her slight nine-and-a-half-stone frame for a second or two, before counting to three and forcing herself to move slowly to her right in a sideways motion, all the time keeping direct contact with the wall and hoping to locate a light switch, or better still an unlocked door through which to escape. But she found nothing on that first wall except for what felt like a large picture frame firmly secured to the hard, cool surface. Was she in a house? It seemed she was in a house… That had to be a good thing, didn't it? Surely it was a good thing… Yes, yes, of course it was. If it was a house, there must be doors, there must be windows, there may be neighbours. There was a way out of there. She could feel her heart beating in her throat and the warm red blood surging through her veins and arteries. She was alive and relatively unharmed. There was hope. There was always hope. Keep moving, Emma. Be brave, girl, and just keep moving. There just had to be a way out of there.

She transferred her hands to the second wall and moved gradually to her right, one step, two steps, three steps, four, another picture frame, yet another frame, and then… a door. Yes, yes, yes! Surely it had to be a door. Come on, Emma, you can do it, girl. She'd be out of there before she knew it, wouldn't she?

Adrenalin surged through her bloodstream as her hope of escape leapt and danced in her mind and left her as excited as an expectant child on Christmas morning. But her newfound euphoria didn't last. The surface of the door was cold, not icy cold like the snow in winter but significantly

6

colder than the wall. It wasn't wood: it was metal. Oh no, it had to be metal. What other explanation was there?

She ran her hands over every inch of that cold, hard, steel door, again and again and again, before finally accepting defeat, slumping to the soft carpeted floor and dissolving into floods of uncontrollable tears that caused her chest to rise and fall as she struggled for breath. There was no handle, no way of opening it, just what felt like an approximate six-by-twelve-inch vent, or serving hatch, at the centre point of the door, at eye level. Like a prison door in the movies. That's what she told herself. Just like a prison door in the movies. Oh God, that wasn't good. It wasn't good at all.

Emma reached up and repeatedly clawed at the surface of the unforgiving metal until her chipped painted nails were broken and her fingertips bled. Suddenly, a dazzlingly bright white light burst into seemingly enthusiastic life and temporarily blinded her one good eye, making her flinch and cower on the floor, overwhelmed by fear.

At first, when she opened her eye and it gradually adjusted to the extreme brightness, the room's comfortably furnished and flamboyantly decorated appearance reassured her in some strange unquantifiable way, as if the bohemian decor somehow introduced an irrational degree of normality to an outlandish situation. But, all too soon, as she slowly swivelled her aching head, taking it all in for the first time, she gasped and spluttered for oxygen as if hit in the gut by a powerful physical blow. There were no windows, not a single one, just four walls covered from floor to ceiling with garish red-and-gold flock wallpaper, adorned with large black-and-white portraits of individual girls of about her age in various states of undress, and a second door in the rear wall to the side of the bed, made of clear, polished and smear-free glass, through which she could see a white porcelain toilet.

Emma sat upright, shielding her face with one hand, and studied each of the photographs in turn. There were five in total, five grinning, pouting girls who Emma thoughtfully observed had an unmistakable air of sadness about them, despite their lipstick smiles. Each of the girls were white, young and slim and had shoulder-length blonde hair cut in a similar style. Just like her. That's what she realised. They all looked just like her! It was too much to take in. Too terrible to contemplate. Where on earth were those five girls now? Would hers be the next portrait hanging on those gaudy windowless walls? Don't think it, Emma. Just don't think it and hope for the best.

As she folded her arms tightly and raised her knees to her chest, in a determined attempt to mask her nakedness and afford herself some small crumb of comfort as she sank into all-consuming despair, a sudden electric hum filled the space with sound. Emma slowly raised her sore and throbbing head, and saw a black plastic and chrome metal wall-mounted video camera located high in one corner of the room, directly opposite the oversized bed. The camera buzzed and swivelled slightly as she moved, focussed on her and only on her. She couldn't actually see the shadow man of her waking nightmare, but she was certain that he was watching her every move.

As she sat there, lost in her thoughts, like a helpless caged creature in a human zoo, a booming disembodied male voice suddenly emanated from two white plastic speakers fixed securely in the ceiling at opposite ends of the room. The voice filled the entire room with vibrating noise that made her flinch, as the camera had only moments before.

'Welcome to your new home, my lovely. I hope you find the accommodation satisfactory.'

She parted her lips as if to speak, but then closed her mouth tight shut when no words came.

'I will refer to you as Venus Six during your stay. I hope that won't be too much of an inconvenience for you.'

She looked up and focussed on the camera despite her injuries, her fear and the brightness of the spotlamps. She desperately wanted him to see her as a real person, an individual with a personality, hopes and dreams. Not some readily available fresh meat served up for him to devour at his convenience, but a girl with thoughts, feelings and a long life to live in that big wide world beyond the room, that now felt so very far away. 'My name's Emma, I'm a student at the university. I'm in my second year. I'm studying to be a sci…'

Even before she could finish verbalising her thoughts, the room was returned to darkness at the flick of an unseen switch, and was instantly filled with the noise of desperate female whimpers that gradually evolved into ear-piercing screams that got louder, louder and louder, causing her to

9

clutch at both sides of her head and tremble. She'd never felt so alone, she'd never felt so helpless, and as if that wasn't bad enough, she'd never been so terrified. She lifted herself onto all fours, crawled forwards and threw up against a wall in a dark corner of the room.

After what seemed like an age, but in reality was no more than two or three minutes, blessed silence prevailed once more and the light shone again and dazzled her for a second time. 'Emma is dead and buried, my lovely. She's gone. She no longer exists. Your name is Venus Six now, although we'll just call you Venus for the sake of convenience. I hope that's clear enough for you. It would not be a good idea to displease me again. I went to a great deal of effort to get you here. Others have made the same mistake and paid a heavy price.'

She just sat there in stunned silence, not knowing what to do or say. The situation was so foreign to her experience, virtually impossible to comprehend or compute.

'What's your name, my lovely?'

She raised her head slowly, looked directly at the camera lens again and forced a less-than-plausible smile in a further effort to be liked and to be seen as a human being with a life to live. It seemed sensible to cooperate, sensible to appease him for as long as she could and in any way she could. Maybe if he liked her, he wouldn't hurt her again. Maybe he'd even let her go. Maybe if…

'I'm waiting for an answer, my lovely. Your life depends on doing exactly what I tell you. I suggest you respond before you anger me any further. Disappoint me one too many times and the last sound you will hear will be your own screams.'

The creeping hand of death reached out, touched her with icy fingers that lingered and caused her blood to run cold, as his words resonated in her mind and unwelcome images played and flickered behind her eyes like a dark cinematic film. 'V-Venus, my name is V-Venus.'

'What was that? What did you say? I couldn't quite hear you despite my excellent hearing. You appeared to be choking on your words, my lovely. I wouldn't go giving me any ideas, if I were you. Strangulation isn't a particularly pleasant way to die. The victim's eyes bulge and dim as their life force slowly drains away.'

She repeated her allocated name, much louder this time, and hated herself for it. But she had to buy time. She had to survive. What else could she do? What else could she say?

'You will call me master for as long as you're here. You'll use the term each and every time you address me. You will never forget to use it and no other term is acceptable. Respect is everything in my eyes. It would be in your interests to remember that and to act accordingly.'

She nodded once, searching her increasingly traumatised mind… Did she recognise his voice? That erudite soft Welsh accent was somehow familiar to her… Surely, she'd heard it somewhere before… But where? Think, Emma, think… Perhaps, if she could just call him by name her plight may change for the better. Or was that a stupid idea? Yes, it was probably a stupid idea.

'I suggest you respond unless you want to live out the remainder of your miserable existence in perpetual darkness, my lovely? I can arrange that for you if you so wish. It would be a minor temporary inconvenience to me, but nothing more.'

She shook her head aggressively and squirmed as the pain in her head escalated from a score of eight out of ten to a resounding nine, becoming virtually unbearable. 'No, please, no, I'm begging you, I really wouldn't want that.'

'Oh, really? If you're sure; I can play the recording again easily enough if you'd like to hear it. I'd raise no objections. I rather enjoy the vivid memories it engenders. It's music to my ears, a pleasant melody that I've come to love, but it seems that's not the case for others. One of my previous guests endured it for nearly three days before finally repeatedly charging the wall and smashing her skull. It was quite a spectacle, as I'm sure you can imagine. Picture it in your mind's eye as I am. It was rather impressive, in a pathetic sort of way… Give me a second, I'll just check my notes. Ah yes, it was Venus Four. I was fortunate enough to catch her entire performance on film for future reference. Perhaps I'll show it to you one fine day. I'm sure you'd find it interesting.'

She couldn't stand to hear that pitiful bawling sound for another second, let alone witness such a horrendous scene on screen. But, was he telling the truth, or just trying to terrify her still further? If he was, it was working. Yes, it was probably true. How did the poor girl stand it for as long as she did? She must have felt so despairing, so desperate to die and escape him. 'Please, master, I don't want to hear it again.'

'Was that a no?'

She nodded and wiped away her tears with the back of one hand. 'Yes, I said no, no, no!'

'You're certain? I was hoping you'd like it. I can give you some time to think, if that helps?'

'Y-yes, I'm certain! A thousand times, yes.'

'Then, I suggest you say it again, but correctly this time with the appropriate degree of veneration and devotion. Come on, I'm listening.'

Was he laughing again? Was that the sound of muffled laughter? Yes, it had to be the sound of laughter. The vicious demented bastard was laughing at her. 'Please don't play it again, master.'

'Now, that was much better. You're learning the way of things here in your new home. Give yourself a robust pat on the back for me… Do it. Do it!'

She reached behind her and did as she was told, like a performing seal in a travelling circus.

'That's it, Venus, pat away, my lovely, pat away. I can see that you're a fast learner. That's to your credit. It may just save your life one of these days. Now, is there anything I can do to make your stay more comfortable? I'm here to accommodate your needs, within reason. This isn't a five-star resort after all.'

Should she plead for her freedom? Should she throw herself on his mercy? No, it was too soon for that, far too soon for that. It wouldn't go well for her. 'I'd like my clothes, please, master.' A reasonable request. Surely that was a reasonable request. Surely it wasn't too much to ask.

She listened as he dissolved into a fit of giggles that angered and unnerved her simultaneously. 'I'm afraid you bled rather badly on your recent journey here, my lovely. I had to dispose of your student bedding for the same reason. Head wounds tend to flow red and create quite a mess in the process. Your clothes were soiled rather badly and have been discarded accordingly. A regrettable inconvenience I'm afraid, but such is life. I feel certain you'll understand and forgive me in the circumstances.'

She raised a hand to her swollen, puffy face and sighed deeply as a single bead of salty sweat ran down her forehead and found a home on her bare chest.

'You've no objection? Can I take that as read?'

She wanted to scream, she wanted to yell and cry like a spoiled child, but instead she said, 'I've no objections, master,' as respectfully as she could.

'Then I suggest we start as we mean to go on. I think it's best if you take a hot shower and attend to that pretty yellow hair of yours. Do it now, please. Come on, straight away, no delays. It's important to look your best if at all possible. If your outward appearance is pleasing to me, I may be less inclined to cut you open and enjoy the internal view. You do understand that, don't you?'

She nodded, but didn't speak. He was insane, completely insane! What other way was there to describe him?

'I require an answer, my lovely. Silence is not a viable option if you wish to survive for very long in this new world of yours.'

He sounded agitated, displeased by her lack of verbal response. She raised her head, looked directly at the camera again, and spoke through her unrelenting tears. 'I understand, master.' That's what the bastard wanted, she was certain of that; her total and utter subservience. Like it or not, she had to play his games.

'You'll no doubt be pleased to hear that I've left some suitable clothing in the bathroom for you, you lucky girl. Now would be an opportune time to indicate your appreciation. I'm a great admirer of good manners.'

Perhaps if she said the right things, she'd get out of there in one piece. Maybe… What was the point of thinking it? It didn't get her anywhere. 'Thank you.'

'Thank you, what? Thank you, what?' There was a steely edge to his voice this time that withered her delicate soul.

'Thank you, master.' The words stuck in her throat, but she felt she had to say them.

'Again!'

'Thank you, master.'

'And again!'

'Thank you, master.'

'Shout it out. Announce it to the world. Shout it, Venus, shout it at the very top of your voice.'

'Thank you, master. Thank you, master.'

'Louder!'

She was yelling now, repeating the phrase again and again and again, like a crazed eastern mantra.

'You can stop now.'

He remained silent for thirty seconds or more before speaking again, as if carefully considering the quality of her presentation and weighing up his response. 'Well, I have to acknowledge that your performance was rather impressive, Venus. Not all my previous guests were nearly so compliant or enthusiastic. Based on my early impressions, I'm inclined to keep you. I do like an intelligent subject. You'll no doubt be glad to hear that they tend to live longer than the more limited creatures I've entertained over the years. I'm easily bored, you see. And who can blame me, eh? I'm sure you wouldn't be critical, what with your circumstances and all.'

She lowered her head and wept as a trickle of warm yellow urine ran down her left leg and soaked the carpet at her bare feet.

'Oh dear, is the pressure getting to you, my lovely? What a sad sight to see.'

She didn't respond. Perhaps silence was best. How could one reason with the unreasonable? What could one say in light of such irrational cruelty? Perhaps if she stilled herself, she'd become less visible. No, that made no sense.

'And don't go thinking that anyone else may have heard your animalistic howling. It wouldn't do to get your hopes up unnecessarily. You can yell away to your heart's content, my lovely. Don't hold yourself back on my account. Your room is suitably soundproofed to the highest possible standards. It was installed by experts some years back, on the pretext of being a recording studio. It proved rather costly, but was well worth every penny. I've had a great deal of fun as a result of their efforts. I think you'll find they did an excellent job. There's no one listening but me.'

'I didn't think there w-was.'

'Oh dear, now you appear to have soiled yourself. Perhaps now would be an opportune time to take that hot shower I mentioned earlier. You can clean up that mess before bedtime. You'll no doubt be glad to hear that I had the foresight to fit a stain-resistant floor covering. It seemed advisable in the circumstances, wouldn't you agree?'

She forced a fragile, quickly vanishing smile and nodded, desperate not to irritate him still further. Perhaps if he grew to like her, he'd be kinder. Perhaps he'd leave the light on rather than return the room to darkness. Perhaps if she followed his instructions to the letter, he'd eventually let her go. Perhaps, perhaps, perhaps! Was she deluding herself? No, no, no! Whatever the odds, there was nothing wrong with hoping.

Emma stood and rushed towards the glass door, acutely aware of her nakedness and the smell of excrement, but there was a second wall-mounted video camera in the small white-tiled bathroom, and she realised that any hope of privacy was lost to her.

Just for a short-lived moment, she was elsewhere, in a happier time and place born of determined denial, as an imagined and beautiful operatic aria filled the room as she

17

turned on the water, stepped into the cubicle and took sensual pleasure in the hot water warming her skin. But the music stopped as suddenly as it began and was replaced by that intangible and unchanging masculine voice that she'd already come to intensely loathe with every part of her increasingly frail being. 'Now would be a good time to switch the water off, dry yourself, attend to your hair and put on the make-up, clothing and shoes I've so kindly left for you in the cupboard directly below the sink. Take your time and make yourself beautiful for me, Venus. I may pay you a brief conjugal visit in an hour or two, if I feel so inclined as the day progresses.' He laughed. 'Not that we're married, of course, not in any legal sense of the word. But, honour and obey, till death us do part. I feel sure you can see where I'm going with this.'

Emma didn't move, lost in crippling indecision born of fear.

'Well, get on with it, my lovely, get on with it. I'm losing patience and that's never a good thing. We haven't got all day.'

Emma took repeated deep breaths, in through her mouth and out through her one relatively unrestricted nostril, in a further forlorn attempt to calm herself before stepping out of the glass cubicle, right foot first, and taking a large fluffy white bath towel from the stainless steel heated towel rail located next to the toilet. She wrapped the towel tightly around herself in a further unhappy attempt to protect her modesty, before stepping to her immediate left and peering into the large wall-mounted mirror secured to the tiled enclave directly above the sink. She was aware of her injuries and had prepared herself accordingly, expecting the worst, but she was still taken aback when she first witnessed the extent of her wounds. Her once pretty face resembled a grotesque Halloween mask with a grossly swollen and discoloured eye, a large purple bruise covering most of the right side of her face, dark congealed blood still smeared around her swollen mouth despite her shower, and a fractured misshapen nose. What had he done to her? What on earth had he done to her poor face? Deep breaths, Emma, deep breaths. Hold it together, girl. No need to panic. What would that achieve? Nothing, nothing at all!

She stood there, staring into the mirror for a few seconds more, reluctantly contemplating her new reality before eventually ensuring the towel covering her nudity was secure and bending gracefully at the knees to open the cupboard with trembling fingers. She was glad of the opportunity to get dressed, glad of the chance to recover her dignity to some degree despite her circumstances. It seemed a small victory, but a victory nonetheless. One small step in the right direction. One small step towards normality and potential freedom. That's what she told herself. That's what she yelled inside her head. But, her raised mood was all too short-lived and all hope suddenly evaporated. All she found in that single cupboard were various items of half-used thrift store make-up, a softwood hairbrush matted with long blonde hairs, black polyester lingerie, sheer stockings with elasticated tops and a pair of matching, ridiculously high stiletto shoes, of a type she'd never have chosen to wear.

Just like those worn by the sorrowful girls in the black-and-white portraits. That's what she told herself. Just like them.

Chapter 2

Detective Inspector Gareth Gravel hung his well-worn but much-loved Harris Tweed jacket on the back of his newly acquired black leather office swivel chair, before slumping at his desk and staring at the seemingly inevitable mountain of paperwork that had appeared as if by magic since leaving his small and cluttered office just a few hours before. It was a part of the job he hated, tedious but essential, and he reluctantly acknowledged that, like it or not, there was no option but to get his head down and get on with it as he had what felt like a thousand times before.

Grav dropped two heaped spoonfuls of instant coffee granules into his chipped but treasured black and white Neath Rugby Club mug and added six sugar cubes and a generous sprinkle of congealed powdered milk, in an unsuccessful attempt to raise his flagging spirits. He swivelled in his chair, reached down behind him, switched on the kettle for the second time that morning and grinned despite himself. Could life get any better? Yes, it fucking well could! A good murder case or an armed robbery, something along those lines would be a welcome distraction. A case he could really get stuck into, utilising the various investigative skills he'd developed and honed in over twenty years of West Wales policing.

He waited impatiently for the water to come to the boil, filled his mug almost to the brim and was stirring the resulting concoction vigorously with a tarnished dessert spoon when the shrill tone of his office phone rang out, causing him to swear loudly and crudely at the untimely interruption. He lifted the mug to his mouth and sipped the hot liquid, leaving a powdery milky moustache above his top lip before picking up the phone and saying, 'Hello' in a hoarse smoker's voice that was familiar to and respected by everyone in the force.

'Hello, sir, it's Sandra on the front desk. I've got an Anne Jones here, who says that her daughter's missing.'

'How old?'

'Oh, I'd say she's probably in her mid to late forties. She could be a little older, I guess. It's hard to tell sometimes, what with the make-up and all.'

Grav took a large gulp of the fast cooling liquid and slowly shook his head back and forth three times. Oh, for fuck's sake! Where did they find these people? 'The missing girl, not the mother, Sandra, the missing girl!'

'Oh, of course. It seems so obvious now that you've said it… Give me a second, sir, I'll go and ask her.'

'How old is your daughter, Mrs Jones?'

The mother dabbed away her tears with a clean white cotton hankie taken from her aged but still stylish blue leather Chanel handbag. 'She's nineteen, just nineteen.'

'She's nineteen, sir.'

'Oh, for fuck's sake, what the hell are you telling me for? She's nineteen not nine. Get someone in uniform to have a word with the woman.'

Sandra took a deep breath and steadied herself before responding. 'It seems the mother's a close friend to the chief constable's missus, sir. They went to some posh boarding school together, apparently.'

'Isn't the desk sergeant available? Surely her majesty would be satisfied with him. He's not a bad-looking bloke from a distance. The girl's probably staying at some friend's house and sleeping off a hangover.'

She grinned, amused by his determined resistance. 'She asked for you by name, sir. It seems you come recommended.'

Grav pushed back his chair with a forlorn expression on his heavily lined world-weary face and cursed his painfully arthritic and overburdened knees as he pushed himself stiffly to his feet with the aid of his desktop. He knew when he was beaten and at least he could kick the paperwork into touch for half an hour or so. It wasn't all bad. Why not look on the bright side of life? Wasn't that how the song went?

He tilted his head back and drained his mug before speaking again. 'Put her in one of the interview rooms and tell her I'll be with her in a couple of minutes. And ask her if she'd like a cup of something. Serve it on a silver tray and don't forget to curtsy. It may win us some Brownie points with the brass when she reports back.'

The young woman laughed, both amused as intended and gratified to end her conversation with a man notorious for his sharp tongue. 'Will do, sir.'

As he pushed open the low-budget, four-panelled door and entered interview room two with flagging enthusiasm, the experienced DI was met by a tearful, somewhat underweight woman with shoulder-length, light brown, tightly curled permed hair, whose immaculate smart but casual outfit and subtle make-up signalled her undoubted membership of the moneyed middle classes. She rose to her feet and reached out to shake the inspector's hand limply with bony fingers as he approached her. 'It's good of you to see me so promptly, Inspector. I'm sure you'll appreciate that I want to get this unfortunate matter satisfactorily resolved as quickly as feasibly possible.'

Grav nodded and smiled warmly in friendly greeting, revealing uneven, yellowed, nicotine-stained teeth that were at least his own. 'Nice to meet you too, Mrs Jones. Please call me Grav. There's no need for formalities in these parts. Now, take a seat, try to relax as best you can and tell me all about it. Perhaps we can start with your daughter's name.'

'It's Emma, Emma Jones.'

Grav took a police-issue pocketbook from the back pocket of his creased trousers, sat himself down, opened it to the appropriate page and made a note of the girl's name in black ink, followed by her date of birth, address and contact telephone number. 'So, your daughter's a student at Cardiff University?'

'Yes, she's in the second year of a Biomedical Science BSc.'

'A bright girl!'

Mrs Jones' eyes noticeably moistened. 'Yes, yes, she is. She wants to be a research scientist after qualifying. It's what she's always wanted to do for as long as I can remember. That's the sort of girl she is.'

'And she's staying in student lodgings?'

The mother took a combined antihistamine and steroid nasal spray from her handbag, looked away and administered two urgent puffs, before steadying herself and nodding her agreement. 'Please accept my apologies, I suffer terribly with hay fever at this time of year.'

'No need to apologise. I get a touch of it myself from time to time… You were telling me about your daughter.'

She returned the white plastic container to her handbag and fastened the clasp. 'She had to move out of the halls of residence after completing the first year of her course. It seems the space is rather limited. She's been in digs ever since. She shares a house with two other girls studying the same subject. I haven't met them as yet, but Emma tells me that they're nice enough and I trust her judgement. She's always been a good judge of character, even as a young girl. I think some people have a talent for such things.'

The DI looked on sympathetically as her tears began to flow. 'Are you okay to continue? I can fetch you a glass of water or a hot drink, if that helps?'

She shook her head frantically and swallowed the excess saliva in her mouth. 'No, no, that's extremely kind of you, but I just want to get on with it please. The quicker we get this done, the quicker you can make the appropriate enquiries and find my daughter.'

Grav raised a hand to his face and scratched his red veined nose with an uneven fingernail. Why so concerned? Why so anxious? Was there more to this than it seemed on face value, or was the woman worrying about nothing very much at all in the way home alone parents sometimes did? 'When did you last see your daughter?'

'I haven't actually seen her since she came home for the weekend two weeks ago, but I spoke to her on the telephone on Friday evening. She never fails to ring at least once a week. We're a very close family. Not at all like some of the miscreants you must have the misfortune to meet in your job. She likes to keep in touch.'

Grav's impatience was betrayed by his voice and body language as he crossed his arms loosely and glared at her. 'Let's see if I've got this right. You spoke to her on Friday night and today's Monday. She's been missing for two days maximum, if she's missing at all. We're talking about a girl of nineteen, not a frigging child.'

Mrs Jones' expression hardened as she leant forwards in her seat and fixed the inspector with a steely glower that left him in no doubt as to both her displeasure and determination. 'I'm very well aware of that, Inspector. But, I think you'll find that the circumstances are exceptional. I wouldn't be here otherwise. I don't make habit of wasting other people's time, or my own for that matter.'

The inspector nodded, unfolded his arms, and reopened his pocketbook. Perhaps there was more to it. 'Okay, I'm listening. Tell me more.'

'My daughter's tutor contacted me at my home first thing this morning to express his concerns regarding her welfare. We've met socially, you understand.'

No surprises there. The middle-class mafia strikes again. Maybe if he'd played the game he'd be a DCI by now, rather than a paltry DI. 'So, what exactly did this tutor have to say for themselves?'

Mrs Jones bit the inside of her lower lip hard before responding. The police officer's tone was bordering on rudeness. Just as he'd been described. He'd better have his compensations as she'd been assured. 'Emma missed the deadline for an important essay this morning. Professor Goddard tried to contact her by phone several times as the morning progressed, but he didn't get a response. It's just not like her, you see. She's an extremely hard-working girl. She couldn't be more committed to her future profession. There is no way she'd jeopardise her future by not handing in an essay, unless it were utterly unavoidable. She'd have rung me if there was a problem. Something has happened to her. I just know it has.'

Grav silently admonished himself for his earlier impatience. He shouldn't be too quick to judge. Maybe the once beautiful woman with her sallow skin and anxious expression had genuine cause to worry. 'Did the professor say anything more? Anything at all?'

'He'd already spoken to her two housemates, who said they last saw her on Friday at about sevenish. That's an hour or so after she'd spoken to me. They tried to talk her into a night out on the town apparently, but she insisted on staying in to continue her work. She mentioned the essay. Neither of them have seen her since, although one of them said she thought she heard someone leaving the house in the early hours of Saturday morning, before turning over and going back to sleep.'

Grav stifled a yawn and began making brief scribbled notes in his barely decipherable handwriting. 'Was there anyone else in the house at the time, that they know of?'

'No, just the three girls, from what I'm told.'

'Neither of Emma's friends brought anyone back from their night out? It wouldn't be that surprising if they had. A boyfriend perhaps?'

She shook her head. 'According to Professor Goddard, they said not.'

'You asked?'

'Yes, I did. The professor was perfectly clear on the matter.'

Grav ran a hand through his sparse greying hair and leant forwards in his seat. Perhaps she should have been a detective at some point in her life. She'd missed her calling. 'Does Emma have a boyfriend?'

She looked at him and frowned. 'There was a young man named Peter Mosely for a few months. I met him briefly on one occasion when visiting Emma in Cardiff at the end of last term. He's a rather diffident and unimpressive individual

28

in his late twenties, who works in the university library in some capacity or other. I thought he was too immature for her. I told her she could do significantly better. He wasn't the man for her. I knew that as soon as I met him.'

'And, she listened to you?'

She nodded once and smiled, but her smile left her face as quickly as it appeared. 'Yes, she did.'

'They're no longer an item?'

Mrs Jones shook her head and shifted uneasily in her seat. 'She finally ended the relationship a few weeks ago to focus on her studies. It was the right decision for her, but he didn't take it well, apparently.'

'Really? Can you expand on that for me?'

'Emma said that he pleaded with her at first: "Please don't leave me, I can't face life without you. I'll change, I promise you, I'll change. Just tell me what to do, and I'll do it." That sort of thing. But when she repeatedly reiterated her intentions he became threatening.'

Grav raised his bloodshot eyes from his notes as the tale took an all too familiar turn. 'Are you telling me he became physically violent towards her?'

Mrs Jones looked unexpectedly shocked at the suggestion. 'Oh, no, no, nothing at all like that. I don't believe he's that type of man, if *man*'s the word for them. She'd have told me if he had. I'm sure of that. The threats were directed towards himself, rather than her: "I can't face the future without you at my side. I'll kill myself if you don't change your mind, and it will be your fault when I do." You know the sort of nonsense such weak-willed people come up with when faced with rejection. It's rather sad in a pathetic way, wouldn't you agree?'

The DI nodded his silent acknowledgement. He'd heard it all before more times than he cared to remember. 'The threats never came to anything?'

'No, he pestered her repeatedly for a week or two as you'd expect he would, but it seems he finally accepted that it was over. I told her to stick to her guns whatever he said and that's exactly what she did. Good on her, that's what I say. She's a chip off the old block if ever there was one.'

Okay, so it seems he hadn't been violent. Time to take a different tack. 'Did Emma seem in any way stressed when you last spoke to her? Breakups are never easy.'

Mrs Jones visibly stiffened, the contours of her face changing as her facial muscles tightened. 'What on earth are you trying to imply, man?'

Just keep asking your questions, Grav. Just keep doing your job, as you always do. 'She's split with this Mosely character, he didn't make it easy for her and she's studying a particularly demanding subject. Science courses aren't exactly easy. It wouldn't be that surprising if she was feeling the pressure.'

She suddenly slapped the palm of her right hand down hard on the desktop and made him jump. 'No, no, no! Don't even think of going down that road, Inspector. She's a happy girl with an IQ in the top two per cent of the population, who thrives in the academic world. She's over Mosely and his antics and was very well prepared for, and confident of passing her essay with flying colours, as she has all the others, by the way.'

She wasn't going to like his next question one little bit, but needs must; he had to ask it anyway. 'And you're certain that nothing's changed? Even the brightest students can sometimes wilt under the pressure. Sometimes when it seems totally out of character. It wouldn't reflect badly on her if she had.'

'Am I not speaking English, Inspector? Do I need to explain myself in simpler terms you can understand? Or, maybe I'm speaking too quietly for your ageing Welsh ears?'

Grav rubbed the top of his head and nodded. Bloody charming! That was a bit full on. 'Okay, I had to ask. Have you got a recent photo of Emma? It's always useful in this type of case.'

Mrs Jones opened her handbag with unsteady quivering fingers, took out a six-by-four-inch colour photograph of Emma smiling sweetly, and handed it to the DI with an outstretched hand. 'Emma is not a case, Inspector, she's my daughter. I'd be glad if you'd remember that.'

'Sorry, force of habit. I didn't mean to imply anything by it… Now, is there anything else you want to say or ask before we bring the interview to a close?'

She stood as if to leave, but remained facing him without walking away. 'Just one thing, Inspector: find my daughter, and find her quickly!'

Chapter 3

The man stared at the screen with unblinking eyes, intensely focussing on the sleeping figure of the girl for a minute or two, before finally looking away and rearranging his handwritten notes on the countertop in front of him. She'd completely lost track of time. Day and night meant nothing to her any more. There was only the room. There was only his voice. He was the centre of her world now and she should be grateful for that. She was alive and had everything she required. He would meet her every need for as long as he deemed it appropriate. He was her god, the reason for her existence, the arbiter of life and death. What more could she possibly want in this life? She was wanted for the moment and that was more than many could claim. Now all she had to do was satisfy his requirements to an acceptable level and survive.

He shuffled through his papers again and leant back in his chair with his slender fingers linked in front of him, as if in contemplative prayer. But, was she the one? Had he finally found her after all this time? His soulmate, the girl with whom he was destined to spend eternity? She could be. It was looking hopeful. She had the right look, the right taste, the right smell. But, would she meet his exacting standards? Would she share his interests in contrast to the crowd? Or, would she let him down and judge him like all the others had? The girls who promised much, but ultimately disappointed before death. She'd better not, for her sake. She could prove no less disposable than the rest of them.

He took a half-empty Irish whisky bottle from the shelf secured to the wall above his head, poured himself an overly generous tot, lifted the glass to his lips and grimaced as the undiluted malty spirit burned his throat. So why her? Why this particular girl when there were so many to choose from? It wasn't an easy question to answer. He'd never targeted a girl within Wales before. That was a first, and maybe he gambled with his freedom. It was a relatively small pond within which to hunt and that increased the risks. He had to accept that and face facts. And he'd never chosen a girl with close family ties in the past, either. He'd ruled out otherwise suitable girls more than once over the years on exactly those grounds. The drug addicts, the sex workers and the homeless who wandered the streets of the northern industrial cities like Manchester, Bolton and Halifax were a much safer option. There was no denying that. Perhaps he should have stuck to them and minimised the risks of detection… So why hadn't he? That was the crucial question, and it demanded an answer.

He sipped the whisky again and cast his eyes over the girl's sleeping form. Because this girl was special. That was why. That explained his deviation from the norm. He'd known it the second he first set eyes on her; the second he spoke to her for the first glorious, wonderful time. She was special. That was it. What other explanation was there? The risks were worth it. It really was as simple as that.

33

He tilted his head back and drained the glass with a self-congratulatory smirk on his face, poured himself a second measure to celebrate what he considered his inspired insight and continued dissecting his past actions with scientific fervour. Yes, he'd deviated from his tried and tested modus operandi for the first time ever, but with very good reason. That was the essential caveat. And, he'd planned her abduction well enough. That was justification in itself. The thrill of the chase had been utterly exhilarating. It always was when the prey was particularly desirable. He'd been meticulous in his planning, as always. He'd considered all the angles carefully and utilised the immense knowledge and range of skills he'd developed over the years to achieve his ultimate goal. That was why he did it. The risks were acceptable and there was nothing wrong with that.

He crossed and uncrossed his legs repeatedly before finally leaning back in his seat with his hands linked tightly behind his nape. It hadn't been easy, of course. He'd had to be patient and bide his time until the circumstances were precisely right. He'd watched her for weeks, he'd established her patterns of behaviour and looked for suitable opportunities until he finally identified the optimum time and place to take her and introduce her to his secret world. And, difficult or not, he'd succeeded in his quest. That was worthy of congratulation. It was a triumph of superior intellect over adversity, and hoorah to that!

He sipped the neat whisky again and smiled contentedly. The long grey wig and unkempt false beard certainly helped maintain his anonymity. As did the dishevelled charity-shop clothing, the walking cane and feigned stooped appearance. No one was ever going to recognise him in that lot. He'd become a reasonably good character actor over the years and an old man was a truly inspired choice. The elderly were largely invisible to others. Even his know-it-all bitch mother wouldn't have recognised him had she witnessed his moment of triumph.

The man's attention returned to the screen of the monitor in front of him as the past faded and he took full advantage of the night-vision lens revealing the girl's every movement. She was still asleep, lying there in sartorial comfort and almost certainly dreaming of him. It would take a bit of time for her to adapt to her new surroundings completely, of course. It always did. But this time it would be well worth the effort. She was wearing the lingerie as instructed. That was to her credit. And didn't she look good enough to eat. The garments accentuated her beauty and made her all the more erotic. She was tottering unconvincingly on the stilettos when moving around the room. That was regrettable, but she'd get used to them given time. She just needed a bit of practice. He'd just have to be patient for as long as possible. Her recent refusal to eat was a little worrying, but she wasn't the first. She'd already lost a pound or two. Her ribs were more visible than before, her cheeks more sunken, but at least she was occasionally drinking from the bathroom tap when she thought he wasn't watching. She'd survive for another week or two on water alone, if he chose to allow her that luxury.

He broke into a broad white toothy smile that belied his age and laughed humourlessly. Now that he thought about it, what did it matter anyway? Watching her slowly starve would be both amusing and informative. Yes, observing her physical and psychological disintegration could prove to be a fascinating process which he could potentially relive time and time again on film at his convenience. Or, alternatively, he could always force-feed her if so inclined. That was always an option worth considering. Why not give her a few days to think about her position and potentially start eating again? That seemed entirely reasonable in the circumstances. He'd always been a generous man. If she ate she may be the one, and if she wasn't, she'd give up on life. What was wrong with that?

He pushed up the sleeve of his bright red woollen jumper and checked the time. Damn it! He'd have to leave for work by eight at the latest if he was going to get there on time, however fast he drove. That only gave him about twenty minutes or so before he had to hit the road. That didn't offer nearly enough time to fully indulge his inclinations as he'd like, but he really mustn't be late again. Drawing further attention to himself was ill-advised at best and should be avoided if at all possible, even for a man of his accomplishments. Why not wake her now and enjoy some stimulating entertainment whilst he had the opportunity? Even twenty minutes, however limiting, were better than no time at all. It would at least give him something to think about and look back on during an otherwise tedious day.

He turned to his right and flicked a switch, causing the room beyond the wall to explode with white light that shone from spotlights in multiple directions and illuminated every inch of the place from floor to ceiling. 'There you go, my lovely, time to rise and shine. Welcome back to the world of the living.'

Emma rubbed her healing eyes and slowly opened them, shielding them from the intense glare with a raised hand. She looked at the camera with her face screwed up tightly, and fought to hold back her tears. Why give the bastard the satisfaction? 'Is it morning, master?'

He grinned and stifled a laugh. 'What time do you think it is?'

'It feels like morning.'

She didn't have a clue. If he told her it was mid-afternoon, she couldn't argue the point with any conviction. How ridiculous was that! 'Are you ready for some breakfast, Venus? Porridge sweetened with a little local cold-pressed honey is a particular favourite of mine. What do you say, my lovely? Porridge and a nice cup of peppermint tea to calm those jangling nerves of yours and settle your stomach?'

She lowered her eyes and whispered, 'I don't feel like eating,' ever so quietly.

Was the bitch trying to enrage him? Would the shrew dare? Had he overestimated her? Was she really that stupid? 'Stop mumbling, girl. And don't forget your manners this time, or you'll pay a heavy price.'

She responded, speaking louder this time. 'I don't feel like eating, master.'

He leant forwards with his nose almost touching the glass screen. Was she displaying a lack of respect with her seeming combination of sycophantic cooperation and passive resistance? Maybe, just maybe! She had spirit, there was no doubting that, but spirit could be broken. It made the process all the more interesting, all the more challenging. Two of his previous guests had demonstrated a degree of noncompliance before eventually attempting to beg and plead and pray and scream their way out of there. She'd not be any different if it came to that.

He sniggered like a bashful child as he pictured the scene and magnified it in his mind. It didn't work for them and it wouldn't for her. She'd crumble in the end, like all the others. Her time would come if she didn't step up to the plate, and soon. It always did. 'I've given you more than enough time to adapt to your new surroundings, my lovely. I've made numerous allowances for your youth and inexperience, but you're starting to try my patience. I would think very carefully before doing that again, if I were you.'

She didn't respond and all was darkness, followed by the wailing female who just wouldn't shut up.

And then sudden silence and light prevailed once more as he leant back in his seat and watched her intently. She was weeping into her hands. Her chest was heaving rhythmically as she struggled for breath: up, down, up, down, in and out, in and out. Those were good things. It was a sight worth seeing. Her resolve was weakening minute by minute, hour by hour, day by day. There was still an identifiable spark of resistance in her eyes, but it was undoubtedly fading. Now was exactly the right time to drive home his advantage before heading for the car. He really couldn't have timed it better. 'This is your final opportunity to fully cooperate, Venus. I'm about to leave for work. Such a shame, I'd love to have stayed and played with you for a little longer, but we all have our responsibilities in this life. The bills have to be paid one way or another. Why not choose the light and the silence that accompanies it whilst you still can?'

Emma sat upright, pulled the increasingly grubby quilt tightly around herself, looked at the camera and said, 'Could I have some toast and a glass of warm water please, master?' as clearly as she could.

The man punched his fist in the air in silent triumph and felt his penis engorge with blood. 'Brown or white? You choose.'

'Brown, please, master.'

'Say it again.'

'Brown, please, master.'

'And again!'

'Brown, please, master.'

He jumped to his feet, turned in a tight circle on the heels of his shoes and began clapping his hands together in a whirl of frantic rhythmic movement, faster, faster and faster, before suddenly stopping to catch his breath. 'Now, that's much better, my lovely. I'm so pleased for you. I was beginning to wonder if we were approaching the endgame far sooner than I'd originally anticipated. Brown it is.'

Chapter 4

DI Gravel finally tracked down his old friend and trusted subordinate, DS Clive Rankin, in the less than impressive police headquarters canteen, where he was sitting alone and enthusiastically tucking into a full English breakfast smothered in copious amounts of brown sauce, which effectively and fortuitously disguised the true nature of the fatty fare.

The DI exchanged well-intentioned pleasantries with the newly appointed, young female cook-cum-chief bottle washer at the counter, before ordering two cheese and onion rolls and a packet of plain Walkers crisps, which he thought would complement them perfectly at that time of the morning. 'Nice to meet you, love. Call me Grav. The food looks terrible as always. You'll fit in brilliantly.'

She looked up and smiled wearily. Another wannabe comedian, that's all she needed on her first day. 'And there I was hoping for a Michelin star by next Tuesday.'

Grav glanced around the room before responding. 'It would be wasted on this lot, love. Just stick to the usual slop. I think that's best.'

'Yeah, you're probably right.'

The DI approached Rankin's table and pulled up a chair directly opposite him. 'Good to see you back in the saddle,

Clive my boy. You're looking suitably bronzed after your holiday in the Costas. How was Spain?'

DS Rankin looked up from his almost empty plate and swallowed a well-chewed piece of salty Danish bacon before speaking, 'The wife's sister came with us.'

Grav grinned mischievously. 'That must have been nice for you.'

'Oh, she's not so bad in small doses.'

The DI's face suddenly took on a more serious persona, as the past closed in and surrounded him mercilessly. 'Don't knock it, mate. An empty house can be a very lonely place. Take my word for it.'

Rankin looked up and nodded, painfully aware that the conversation was taking an all too familiar turn. 'Heather was a great girl.'

'The best!'

'Fucking cancer!'

'You've got that right.'

Rankin wiped the grease from his mouth with a shirtsleeve, picked up his mug and drained the sweet, dark lukewarm liquid at the bottom. 'Have I got time for another coffee, boss?'

The DI checked his digital Casio wristwatch. 'Yeah, knock yourself out. Tea with four sugars for me, if you're feeling generous.'

'I can see the diet's going well. It was five sugars before the holiday.'

Grav laughed, causing his overhanging beer gut to wobble like a birthday jelly. 'Yeah, I'm starting ballet classes next week. My saggy arse will look good in the tights.'

'Now, there's a mental picture I'm keen to get out of my head.'

'You're not getting a hard-on, are you, Clive?'

Rankin laughed in response to his boss's crude and familiar lighthearted banter. 'I may well never want sex again. How would I explain that one to the missus?'

'There you go, boss. You can stand the spoon up in it if you try hard enough.'

'Thanks Clive, it's appreciated.'

'So what happened when I was away?'

'Same old same old, the usual delights, nothing major. We've got a missing student at Cardiff University, I want you to check out for me as a matter of priority.'

Rankin adopted a puzzled expression, his eyes narrowing. 'Cardiff? Wouldn't it make more sense for the South Wales force to look into it?'

'Yeah, you'd think so, wouldn't you? If only life were that simple!'

'So what's going on?'

Grav looked away momentarily, contemplating his choice of words carefully before speaking again. 'I had a personal visit from the chief constable, no less. Doff my cap, and all that shit. He's the girl's godfather.'

'Ah, I'm beginning to get the picture.'

'I'd done the usual as per the standing orders: circulating a missing persons notification to the relevant people in Cardiff, asking them to make a few phone calls to local hospitals and the like, but he made it crystal clear that wasn't good enough for this particular young lady. He wants her found and quickly.'

'Couldn't you have a word with the local police and ask them to treat it as a priority case? I'm sure they'd understand.'

Grav shook his head, resigned to the unrelenting realities of top-down policing. 'The chief's already spoken to his opposite number at the Cardiff end. We're taking the lead on this one despite the geography. It's a done deal.'

'Oh, for fuck's sake! Different rules for different people. What's that about?'

'I know, mate, I know, but needs must. We've got to keep the old man happy in the interests of an easy life. Make some enquiries and with a bit of luck you should have it cracked before the end of the week. South Wales have made a PC Laura Williams available to help you with the basics as and when needed, if that helps?'

'Have you got the case's details?'

Grav drained his mug, flicked his empty crisp packet aside and stood to leave for his small cluttered office on the first floor of the 1960s concrete building. 'There's an orange cardboard file on my desk on top of all the other crap that should tell you what you need to know.'

'Okay, boss. Have I got time for one last coffee before heading off?'

'Yeah, why not live a little?… Oh, and keep me in the loop. I'll be reporting back to the chief just as soon as you come up with anything useful.'

'Will do, boss. She's probably shacked up with some hairy arsed bloke somewhere and having the time of her young life. You know what these students are like.'

The experienced DI looked back on approaching the door and shook his head slowly and deliberately. 'I'm not so sure, Clive. I've got a strange feeling this one's going somewhere.'

It took DS Rankin just over an hour to drive the seventy or so miles down the M4 motorway to the pleasant seaside city of Cardiff, Wales' bustling, multicultural, rugby union-obsessed capital. He listened and sang along to one of his wife's favourite Hall and Oates CDs, as he inexpertly navigated the seemingly endless traffic, past the fast-developing new stadium and the equally impressive Victorian Gothic castle. Then after locating his destination of choice, he found an adequate parking space almost directly outside the university's main modernist building.

Rankin made a superfluous adjustment to his much-prized red and blue-striped polyester Caerystwyth Rugby Club tie, locked the car with the press of a button, strolled casually in the direction of the main entrance and wandered through the unfamiliar corridors for ten minutes or more, before eventually finding Professor Goddard's generously proportioned second-floor office, piled high with academic papers on every conceivable surface.

'Professor Mark Goddard?'

The tall, slim, distinguished-looking man in his early forties stood and smiled warmly in greeting. 'Am I correct in assuming that you're Detective Sergeant Rankin?'

Rankin nodded and considered delving in his pocket for his warrant card, but decided against. The man knew who he was. Why bother with protocol? 'Good of you to see me so quickly, Professor. I appreciate that you're a busy man.'

The professor shook Rankin's hand with a surprisingly firm grip for a man of his lean stature, and smiled for a second time. 'I don't know if I can tell you any more than I've already said on the phone, to be frank, but I'm more than happy to help if I can. I'm delighted that you're treating this unfortunate situation with the priority it deserves. I did wonder if such cases were taken seriously, what with everything else you've got to do with your time. Have you made any progress since we last spoke?'

The DS sat on a hard wooden chair without waiting to be invited and took a notepad and biro from the black plastic Samsonite briefcase, received as a gift from his long-suffering wife the previous Christmas. There was little purpose in sugar coating this particular pill. It wasn't as if he were a relative or close friend of the girl. 'She hasn't been seen for five days, she's not answering her mobile, we've checked the local hospitals without success and she hasn't withdrawn any cash for over a week. It's not looking good at this stage.'

The professor raised a hand to his face and slowly massaged his lower jaw between thumb and fingers. 'Ah, that doesn't sound particularly hopeful… What are the chances of you finding her?'

Not an easy one to answer with any degree of certainty, but he'd give it a try as best he could. 'It's hard to say. Over 200,000 people are reported missing in the UK every year. A lot of them turn up, but not all of them.'

'Really, that many?'

Rankin nodded his assured confirmation. 'Yeah, I'm afraid so.'

'I had absolutely no idea.'

'Why would you?'

The professor glanced at the wall clock above his desk before refocusing on the plain-clothes officer with keen eyes. 'I'm due to give a lecture in approximately twenty minutes, Sergeant. Perhaps we can progress matters.'

Rankin opened the notepad and rested it on his briefcase before asking his first question. It was time to get on. 'Was Emma struggling with any aspects of the course? Anything at all?'

'Um, no, no, as I said on the phone, she really is a first-class student. She pushes herself hard and sets herself particularly high standards, but then all the best students do. I did much the same thing myself when at Oxford as a young man. There are stresses, of course, there are always stresses, it comes with the territory, but she's one of those rare individuals who thrive on the pressure and excel, as I did.'

'So, you have a high opinion of her?'

He nodded assuredly. 'Oh, yes, Sergeant, I can say that without hesitation. I expect great things of her. She's an impressive young lady.'

Okay, so it seemed the pressure of work hadn't led to her disappearance. 'Have you seen any changes in her recently, any clue that something may be amiss: anything she's said, anything she's done which was in any way out of the ordinary, any change in her appearance, any suggestion of health issues that may be worrying her?'

The professor paused, considering the questions carefully for a second or two before saying, 'No, absolutely not!' in an unequivocal tone, he thought would most effectively get his message across. 'She's been her usual cheerful and hard-working self from what I've seen. Emma's the sort of young lady who brightens your day by her very presence. She lights up a room.'

'Has she ever fallen out with any of the other students?' He knew he was clutching at straws, but he asked the question anyway.

The professor raised his eyebrows, frowned and shook his head. Hadn't he already clarified that wasn't the case, in one way or another? Maybe the methodical approach adopted by the officer was the best way of establishing the facts. Or maybe the miserable pleb really was as limited as he appeared to be. 'She's a very popular girl, who's fitted in extremely well from the very beginning of the course. The staff like her and the other students like her. I really can't make it any clearer than that.'

The man was losing patience. Just for a fraction of a second it had shown on his face. His voice had taken on a harder tone. Maybe he wasn't quite as dedicated to his students' welfare as he liked to make out. 'Her mother mentioned a boyfriend. Were you aware of the relationship?'

The professor nodded his head. 'I assume you're talking about young Peter? Emma mentioned him in passing during one of our weekly tutorial sessions.'

Rankin quickly scribbled the response. 'So, what exactly did she say about him?'

'Um, now let me think… Not a great deal, really. Simply that he was helping her locate some particular research material pertinent to an assignment she was finding especially stimulating.'

'Nothing more?'

'No, not that I can recall.'

It was probably worth pursuing the line of questioning further before moving on. Everything had to be ruled in or out, however seemingly unlikely. 'I believe he's one of your co-workers?'

Professor Goddard smiled sardonically and visibly stiffened, signalling his displeasure loud and clear. 'Oh, I wouldn't go as far as to say that, Sergeant. He's employed by the university as I am, that much is true, but he's not one of the academic staff.'

The pompous prat! If his ego were any bigger, it would fill the entire room. 'Okay, point taken. Tell me more about Peter Mosely.'

The professor looked at the clock again, more pointedly this time. 'What exactly are you asking me?'

'What kind of man is he?'

What a preposterous question! As if a man of his high status and intellect would interact with a common underachiever like Mosely in any meaningful way. He had far more important things to do with his time. 'I've seen him at the library once or twice, but I've had no cause to speak to the man at any length. If I need particular texts, the head librarian invariably sees to it for me.'

This time it was Rankin's turn to check the time. Was there really any point in continuing the interview? The self-important prat seemed more interested in expounding his own importance, than anything else. 'Do you know anything of Mosely's background?'

'I believe he had aspirations to study science at some point in the past, but he wasn't up to it academically. His boss said something along those lines. Not many people are.'

It seemed he knew more of Mosely's history than he'd originally let on. 'Is that something he resents?'

Professor Goddard stood to leave and made a show of gathering some papers from his desktop, before turning to face Rankin again. 'I suggest you ask him yourself, Sergeant. You'll find him in the small reference library on the third floor, if I'm not mistaken. Now, unless there's anything else that can't wait, I really do have to make a move. The lecture's not going to present itself.'

'Oh, there is one more thing.'

The professor sighed noisily. 'Let's talk as we walk.'

Rankin hurried to keep up, as the lecturer strode purposefully down the long narrow sunlit corridor. 'Where can I find Emma's housemates?'

'They'll both be attending my lecture; I could pass on a message if required.'

'Tell them I'll meet them at their digs at five thirty sharp.'

'You could speak to them here, if that helps.'

This time it was Rankin's turn to sigh. 'Just tell them, Professor, just tell them.'

Rankin held up his plastic warrant card at eye level and approached a pencil-thin, nervous-looking, black-haired young man standing behind a highly polished wooden counter, which was festooned with various multicoloured textbooks covering every imaginable scientific subject. 'DS Rankin, West Wales Police. I'm looking for a Peter Mosely.'

The young man looked up, pushed his long dyed black fringe away from his eyes with delicate white fingers and looked past Rankin, as if speaking to someone standing behind him, rather than focussing on his face. 'I wasn't intending to keep the books! I was always going to…'

Well, hello Peter. Sorry to spoil your day for you. Rankin held an open hand in the air, as if stopping traffic in a busy street. The poor boy looked ready to shit himself at any second. 'Stop right there, Mr Mosely, you don't want to talk yourself into a theft charge. I couldn't give a toss about the books. I'm here to talk to you about Emma.'

Mosely looked close to panic, as he gripped the counter with both hands, supporting his weight. 'Oh, my God! Has something happened to her?'

'I'd sit down before you fall down, if I were you, Mr Mosely.'

He lowered himself into his seat as instructed and held his head in his hands. 'She is all right, isn't she?'

'You weren't aware she was missing?'

Mosely pulled a scrunched up paper hankie from a trouser pocket and blew his nose loudly as the tears began to flow down his increasingly morose face.

'Take a second, Mr Mosely. There's no rush.'

He blew his nose for a second time and returned the tissue to his pocket. 'Thank you, give me a second.'

'Are you ready to continue?'

Mosely nodded quickly and repeatedly. 'Yes, I guess so.'

'When did you last see Emma?'

'I haven't spoken to her for two weeks or more.'

Was he trying it on, or just confused? 'I asked you when you last saw her, not when you last talked to her. There's a difference.'

Mosely focussed on the floor and shifted uneasily in his seat as tiny fresh beads of sweat formed on his prominent forehead. 'She was in the library one day last week. I think she's avoiding me.'

'Which day was it?'

Mosely opened a drawer, searched through the contents with overwrought fingers and urgently pulled out a five-by-four-inch, handwritten, white cardboard index card. 'She signed out a quantum physics textbook. It's an area of science that particularly interests her.' He examined the calendar hanging on the wall behind him. 'It was Tuesday morning.'

Rankin held out a hand and took the card from Mosely, who was only too pleased to confirm his version of events. 'Okay, so you last saw her on April the twenty-eighth.'

'Yeah, that's right.'

'And you haven't seen her since then?'

He shook his head forlornly. 'I still love her.'

'I've no doubt that you do, Mr Mosely, but from what I'm told she doesn't share your feelings.'

Mosely's nostrils flared as he jumped to his feet. 'It's not like that! She needs to focus on her studies. She told me that herself. Things will be different when she finishes her degree.'

Rankin rested his elbows on the wooden counter and held Mosely's angry gaze until his newfound bravado melted away. The boy's reactions seemed genuine enough, but he had to be sure. 'So, how did you feel when she dumped you, Peter? It must have stung a bit. The love of your life ending the relationship like that.'

Mosely looked ready to explode and he hissed his subsequent words through gritted teeth before gradually composing himself. 'She still loves me, but she needs to focus on her course for now. We'll be together again one day. I'm going to ask her to marry me.'

The boy was either deluding himself, or Emma had made promises she had no intention of keeping. 'Were you angry with her? It wouldn't be surprising in the circumstances. You seem angry enough to me.'

Mosely shook his head, his long hair seemingly flying in every conceivable direction at once. 'I love her. I'd never hurt her! I'd do anything for her, anything at all.'

Rankin paused briefly before speaking again. 'Who said anything about hurting her?'

'It was implied.'

The boy had a point. Maybe he shouldn't push too hard given Mosely's recent talk of suicide. 'Can you think of any reason why Emma may have chosen to leave the university without telling anyone?'

The blood visibly drained from Mosely's already pasty face and he flopped back into his seat with an audible thud as his legs gave way. 'There is no way she'd do that. She absolutely loves the course, she loves Cardiff and she loves…'

Well, at least he was right on two counts. The boy was kidding himself. You could convince yourself of almost anything if you tried hard enough. 'Was she experiencing any problems you're aware of? If not the course, something else, anything at all?'

Mosely shook his head again, more slowly this time. 'She was upset after our break up, but she was getting on with her life. Oh, and she sometimes complained of pain in her coccyx after a fall on ice last winter, but it wasn't a big deal. She just used that anti-inflammatory gel occasionally if it flared up. If there was anything amiss, anything serious, I'm certain she'd have told me.'

Rankin cursed silently under his breath. English wasn't his first language nor spelling his greatest strength. He resorted to writing *Tail Bone*, before moving on. 'Is there anything else? Think hard, even the most seemingly insignificant detail may help us find her.'

Mosely stared into space, lost in his thoughts. Should he say something? Would the detective get the wrong idea? It was a significant possibility, but he'd never forgive himself if he remained silent and something happened to Emma.

'Spit it out, Peter, I know there's something you're not telling me.'

It was now or never. Time to bite the bullet, as the old saying went. 'She told me to stop following her.'

Here we go, maybe he was onto something. 'When exactly was this?'

Mosely hung his head, focussed on the red-carpeted floor and mumbled, 'It was Tuesday morning.'

Was that Tuesday? Did he say Tuesday? So they had talked. The manipulative little git! 'Speak up, Mr Mosely. Now is not the time to hold anything back.'

He said it again, enunciating his words more clearly this time.

'So you did talk to her! Why the earlier denial? What the hell was that about?'

Mosely appeared close to panic as he struggled to compose himself. 'She just yelled at me as I handed her the book. I'd never seen her like that before. I'd never seen her so angry.

She just snatched the book from me, turned and walked away before I had the opportunity to engage her in conversation. I called after her, I said I had absolutely no idea what she was talking about, but she didn't even look back at me as she left. I really don't think she believed a single word I said to her.'

Rankin turned the page of his notebook. 'So, had you been following her? She obviously thought so.'

'I know what you're thinking, but no, absolutely not! I'd never do that. Why would I do that?'

'You loved her. You wanted her back. It wouldn't be that surprising.'

Mosely began weeping uncontrollably, the tears rolling down his ashen face. 'I d-did not follow her. I never f-followed her. I've told you, I w-wouldn't do that!'

'So, if you didn't follow her, why would she say you had?'

'I don't know. I swear I d-don't know. I've got no idea.'

'Are you saying she was lying?'

'No, no, I'm not saying that. Emma's not a liar! I just don't know why she'd say something like that. She must have had her reasons.'

Rankin paused for a beat. The story had the ring of truth to it. The boy could have kept his mouth shut. Surely, a guilty man would keep his mouth shut. Why volunteer the information in Emma's absence? 'Do you think someone else was following her? Someone she thought was you.'

Mosely's tears stopped in an instant and he swallowed hard before responding. 'Oh my God, I hadn't considered that. But, I guess that makes sense. But, who the ...'

'So, you haven't seen anything suspicious? Think Peter, anything you've seen may help.'

Mosely remained silent for a second or two, deep in thought. He wanted to help. He really wanted to help, but what could he say? 'There's nothing. I wish there was, but there's nothing.'

Rankin closed his notebook and returned it to his briefcase, before handing Mosely a white card embossed with his contact details in black print. 'We're done for today. If you think of anything, anything at all, don't hesitate to give me a ring, day or night. Someone can always get hold of me or pass on a message.'

A thin smile crossed Mosely's face. 'So you believe me?'

'Don't quote me on this, son, but, yes I believe you.'

'Thank you, that means a lot.'

Rankin grabbed a quick prawn and mayo sandwich in a pleasant local café close to Queen's Street station, before making his way through the busy city streets to Cathays Road, the heart of Cardiff's studentville.

He slowed the unmarked blue Mondeo on arrival in the wide suburban street and repeatedly glanced left and right towards passing houses, whilst choosing to ignore the increasingly irate driver of the vehicle directly behind his. Shut the fuck up you obnoxious prat… Number fifty-two, number fifty-two, where the hell was it?

The DS knocked and kept knocking until a strikingly attractive girl with unkempt curly brown hair and wearing a baggy, dark blue sweatshirt with the Cardiff University logo

56

emblazoned on the front, finally opened the front door and said, 'Where's the fire?' in high-pitched musical West Country tones, that Rankin found strangely captivating. He grinned self-consciously, despite the sombre nature of his visit and silently acknowledged that he'd always been a pushover for a pretty face. Come on Clive, get a grip man, and get on with the job. His days of flirting with nineteen-year-old girls were long gone.

Rankin ran a hand through his short cropped hair, introduced himself and explained the purpose of his visit.

The young girl's face took on a more subdued persona, her amusement at his reaction to her appearance suddenly muted. 'You'd better come in then. My name's Helen. I'm one of Emma's housemates.'

Rankin followed her into the magnolia-painted hall, back in business mode. 'Nice to meet you. Professor Goddard gave me your details earlier today. Is Dianne in?'

She turned to face him. 'She's in her room upstairs. Shall I call her?'

'I'd like to see Emma's room first, if that's okay with you? I'll have a chat with you both after that. Perhaps you could give me a guided tour.'

She frowned as she turned and headed for the stairs. This had to be serious, despite the officer's friendly nature. Surely the police wouldn't send a sergeant unless they were genuinely concerned. She'd watched enough detective dramas on TV to realise that. 'Emma's room is on the third floor. I'll take you up.'

Rankin followed on. 'Thanks, that's appreciated.'

The DS pushed open the door with his foot and entered a seemingly unremarkable and sparsely furnished bedroom, typical of a thrifty student's abode. Emma had adorned the walls with brightly coloured posters of various iconic stars of music and screen, in an obvious attempt to brighten the place up, but even they failed to fully overcome the landlord's general penny-pinching and lack of attention to detail.

Rankin manoeuvred himself to the approximate centre of the room and turned slowly in a circle, looking for even the slightest clue that might offer any degree of insight into Emma's vanishing. He turned, stopped, then turned again, examining every inch of the place, but nothing drew his attention, which didn't surprise him in the slightest.

The DS approached a chest of drawers topped with various items of make-up, a free-standing mirror and two silver-framed, glossy colour family photos, featuring several smiling individuals in happier times. He picked one up and focussed on Emma's glowing image. If only it could speak. Where are you girl? Where the hell have you gone?

Rankin began rooting through the bottom drawer, but only found socks, variously coloured tights, and several white bras and briefs mixed together in no particular order. It was a similar story with the middle drawer, which was filled with t-shirts, sleeveless vests and the like, but the top drawer was much more interesting. Amongst the pens, papers, hair clips, tampons, contraceptive pills and non-prescription painkillers, he immediately spotted a grey leather purse.

When he took it in his hands and slowly opened it, his worst fears were realised.

Rankin sat on the single bed and took one item at a time from the purse, placing them on the mattress immediately next to him: a National Westminster student bank card, a solitary five-pound note folded at the centre, three shiny pound coins and various copper change, two first-class stamps and a Students Union 10% discount card pertaining to local shops and eateries. Why would she leave the house without them? Surely she wouldn't leave without her purse unless rushed, intoxicated, unwell, or worse still, forced.

He returned to the centre of the room and turned again, even more slowly this time, paying close attention to detail, searching for any sign of room invasion, but nothing, again nothing. The window appeared secure and fastened on the inside and there were no signs of a struggle. If someone had gotten into the place, they knew exactly what they were doing.

As soon as Rankin was satisfied there was nothing significant to see, he approached the large Victorian wardrobe at the side of the bed and opened both doors wide before peering in. He found nothing very remarkable, although the clothes were all pushed to one side. He pondered this for a second or two, wondering if it were of any potential significance, but decided the answer was very probably not. It seemed that with the exception of the purse, the room offered nothing potentially useful or informative.

The DS placed the items back in the purse as originally located and went to leave the room in search of the girls. But as he was approaching the door something caught his eye, something on the worn, multicoloured-carpeted floor below the edge of the single bed that told him this was more than a missing person case.

Rankin knelt down, reached out, clutched the black Nokia pay-as-you-go mobile phone in his right hand and stared at it for a second or two, pondering its likely implications. No nineteen-year-old he'd ever known would go out without their cash and flash new phone. Why should Emma be any different? Something had happened. Something was very wrong. She'd either harmed herself, or someone had harmed her in some way.

When Rankin emerged from the bedroom, he found Helen waiting patiently on the communal landing.

'Any joy?'

'I noticed there are no bedclothes or pillow, any ideas?'

'No, I noticed that myself. I thought they must be in the dirty washing, but it seems not.'

'Seems strange.'

'I thought so.'

'And I didn't find a door key.'

'It's on the hook in the kitchen, next to the fridge.'

'Ah, okay, did she usually leave it in the house?'

She shook her head silently whilst chewing her top lip.

He held up the purse in one hand and the phone in the other. She'd been hopeful, optimistic. It was a shame to rain on her parade. 'Are these Emma's?'

The young girl looked from one to the other and nodded, her world a darker place. 'She was virtually glued to that phone. She's the first of the three of us to get one. It was always in one pocket or another. Something's happened to her, hasn't it?'

'One step at a time, love… Give Dianne a shout for me and I'll have a chat with you both downstairs.'

The girl nodded again, keen to cooperate and help her friend if at all possible. 'We usually talk in the kitchen.'

Rankin began descending the staircase, which creaked loudly under his weight. Okay, so that was hard to miss, pissed or not. 'The kitchen's just fine with me.'

'It's the second door on the left. Help yourself to coffee or wait for me if you like, whichever suits you best. I'll just explain things to Dianne and we'll join you in a minute or two.'

'Take your time, love, I know this isn't easy.'

'Take a seat girls, this shouldn't take too long.'

Helen forced a transient smile in an attempt to lighten the obvious tension. 'Shall I put the kettle on?'

Rankin pushed up his sleeve and noted the time. 'Yeah, why not? I'll have a cup of tea, if there's one on offer.'

Dianne sat at the kitchen table and repeatedly wrung her hands together, whilst Helen took three unmatched cups from a cupboard and placed a single teabag in each of them. There was comfort in familiar ritual, whatever the situation. 'Milk and sugar?'

'Just one sugar for me please, love.' He patted his midriff. 'I'm trying to keep the weight off. Middle-age spread and all that.'

Both girls smiled, warming to the officer and his self-deprecating convivial banter. 'There you go, Sergeant.'

He accepted his drink gratefully, smiled and nodded. 'Thanks love, now take a seat next to your friend and we'll make a start.'

Helen sat as instructed.

'Am I right in thinking that the last time you saw Emma was on the Friday evening, before a night out?'

Both girls nodded and said, 'Yes,' in unison, followed by Dianne adding, 'It was sometime after seven but before eight.'

'And one of you thinks she heard her leave the house in the early hours of Saturday morning, correct?'

Dianne played with her silver bracelet, leant forwards in her seat and said, 'Oh, I definitely heard her. The stairs were creaking even louder than usual for some reason. You heard what they're like just now when you came down.' She glanced sideways at her friend. 'I definitely heard them creaking. I hadn't drunk as much as Helen.'

Helen raised her eyes and smiled thinly. 'Guilty as charged, I'm afraid. I was seriously pissed. I don't think I'd have heard a bomb go off in the next room.'

Rankin refocussed on Dianne inquisitively and held his gaze. 'Any idea what time it was?'

She shook her head and scowled. 'I think we got in at about twoish and it was still dark when I heard her go downstairs, so I guess it must have been sometime between then and dawn. It's hard to keep track of the time when you're half asleep.'

'And you're certain it was still dark?'

'Yeah, absolutely! I can remember looking through my partially open curtains and seeing a yellow moon against a dark sky, before closing my eyes again and telling myself to go to sleep. I wish I'd got up now. Maybe if I had, Emma wouldn't be missing.'

Rankin noted her response in his usual scribbled script. 'Don't beat yourself up, love. You can't have known what would happen. What's the point in recriminations?'

She smiled. 'I still can't help blaming myself.'

Helen reached across and squeezed her friend's hand in silent support, as Rankin continued, 'Can either of you recall her leaving the house at that sort of time previously? I need to know if it was out of character. Do you think she may have gone for a nighttime walk?'

Both girls shook their heads together, as Helen spoke up and said what they were both thinking, 'I guess she could have gone for a walk if she couldn't sleep; it was a pleasant enough night. But I don't think it's very likely, because Emma's afraid of the dark.'

'Was she worried about anything you know of?'

This time it was Dianne who responded, as Helen looked on. 'I think she's the most chilled-out person I've ever met. She meditates, does yoga regularly, eats healthily and generally cruises through life. Nothing seems to get to her. I wish I had half her self-confidence.'

'Are you of the same opinion, Helen?'

'Yeah, I'd say so. She was a little rattled by that business with Peter for a few days, but she didn't let it get to her for very long. She doesn't tend to dwell on the negatives.'

Rankin raised the cup to his lips and gulped his tea greedily. 'Yeah, I heard about that. What do you make of Mosely?'

Helen rested her elbows on the tabletop and linked her hands together in front of her. 'I never understood what she saw in him. But, I guess he's harmless enough.'

Rankin drained the remainder of his tea. 'So you've no reason to think that Peter posed any threat to her?'

Both girls laughed despite, or perhaps due to the onerous nature of the discussion.

'Yeah, I've only met him briefly, but that's my impression too. Were there any other men in her life who I may not know about?'

Helen turned in her seat, looked at Dianne and smiled nervously. 'There was that old guy she kept mentioning.'

This could be interesting. 'Who exactly are we talking about?'

'You can tell him, Helen. She shares more with you than she does with me.'

'Helen?'

She was wishing she hadn't opened her mouth in the first place. 'Oh, it's nothing really. I don't think it matters a great deal. We were just messing about to relieve the tension.'

The DS tapped the tip of his pen on the tabletop. 'Just say it and let me be the judge of that. The quicker we can get this done, the quicker I can get home to the missus.'

Now she was really wishing she hadn't said anything in the first place. 'Emma said she kept seeing this really old guy with a walking stick, in the street wherever she went. She joked that he must fancy her or something. She even recalled seeing the same man in Caerystwyth once or twice before coming to college.'

'Has either of you ever seen him?'

The two girls said, 'No' together.

'So, how do you know about the stick?'

Helen rose to her feet and mimicked an ancient and bent over individual, shuffling along with obvious difficulty, imaginary cane in hand. 'Emma used to do an impression of him to make me laugh when she'd had a drink or two. "Hello, my lovely. Marvellous to see you again. Your hair's looking particularly attractive today, blonde, and styled just as I like it. It's almost as if you prepared it just for me. I hope your boyfriend realises what a lucky man he is."' She paused. 'Well, you know the sort of thing.'

Rankin closed his notebook, slipped it back into his briefcase and chuckled to himself as he stood to leave. The interview was going nowhere fast. If being a decrepit and sex-starved old lech was an arrestable offence, they'd have to build a lot more prisons.

Chapter 5

Emma was understandably reluctant to acknowledge the fact, but she seriously considered starving herself to death for a time, when depression and hopelessness closed in and engulfed her. She had absolutely no idea how many days had passed before finally deciding to eat. But she did, in what she considered a stoic drive to survive. If she was going to die, it wouldn't be without a fight.

He, the man whose faceless voice she now knew so very well, piled on the pressure, as was his custom. He didn't want her dead, or at least not yet. But as unlikely as it seemed, it wasn't his toxic persuasive tactics that eventually changed her mind for her. It was a determined spark of life somewhere inside her that changed her attitude. With every hour that passed she came to hate him with ever increasing intensity and became more determined than ever to survive, despite his best efforts to destroy her psychologically. She discovered an inner strength she had not known existed. If she was to have any chance of escape, she had to eat, she had to exercise, she had to gain strength. It really was that simple. She was a scientist, after all. If she didn't understand the need for regular sustenance and movement, who on earth did? And so she began eating when he offered food, however unappetising the meal, however hard it was to force one mouthful after another down her throat, and she performed regular weight-bearing exercises such as press-ups and sit-ups or yoga when the room was in total impenetrable darkness and she thought he couldn't see her.

She still had absolutely no idea who her captor was, or even what he looked like. The voice was still strangely familiar, but that's all it was. She just couldn't put a name to it, however hard she tried. He offered food and drinks via the damned speaker system installed in the ceiling prior to her arrival, and every time she asked herself: who is he? Who on earth is he? But, so far, as hard as she tried, she didn't have an answer.

Meal times, or feeding times, as he referred to them, were always the same. First he'd announce that it was time to eat, then, after a few minutes' delay, he'd rap on the steel door with some indeterminate object or other and tell her to approach the hatch. Whatever he deemed suitable was then handed to her through the gap as she stretched out her hand to accept it. She'd peered through that opening more than once in an attempt to identify him, but all she glimpsed was a face seemingly covered in what appeared to be a brightly coloured clown's mask, with emotionless eyes and topped with wild, black curly hair, which may or may not have been his own. She found the sight of it horrifying initially, but finally decided that it may be to her advantage. Maybe his anonymity was a good thing. Maybe he planned to release her back into the world outside the walls at some point in the not-too-distant future. Maybe he was thinking of his continued freedom when that happy day dawned. Or was she deluding herself? Was she clinging on to hope born of denial, as she had previously? She had no way of knowing.

At first she thought the meals in themselves were reasonable, if the use of such a word had any place in her dark and claustrophobic world. Again, she found solace in that fact, telling herself insistently that he wouldn't bother providing varied nutritious food unless he intended to keep her alive. But, her positive interpretations were short-lived. She soon came to realise that feeding time was an intrinsic part of his game as he repeatedly toyed with her sanity. He hid things in her meals and squealed with delight when she found them. She discovered a large black beetle in a dollop of lumpy mashed potatoes the first time, followed by a rat's tail amongst long strands of pasta smothered in tomato sauce. And then, just when she thought things couldn't possibly get any worse, he proved her horribly wrong. She could imagine him staring at her through the camera lens when she pictured it. She could see him sitting there in her mind's eye, savouring the moment and cackling in delight as she discovered a semi-frozen severed human toe amongst the chunks of fatty roast pork and soggy white rice on her half-empty plate. Laughter exploded from the ceiling-mounted speakers as she gagged, spat a half-chewed mouthful of meat from her mouth, leapt from the bed, and ran for the toilet to urgently throw up what she'd already eaten of her meal.

And after all that, he ordered her to dance as she returned to the room with tears flowing down her sullen face. He did that sometimes, when it pleased him. 'Dance for me, Venus. Turn slowly in a circle with elegance and grace. Bend at the waist, my lovely. Face away from the camera. That's it, that's it, bend at the waist and remain still for a moment or two whilst I appreciate your beauty.'

And, like it or not, she'd dance to his preposterous tune, time and time again, following his precise instructions, sometimes in the black underwear provided and sometimes naked, but always tottering on those crazily high shoes, that he appeared to appreciate above almost all else. What was it he said? What were his exact words? 'They extenuate your eroticism, Venus. I fail to understand why you didn't wear such things in your previous life. You lacked intrinsic style in those far-off days. I'm helping you evolve into the woman you were always meant to be. You're transforming into a butterfly. An ugly duckling is becoming a swan. I hope you've come to appreciate that, my lovely. I'm doing this for both of us.'

And she'd replied, 'Yes, master,' and continued dancing and hating every ludicrous moment, before falling to her knees and thanking him for his patience and care when he demanded it of her.

She'd examined every inch of the room as she pranced and swirled to his tune. She'd searched for any sign of weakness, any potential means of escape, however remote, but she'd found nothing. Nothing, except a bright-red-painted, broken and bloodied fingernail that must once have adorned the hand of a previous victim. She considered stopping eating again when she found it. Maybe death would be a welcome release after all.

Chapter 6

House-to-house enquiries were always onerous and seldom productive in PC Laura Williams' humble opinion, but at least it was a pleasant enough day to stroll the streets of Cardiff in shirtsleeves, with the birds singing in the life-enhancing, green-leafed urban trees. Here was hoping the weekend would be just as nice. The kids could do with a nice day at the beach. Perhaps the Gower was worth considering.

The constable pressed the single bell to the left side of the dark blue front door of a three-storey house located almost directly opposite Emma's student residence. She noted that it was one of the few houses in the wide street retained as one dwelling, rather than being adapted for multiple occupancy to maximise rental income, as in the case of the vast majority. Maybe the owner actually lived there. That would be something of a novelty in that once upmarket part of the city.

She rang the bell again on virtual autopilot and was about to stroll away with her hands linked behind her back, when the door was suddenly opened by an excessively muscular, steroid-fed man in his mid-to-late-thirties. He looked dishevelled, wearing nothing but a grubby white vest, a ridiculously inadequate pair of shorts that barely covered his modesty and a pair of red flip-flops that looked close to falling apart.

She met his gaze less than enthusiastically and introduced herself with a forced smile that melted away as quickly as it had appeared. 'Good morning, sir, are you the householder?'

He looked her up and down hungrily without making any effort to hide the fact. 'If you're wondering how a lowlife like me can afford this place, it's none of your fucking business.'

Well, he had that spot on. Not that she cared one way or the other. 'Not at all, sir, we're making enquiries regarding a missing student.' She reached out and pointed in the direction of Emma's digs. 'She's one of the three girls who live opposite. You must have seen them from time to time.'

He couldn't have looked less interested if paid to. 'Is this going to take long? I've got to sign on in about half an hour.'

Oh, the joys of police work. The PC handed him a copy of that same head and shoulders colour photo of Emma with a beaming smile on her pretty face, as provided by her mother. 'Do you recognise her?'

He handed it back almost immediately and scratched his large sunburned balding head before responding. 'Yeah, I've seen her out and about once or twice. She's not a bad-looking girl if you like that sort of thing. Not nearly enough flesh on the bone for my tastes. I like something to hang on to.'

Like he could afford to be so fussy. What it was to be so deluded. 'So, how well do you know her?'

'I didn't say I know the snooty cow. I've just seen her going back and forth to the house with her posh stuck-up mates, but that's all.'

PC Williams took a single urgent step backwards as the man burped loudly without shielding his mouth, causing his pungent beer-soaked breath to fill her nostrils. What a charming man! She should check his record when she returned to the station. The prison tattoos were a dead giveaway. And those had to be needle marks on his arms. A junkie, if ever she'd seen one. 'When did you last see her?'

'Why do you want to know?'

'Just answer the question.'

He glared at the officer and shook his head aggressively. 'If that bitch has said I've done something to her, she's fucking lying!'

Definitely a man with a history; he very probably had a crime sheet as long as your arm. 'You're not a suspect, sir. This is a missing person enquiry, not a criminal matter.'

He visibly relaxed, the lines on his face melting away and virtually disappearing. 'I should fucking well hope not. Are we done here? I've got about ten minutes before my bus goes.'

PC Williams stood her ground. 'I asked you when you last saw her. The DSS will understand if you're late. I can give you a note of explanation, if that helps.'

He looked less than convinced. 'When's the last time you signed on? The bastards will use any excuse to hold back the cash.'

The lazy uncooperative git! Maybe a paying job wouldn't be a bad idea. 'Just answer my questions, sir, and I'll be on my way.'

Okay, so she wasn't inclined to give up easily. 'I saw her about two months back.'

Why not just say that in the first place and stop wasting her time? 'And you haven't seen her since?'

'No, I fucking well haven't. Is that it?'

She considered telling him exactly what she thought of him, but decided against and reluctantly ate her words. 'Emma was last seen on Friday, May the first between seven P.M. and eight P.M. Did you see anything unusual that day? Anything that could give us some clue as to her whereabouts?'

He shook his head. 'I'm no grass.'

She was losing patience fast. The confused morality of the criminal classes never ceased to amaze her. 'As I said, sir, this is a missing person enquiry, not a criminal matter.'

He laughed, head back, multiple dark amalgam fillings in full view. Hopefully, if he gave the pig something she'd piss off and let him get to the pub before the racing started on the telly. 'There was that old sod carrying something or other to his car in the early hours.'

Don't say she was actually going to find out something useful for a change. Wonders never ceased. 'Carrying something from where?'

This time it was the interviewee's turn to point towards Emma's lodgings. 'From the three girls' place.'

This was beginning to get interesting. 'And it was definitely that night?'

'Yeah, I went down the boozer to watch the boxing on Sky. There was a title fight on involving a local boy.'

'Can we take a seat inside the house, sir? I need to ask you a few more questions and get something down on paper.'

He appeared crestfallen, his plans for the day blown right out of the water. He'd miss the start of the first race at this rate. 'I haven't got time for this shit, love.'

She glanced past him into the hall as he went to close the door. 'Be a shame if the drugs boys decided to pay you a visit. I'm sure they could find something interesting if they tried hard enough.'

He turned and glared at her. 'You wouldn't do that!'

'Try me. I'm not as nice as I look.'

'I'd avoid the settee if I were you, love. One of my mates pissed himself after a particularly heavy night.'

She chose a well-worn armchair that was at least dry and relatively unsoiled. How the other half lived!

'I would offer you tea or coffee, but the butler's got the morning off.'

She smiled in response to his effort to lighten the mood. 'Let's start with your name and date of birth?'

Questions, questions, the pigs were always asking questions. 'Do you really need those details?'

She opened her pocketbook at the appropriate page and poised the tip of her Parker pen above the paper. 'You know the answer to that one.'

He shrugged. Best to get it over with. 'Lee Price.'

You had to love a trier. 'And your date of birth, Mr Price?'

'It's the twenty-eighth of May, seventy-one, if you must know.'

74

He looked a lot older. The drink and drugs had aged him prematurely. They had a habit of doing that. 'So what exactly did you see?'

He began picking his nose, knuckle-deep, before flicking the green snot onto the threadbare carpet before speaking again. 'They had a lock-in at the Black Lion. I walked back to the house sometime after midnight with some slapper I met in the bar.'

What a charming man! Such good manners and a nice way with words. 'What was the young lady's name?'

He shook his head dismissively and laughed. 'I haven't got a clue. I can't remember what she looked like, let alone anything else.'

'Her age, build, hair colour, anything?'

'Nope, I found an orange thong and an empty Embassy fag packet in the downstairs bathroom, if that's any good to you?'

'Not really, can't you recall anything about her at all? Surely there must be something you can tell me, if you spent the night together.'

'I'm pretty sure she had a tattoo of a butterfly on her arse.'

'Tell me more.'

'I've got nothing. It could have been a moth for all I know.'

She smiled despite herself and resisted the impulse to laugh. There was a comic madness to it all. The lives people chose to live never ceased to surprise her. 'So what exactly do you remember seeing?'

He paused briefly and blew the stale alcohol-impregnated air from his mouth with an audible hiss. 'Like I said, when we were walking back to the house, I'm pretty sure I saw some old bloke carrying something out of the girls' place opposite.'

Maybe he was choosing not to remember the woman's name. Maybe she was on the game. Yeah, that was probably it. The pub was popular with prostitutes. But, there was little point in pushing it. 'So what was he carrying?'

He shook his head again. 'I haven't got a fucking clue.'

Be patient, girl, be patient, keep asking the right questions and you'll get there in the end. 'Try to think, Lee, this could be important. Was it something big or something small?'

He sat bolt upright in his seat and thought back to that night. 'He was carrying something over one shoulder. Could have been a rug, or something along those lines, I guess.'

Was it Emma? It could have been Emma. That would certainly up the ante. 'That's good, Lee, looks like the drug squad may not be calling on you after all.'

'Well, thank fuck for that.'

'I want you to think carefully before answering my next question, or I might have to change my mind… Do you think he was carrying the missing girl?'

He leant forwards in his chair, keen to emphasise his point. 'Look, the guy was ancient. It's surprising he could carry anything at all.'

'So he didn't appear to be struggling under the weight?'

'Not that I noticed. It's not as if I was planning to help the bloke. I had more important things on my mind.'

It didn't make a lot of sense. An old man carrying a nineteen-year-old woman with effortless ease. Maybe the entire story was fiction. 'Are you sure about what you saw?'

'Yeah, I'm sure. I've never been more sure. Do you want to know what I actually saw, or something that suits you better? I'll say he rode down the path on a silver unicorn if you'll piss off and let me get on with my day.'

Time to move on. 'Just tell me the truth, Lee, nothing more, nothing less.'

The silly cow had had a sense-of-humour bypass. 'I was just having a joke with you.'

'So what did he do with whatever he was carrying?'

Now, that was one he could answer with confidence. 'He threw it in the back of one of those Swedish estate cars.'

She noted his response. Things were looking up. Maybe she'd make a detective after all. 'Are you talking about a Volvo?'

He nodded with growing enthusiasm. 'Yeah, that's it, a Volvo, the flash git!'

This could be absolutely crucial, a game changer. 'What colour was the car?'

'It was hard to tell under the street lights.'

Here we go again. 'Light or dark?'

'Dark, I think.'

All of a sudden he wasn't doing quite so well. 'But you can't be sure?'

'Not really, I was pretty hammered.'

Oh, bollocks! 'But, you're certain it was a Volvo? That's what you're telling me?'

He shifted nervously in his seat, repeatedly transferring his weight from one buttock to the other. 'Well, not one hundred per cent to be honest, but pretty sure.'

This was going downhill fast. 'You're saying it could have been a different make?'

'Well, yeah it could have been, now that I think about it: a Passat or a Cavalier maybe. It's hard to remember with any clarity.'

'Put a number on it for me.'

He appeared puzzled. 'What do you mean?'

'In percentage terms.'

He paused briefly and then said, 'Fifty-fifty, I guess.'

Oh shit! She knew the answer would be 'no' before asking the question, but she asked it anyway: 'Did you see the number plate?'

'No, why would I?'

He had a point. He was thinking about sex, not cars. 'Which way did he go when he drove off?'

Now, that was one he could definitely answer with certainty. 'Back in the direction of the Black. Are there any of those newfangled CCTV cameras in the area?'

So, he wasn't quite as stupid as he seemed on first meeting. 'There will be soon, but not as yet. Let's move on to the elderly guy's description. What can you tell me about him?'

'Long grey hair, beard, glasses.'

'That's helpful, Lee, how tall was he?'

'Average, five-eight, five-ten, possibly.'

'Heavy build, average build, light build?'

'Eleven and a half, twelve stone.'

It looked like he'd seen a lot more than it first seemed. It was surprising what a bit of pressure could achieve.

'So, how long was his hair?'

'Shoulder length, like an old hippy.'

'And the beard?'

'Long, scraggy, a right mess. If there was ever a bloke who needed a decent barber, that was him.'

'What about the glasses?'

He laughed, amused by the line of questioning. 'Give me a break, love. Who am I, the fashion police?'

'So, you can't remember what they looked like.'

'No, I fucking well can't! I was focussed on the tart at the time.'

'What about his clothes?'

He snorted like a suckling piglet on the teat. 'You have got to be kidding me. I don't know what *I* was wearing, let alone the old git. Now, if you ask me what the tart was wearing, you might get an answer.'

'So why do you remember the beard and hair? That seems a bit unlikely given everything else you've said.'

For fuck's sake! You tried to help some people… 'ZZ Top are one of my favourite bands. The old bloke looked a bit like one of them. It stuck in my mind.'

This time it was her turn to laugh. 'Have you seen him before?'

'Nope.'

'You're certain of that?'

'Yeah, yeah, I said so, didn't I?'

'Is there anything else? Anything at all you can tell me?'

'That's your lot!'

She stood to leave, glad of the opportunity to breathe the fresh air again. 'I appreciate your cooperation. If you think of anything more, you know where to find me.'

'Good luck with that.'

The cheeky sod. 'I won't hold my breath, Lee, but no doubt we'll meet again one way or another.'

He opened the front door, and stood to one side to facilitate her departure. The quicker she was out of there the better. 'Oh, that is good news. I'll count the days.'

'As I said, Lee, you know where to find me.'

PC Williams called at one place of residence after another for another two hours or more, before finally accepting defeat. In the unlikely event that any of the other residents of studentville knew anything significant, they weren't telling her about it. She'd have to call back at the empty houses, of course, but such things would have to wait. It was time to head back to the station. Another hour or so and she'd be home with the children. That was something to look forward to. Hooray to that!

'Hi Sarge, is it okay if I use your office to give West Wales a ring before I head off home?'

'Yeah, no problem, how's the investigation going? I heard you'd applied to join CID.'

PC Williams smiled. He'd recommended her. 'Not bad, as it happens. Do you know a charmer named Lee Price? He lives in one of the big houses in Cathays Road.'

The long serving and experienced career sergeant nodded resignedly. 'Yeah, I've known him since he was a teenager. His mother left him the house, poor cow, when he was nineteen. He wasn't a bad lad early on, but he went off the rails after she was killed in a head-on car crash in the Penarth area. You know, drugs, drunk and disorderly, that sort of thing.'

'Is it worth me running a PNC check?'

He laughed. 'I think I can tell you as much as the computer can. Lee's been convicted of a string of drug offences, both possession and dealing. Cannabis in the main, but I'm told he's moved on to class As. He did a six months stretch in Swansea nick a couple of years back.'

'That's really helpful thanks, Sarge. Has he got any history of violence or sexual offences?'

He shook his head. 'Na, nothing like that. He's a waste of space, but he's not one of the evil bastards out there. Why do you ask?'

'Oh, it's this missing student. He may have seen something.'

'I don't think Lee's the most reliable witness in the world, to say the least. He's away with the fairies half the time.'

She walked past him and into his shared office. 'Yeah, you're probably right, Sarge, but he's all I've got at the moment.'

'You're doing your best, girl. West Wales will have to be happy with that.'

'Yeah, let's hope they see it that way. Why I'm reporting to them at all, is a mystery to me.'

'Don't ask me, no one tells me anything around here.'

The phone rang and rang before Laura Williams finally heard Rankin's newly familiar voice at the other end of the line. 'Hello, DS Rankin, it's Laura in Cardiff, I wanted to update you on my progress at this end.'

Progress! That was more than he'd managed. Here was hoping she was getting somewhere. 'Call me Clive, love, there's no need for ceremony. What have you got for me?'

The PC outlined the day's events as Rankin listened in contemplative silence.

'How reliable is this Price bloke?'

'Like I said, he's got a history of drug use, cannabis, steroids and the heavier stuff, but I get the impression he's telling the truth on this occasion. Why would he lie to us? He's got nothing to gain.'

'Unless he's involved. He could be pointing us in the wrong direction.'

'My desk sergeant's known him since he was a kid. He doesn't think it's likely.'

'Thanks, a bit of local knowledge is always useful, but I might pay him a visit myself anyway.'

'So you think it could be significant?'

'It seems an unlikely scenario; some old bloke carrying her from the house in the early hours, but we've got nothing else to run with. It would make sense to send your local scenes of crime people around to check the girls' place for known fingerprints, or any signs of blood. I'll have a chat with DI

Gravel, ask him to link in with someone your end and we'll go from there.'

'Okay, Sarge, I'll be back in touch if I come up with anything else.'

'You do that, Laura, I appreciate your help.'

Chapter 7

The man searched through the large and lockable 675-litre chest freezer for a full five minutes or more, before finally locating his particular clear plastic bag of choice amongst all the others. He closed the lid carefully, held the bag up to the light of the window to confirm its contents and smiled contentedly as he felt his pulse race. Trophies brought back such wonderful vivid memories. Big, bright and loud memories that took him back in time to visit the dead. He really should make the time to appreciate his collection on a more regular basis.

He loosened and removed the tight elastic band securing the top of the bag and tipped out the contents on top of the freezer: four frozen fingers of varying sizes with red, perfectly painted nails. Four glorious reminders of happy times past, four prized possessions to be treasured.

He picked up the index finger and held it to his lips, sucking at it like a baby on its mother's nipple, before slowly lowering himself to the floor and unfastening his trousers. Maybe Venus Six would add to his collection and maybe she wouldn't… Maybe she'd understand his vision… Maybe she'd contribute to his project… Maybe she'd become the assistant he'd always craved. Someone to do his bidding. Someone to appreciate his many admirable accomplishments… Or maybe he'd have to kill her as he had the others: those false messiahs who'd promised much but ultimately delivered little. Either way, he'd have some fun along the way. And, anyway, there were plenty more fish in the sea.

The man rose easily to his feet, wiped himself with a Kleenex tissue taken from a box kept on a shelf for the specific purpose, refastened his trousers and nibbled at the ragged boney end of the finger for a second or two, savouring the taste and texture, before returning it to the bag with the others. Body parts began to melt surprisingly quickly once subjected to the comparative warmth of the room. He really should resist the temptation to chew if his collection were not to become depleted before he had the opportunity to replenish it.

He closed the door of the utility room and strolled casually into the generously proportioned but increasingly dated kitchen. His collection was a testament to his efforts, a physical reminder of his accomplishments. He'd done well, really well, and a celebratory glass or two of chilled Chardonnay was entirely justified in the circumstances. He took the bottle from the fridge, removed the cork, filled a crystal wine glass to the halfway point and lifted it to his lips, enjoying the familiar acidic tang, but mourning the loss of the finger's lingering fleshy remnants on his breath. The wine was delicious, but second best. If only everything could taste as good as human flesh. Nothing even came close. Nothing else held the same visceral fascination… Oh well, *c'est la vie*, that was far too much to ask for.

The man reached to his right and switched on one of several monitors located in various locations around the ground floor of the house for convenience of use. The bitch was sleeping again, maybe he'd give her another fifteen minutes or so before disturbing her. A second glass of vino and the opportunity for some relaxation wouldn't do him any harm at all. There was a time for impulsiveness, but there were things to decide. It was important to think things through and consider all the angles before acting. He possessed a superior intellect, why not make full use of it?

He sipped at the wine and relaxed back in his easy chair, lost in his thoughts. Time had passed surprisingly quickly since her arrival. But then, it always did. He'd followed his usual well-established protocol with reasonably positive results. Venus Six was ticking most of the required boxes up to that point. She was beautiful, that was certainly true. She was relatively compliant, but with an admirable spark of defiance that would be amusing to extinguish. As long as she didn't push that defiance too far, he'd let her play her transparent and predictable games for a time, until he finally lost patience. A degree of independent thinking may serve his future purpose if she proved to be a potential partner. And her dancing was improving with every single day that passed. That was to her credit. She was becoming more familiar with the shoes and more eager to please. And the way the sweat shimmered on her body when he turned the heating right up to maximum was truly exquisite, like a pink and moist open wound. She was still a little erratic at times, her movements somewhat robotic occasionally, but there was nothing fundamentally wrong with that. At least she was trying to the best of her ability when properly encouraged.

86

And she had a derrière to die for. It looked so succulent and particularly tender. Maybe she really was the one. Maybe he'd actually found her this time. Yes, the hunting was enjoyable, the capture rewarding, the imprisonment interesting in an increasingly repetitive sort of way, but it was about time one of them actually met his required standards to the letter. That was reasonable, wasn't it? That wasn't too much to ask after all his efforts. No, of course it wasn't. She could be the one, she really could. Maybe, just maybe, he'd keep her alive long enough to find out.

'Good morning, Venus, time to wake up and face the new day. How about a little breakfast?'

She shielded her face with an open hand as her eyes gradually adjusted to the intense glare of the spotlights. 'What time is it, master?'

'Oh, let's not go down that rocky road again. Time has no meaning in your new world. It's time for you to accept that. There's just you, me and the room. That's your world, that's your universe! Time is an irrelevance. Now, tell me, porridge or cereal? Or are you an enthusiastic meat eater like me?'

'Cereal please, master. If you let me out, I could help you make it. I'd like that.'

He clenched his hands into tight fists and rocked to and fro on his high stool. Was she trying it on? Would the bitch dare? Would she really be that stupid? Or, did she genuinely want to help him? Maybe she was reaching out with well-intentioned affection. 'Why would you want to do that?'

She took a deep breath, sucking in the fetid air to steady her jangling nerves. Was he falling for it? Would he unlock the door? 'I just think it's about time we got to know each other a little better, that's all, master.'

He relaxed his hands, giving her the benefit of the doubt at least for the moment. 'Oh, we will, Venus, we definitely will, but now is not that time.'

Chapter 8

Emma had completely lost track of how long she'd been imprisoned in that windowless concrete box and she silently acknowledged that her new reality was impossible to accept. It could be days, it could be weeks, or it could be months, God forbid. She'd thought about it, focussed and thought about it some more, but she still didn't have the slightest clue. She had no way of knowing and no one to ask. There was just the room, the dazzlingly bright white light or total impenetrable darkness, the pervasive ear-shattering noise or lonely silence and his voice: that erudite, educated voice that in any other circumstances would have the spark of middle-class normality about it. The man, whoever he may be, was totally insane, of course. She had absolutely no doubts about that. Reason was lost on him. He considered the abnormal normal and the indefensible acceptable. He was a man devoid of empathy or virtue, incapable of sympathy or understanding. Something was missing in him. Something that made us human. Maybe, if she'd studied psychology rather than the physical sciences, she'd have a better chance of understanding his psychopathy and manipulating him to her advantage. Either way, she had to attempt to outthink him and save her life. One thing was certain: she was going to give it her best shot. That was reason to hope in itself. And the police would be looking for her. Her lovely mum would make sure of that. She just wouldn't let up until she got exactly what she wanted. But, like it or not, she couldn't rely on their efforts, however tempting. There were no guarantees they'd find her. Where would they look? She had to accept that she could be almost anywhere.

Emma rolled over on the bed and rubbed her head gently, whilst deep in meditative thought. She'd tried to hold it together as best she could. She'd tried to ignore and overcome the almost irresistible impulse to panic and to retreat into a dark downward spiral of despair. She'd learned to meditate on and direct her anger, frustration and loathing towards her will to survive and escaping her private hell.

Emma closed her eyes and smiled, as she pictured herself opening the steel door and walking out into the sunshine to breathe the fresh air. She imagined the monster man being dragged away by the police, his hands handcuffed behind his back. If only it were that simple! If only she could click her fingers and make fantasy reality.

But she couldn't and she frowned as the fantasy faded and her thoughts darkened again. She still hadn't met her captor or seen the bastard's face, but she knew he came into the room, unseen and unheard, because he left fresh towels and toiletries from time to time.

It had puzzled her for a time: the unexplained appearance of various items at indeterminate intervals. He certainly didn't enter her concrete box whilst she was awake, and she'd slept fitfully since her imprisonment, always on alert and waking at the slightest sound. So, if that was the case, how could he sneak in undetected? She just couldn't work it out initially. The soap, shampoo, perfume and the likes weren't materialising from thin air. That much was obvious. Was there a second clandestine door somewhere in the bathroom? She'd looked again and again, whilst careful to disguise her activities. But, if there was a second door, she certainly hadn't found it. She really didn't think that hypothesis offered a viable explanation. And anyway, she'd thought about it at length and had decided that she finally had an answer that made sense. She'd noticed that sometimes, after one of his revolting meals so full of amusing surprises, she drifted off to sleep. Not the normal and reinvigorating sleep with which most of us are happily familiar, but immediate and total oblivion from which she awoke with a pounding headache and unsteady legs. The bastard was drugging her when it suited him. She had no doubt about it. She was totally at his mercy.

When she woke on the last occasion, she finally realised just how vulnerable she was. There was blood on the sheets, deep scratch marks on her back and buttocks, and human bite marks on her inner thighs and on one breast close to the nipple. The realisation was truly horrible and utterly demoralising, but on a positive note, he had sexual desires. Deviant and twisted desires, but desires nonetheless. That's something she planned to use to her advantage if she got the chance. Sex was a potential weapon she could utilise, if given even the slightest opportunity to act on her intentions. It may or may not work, but there was only one way to find out. She had everything to gain, and very little, if anything, to lose.

91

For as long as she could remember, all she'd wanted to do was to become a research scientist. But for now, such thoughts would have to be put on hold. All those small things that concerned her in her previous life now seemed so utterly unimportant. Her priorities had changed by painful necessity. She wouldn't be giving up her life without a fight. She was a proud and brave lioness, not a twitching and cowering mouse.

Chapter 9

Grav was striding across the landing in the direction of the bathroom to empty his bladder for the fourth time that night, when the phone rang out loudly in the hallway. He cursed crudely as he descended the stairs one slow step at a time and picked up the receiver from its wall-mounted cradle next to the front door. Why the hell was someone ringing him at three in the frigging morning? It had better been good.

'Hello, boss, sorry to disturb your beauty sleep.'

Grav yawned expansively. 'What the hell do you want, Clive? Have you seen the time?'

'We've got a body.'

Grav was fully awake and alert in that instant. 'Where?'

'Caerystwyth Wood, near to the old ruined mill at the edge of Trinity Fields.'

'Who found it?'

'Some bloke rang in anonymously about forty-five minutes ago. He claimed he was in the wood hunting badgers when one of his lurchers ran off and started digging and worrying at something in the soft wet ground about twenty yards away from where he was standing. When he went over to take a look, he found a decaying human foot protruding through the earth, minus toes.'

'Male or female?'

Rankin paused before responding. 'Female… I brushed the earth away from her face. She meets Emma's description. I'm pretty sure it's her.'

'Oh, for fuck's sake!'

'I know. What a way to end up at nineteen.'

'Have you done the necessary?'

'I asked the control room to try to identify the origin of the call, but it doesn't help us a great deal. He rang from the phone box on the estate, but just said what he had to say quickly and put the phone down.'

'It shouldn't be too difficult to track him down. Doesn't Ben Marsh have a couple of lurchers? He does a bit of poaching.'

'I'll pay him a visit sometime tomorrow and put a bit of pressure on if you think it's worth the time and effort.'

'And you've secured the area?'

Why did he always feel the need to ask? How many years was it? 'Yes, boss, it's taped off. And the on-call pathologist's on her way here as we speak. I've asked the scenes of crime boys to bring some lighting. I can hardly see a thing with a torch, now that it's clouded over again.'

'Makes sense. Is it Dr Carter, or that new woman who's up her own arse?'

'Yeah, it's Sheila Carter.'

'Well, thank fuck for that. Hang on there, Clive, I'll be with you in about twenty minutes maximum. Don't let anyone disturb the scene more than you and the dogs already have. I'll leave seeing the parents until first thing in the morning.

There's nothing to gain by paying them a visit at this hour. I'm going to wreck their lives soon enough anyway.'

'Okay boss, you might want to bring an umbrella with you, it's just started pissing down.'

DI Gravel parked in the small council housing estate close to the most convenient access point to Caerystwyth Wood, and left the car just as the previously heavy rain was turning to light intermittent drizzle that seemed to come from every direction at once. He opened the racing-green Volkswagen Golf's rear hatch, pulled on a pair of well-worn size-ten black wellingtons and set off in the direction of the bright lights illuminating a section of trees about three hundred yards away.

'All right, Clive? You look like shit. Any sign of Sheila?'

Rankin swivelled on the spot and pointed to his left. 'She's over there behind those bushes. We've found several other areas of disturbed earth. It's not good, Grav. I think this may be some psycho's dumping ground.'

The DI stared down at the young girl's recently uncovered body and felt a cold shudder run down his spine. Fucking terrible! Her skull was caved in. What a waste of a young life! If he ever got used to this shit, it was time to give up the job for good. 'How long has the girl been here?'

'The doc thinks two weeks maximum, but don't quote her on it, you know what she's like, her usual caveat.'

The DI nodded his acknowledgement. 'So, if it is Emma, she was killed very soon after her disappearance.'

'It seems so.'

Grav looked up and smiled in familiar friendly greeting as Dr Carter appeared from behind a bush and walked briskly towards them despite the uneven and slippery ground. 'All right, Grav? Sorry to hear about Heather.'

Reminders, always reminders of his deepest sorrow. 'Thanks Sheila, it's appreciated.'

'Cancer?'

'Yeah, bowel cancer, her passing was a blessing in the end.'

She nodded twice, knowing exactly what he meant without the need to discuss it further. 'There's another girl buried about thirty feet from here.' She pointed behind her. 'Can you see the holly tree to the right of the two?'

'Yeah.'

'She's just behind it in a shallow grave. Whoever buried her didn't spend much time digging. There were about three feet of earth covering the body at most. Could be a coincidence, but it's the ideal depth to aid rapid decomposition.'

Grav began walking in the direction of the tree with Rankin following close behind. 'Show me.'

Rankin bent down and gently brushed the earth from the young woman's skull with the gloved fingers of his right hand, as he had earlier, whilst fighting to suppress his gag reflex. The girl was in a far more advanced state of decay than the first body found with all that entailed, although her fractured skull, dyed platinum-blonde hair, and prominent teeth were still obvious features that stood out alarmingly in the glare of the torchlight focussed on the face. He stood, took a small blue bulbous glass jar of Vicks menthol vapour rub from the side pocket of his lightweight Kagool, unscrewed the plastic top, dipped in a finger and urgently rubbed it around the inner edge of both nostrils, before offering the jar to Grav and the doctor to do likewise. He placed it back in his pocket when they both declined with thanks. 'How old is she?'

The doctor looked down at the woodland grave, silently contemplating man's seemingly unlimited capacity for evil as she had so many times, before finally raising her head and meeting Rankin's eyes. 'I'll be able to tell you more after the post-mortem.' She was nothing if not predictable.

The DI placed a hand on each of her shoulders and grinned. 'Come on, Sheila, what's your best guess, girl? You can tell your uncle Grav.'

'Okay, okay, I'd say early to mid-twenties, similar to the first girl, if you have to know right now. But don't quote me on that until I've got her back to the lab for a proper examination. I may just change my mind.'

'All right, message received loud and clear.'

'It might seem obvious, but do you think this is the work of a single serial killer?'

Grav lowered his arms and took a backward step, sliding in the mud and almost falling to the ground before steadying himself. She knew the answer was 'yes', so why ask? 'It's certainly looking that way. It's a first for this area. I think it's time for me to wake up the chief constable. His life's about to get a lot more interesting.'

Chapter 10

DI Gravel wasn't looking forward to informing Emma's parents of the developments in the case, far from it in fact. He seriously considered delegating the task to one of the division's female family liaison support officers for a time, but eventually decided it was a job he shouldn't and couldn't avoid, however strong the temptation and whatever excuses he could come up with. He owed them that much and rank carried its responsibilities as well as its privileges. It was something he had to do himself.

Grav pulled up directly outside the Jones family's large and impressive detached Georgian house at approximately 7:00 A.M., and quietly pondered that no amount of money could protect you from life's inevitable tragedies: taxes, death and much else along the way. He knew that as well as most, and he missed Heather every minute of every single day. No wonder he was hitting the bottle a little harder than usual, no wonder his headaches were a more regular feature of his life, no wonder his chest ached when he was particularly stressed, and no wonder he'd taken up the fags again. All that talk of the future, all those cherished plans: the Mediterranean cruise, the trip to Barbados to see their son, and all the other places they looked forward to visiting after his retirement, but never did. It all came to nothing. If only he'd made the most of their time together whilst he had the chance. What was the point of savings if they didn't enhance your life and those of your loved ones? He was left with nothing but fading memories. The circle of life could be hard to bear when you were on the receiving end.

Grav met his reddened and moistened eyes in the car's rear-view mirror and loosened his white-knuckle grip on the steering wheel. Come on Grav my boy, time to get on with it. He had a job to do and it needed doing. There was no point in wallowing in the past. Regrets achieved little if anything at all. The quicker he pulled himself together and told the parents what they needed to hear, the quicker he could get back to the investigation.

The DI knocked and kept knocking until the red velvet curtains of a first-floor window were flung open and a grey-haired man he didn't recognise, but assumed was Emma's father, opened the window and poked his head through. 'What the hell do you want at this time of the morning?'

'Mr Jones?'

'Who's asking?'

Grav reached into the inside pocket of his Harris Tweed jacket and held up his warrant card in plain view. 'DI Gravel, I met your wife at Caerystwyth police station.'

'DS Rankin's not with you?'

'He's otherwise engaged.'

'Any news?'

It was always the same. He was a purveyor of doom and gloom, the dark-clad angel of death, and the unfortunate recipients knew it as soon as they saw him. 'Can we talk inside, Mr Jones?'

The window was closed as quickly as it had opened and within seconds there was the unmistakable sound of a key turning in the lock. The door opened and Grav stood face to face with both parents, standing and staring at him with anxious expressions on their pale waxen faces. Ray Jones clutched his wife's hand tightly in his and took the lead as he felt obliged to. 'What's happened? Have you found our daughter?'

Grav took a deep breath. This was one task that never got any easier. 'Can we go inside and talk?'

The parents turned in unified silence and led the DI into a beautifully appointed lounge that screamed affluence and carefully considered good taste. Mr Jones invited Grav to take a seat in a dark brown leather Chesterfield armchair and gently guided his wife towards the matching settee, whilst struggling to devour his sadness as best he could. 'Just say what you're here to say, Inspector. It can't be any worse than our ruminations.'

Grav didn't have the slightest clue what ruminations were, but he got the gist anyway. They wanted the truth. They needed the truth. They deserved the truth. 'This isn't good news, I'm afraid.'

Ray Jones placed a supportive arm around his wife's shoulder and pulled her closer to him. 'We've already realised that, Inspector. For God's sake man, just tell us what you know before we explode!'

Grav nodded his resigned agreement. 'The bodies of two young women were found in Caerystwyth Wood. There may well be others to find. One, the first body discovered in the early hours of this morning, meets Emma's description. We can't be one hundred per cent certain it's her at this stage, but I think it's likely. I'd say you need to prepare yourself for the worst.'

The father leant forwards in his seat, whilst the mother raised her hands to her face and broke down into all-consuming sobs that caused her chest to heave as she gasped for breath. 'I want to see her.'

The DI shook his head slowly and deliberately. 'I really don't advise it, Mrs Jones. There's no easy way of saying this. The body's been in the ground with all that entails. We'll need to rely on DNA testing for a definitive identification.'

Both parents shuddered as unwelcome mental images invaded their troubled minds and refused to fade. 'You say the girl's body is in a state of decomposition? That's what you said, yeah?'

'That's correct, Mr Jones.'

He looked more hopeful, increasingly optimistic and desperate to rewrite the future. 'So it may not be Emma?'

He was clutching at straws. Understandably keen to deny an unwelcome reality that was staring him in the face. 'Look I'm sorry, but if Emma was killed very soon after her disappearance, the timescale fits. I'll seek to clarify matters as quickly as feasibly possible. I can get the DNA results within a few days, but we should be able to get a forensic dentist to compare the dental records sometime today. I'll be in touch the second I have the results. That I guarantee you.'

Ray Jones focussed on the royal-blue Axminster carpet at his feet and pulled his wife towards him for a second time. 'Is there anything else you need from us?'

The inspector took a small clear plastic tube from an inside pocket of his jacket and removed the stopper. 'I need to swab the inside of your mouth. It will only take a second.'

Mrs Jones suddenly pulled away from her husband and stood to leave the room. 'Just get it done, Ray. I'm going to phone my mother. Someone's got to tell her.'

'All right, dear. If you think that's best.'

He turned his head back to face the DI and opened his mouth wide.

'Hold still… That's it, we're done. As soon as I know something definite, you'll be the first to know.'

'Where is she?'

Just say it Grav. Just say it and get it over with. 'She's at Caerystwyth Mortuary. There's going to be a post-mortem later today. I know the pathologist; she'll treat the body with the utmost respect.'

Oh, God, as if things weren't bad enough already. 'Is that really essential? How can I tell my wife that her little girl's going under the knife?'

'I'm sorry, Ray, there's no alternative. If we're going to put this man away, we have to establish exactly how she died.'

Ray Jones began weeping silent tears. 'Who'd do such a terrible thing? I'd tear the bastard limb from limb if I got hold of him.'

And who could blame him. He'd do much the same himself in the same circumstances. 'I can't answer that as yet, but I won't rest until I nail him. That I can promise you.'

The distraught father met Grav's bloodshot eyes and held his gaze. 'I want you to swear to that. I need to know you mean what you say.'

Grav reached out and shook the father's hand firmly. 'You have my word. I'll put the bastard away for the rest of his miserable life.'

Grav was back in Caerystwyth Wood by 8:40 A.M. and both pleased and relieved to see that a team of detectives were carefully examining every inch of the relevant area under Rankin's direct supervision. 'All right, Clive my boy? Glad to see it's finally stopped raining.'

'How did it go with the parents?'

'Fucking terrible!'

'Poor sods.'

Grav nodded once as he surveyed the scene. 'Yeah, you've got that right... What exactly are we dealing with?'

'We've got five bodies, all female, all of a similar height, all blonde, all minus their toes and fingers. The pathologist says it looks as if they were cut off whilst the girls were alive.'

The DI blew the moist morning air through pursed lips with a noticeable whistle. 'Are you serious?'

'Yeah, I'm afraid so. We're looking for one sick bastard. If it is the Jones girl, she never had a chance.'

'We'll know one way or the other later today.'

103

Grav glanced to both right and left. 'Have you found anything useful?'

'A couple of fag butts, but they could be anyone's.'

'They've got to be worth looking at. We've got fuck all else at the moment.'

Rankin massaged the back of his increasingly cold and stiff neck with one hand. 'Yeah, you've got a point there. Have Cardiff had a good look at the girls' digs?'

'I had a chat with the local DI late last night. The SOCOs have been over every inch of the place based on Price's claims. There were spots of blood leading from the bedroom, down the stairs and into the hall in the direction of the front door. How the hell did you miss that lot?'

Rankin's face turned a darker shade of pink. 'The place is fitted with multicoloured flowered carpets. There's a lot of red. I just didn't see it.'

'For fuck's sake, Clive!'

'I guess that explains why the bedclothes were missing. The bastard's taken them with him! Any blood splashes on the bedroom walls?'

'Nothing reported… Any other developments this end?'

Rankin nodded twice. 'Two bodies are already at the morgue. The other three will follow shortly. Dr Carter's going to start the first post-mortem at about eleven o'clock, when she's had a couple of hours' shut-eye. She's cast a quick eye over the bodies at the morgue and mentioned seeing saw marks on several bones, as if areas of flesh had been removed. You can draw your own conclusions.'

'It doesn't get any better, does it?'

'No, it doesn't.'

'Is she doing all the post-mortems herself?'

'Na, she's doing three, but a second pathologist's available to give her a hand with the other two this afternoon. She reckons we'll have their initial findings by sometime tonight, with reports to follow as soon as possible after that.'

'Okay, makes sense. I'll head over there in a couple of hours and ask her to start with the first body found. If it's Emma's, I want to let the parents know as soon as feasibly possible. At least then they can start mourning her loss.'

'Okay, I'll leave it with you.'

'I'm going to head off and bring the chief super up to speed before heading to the morgue. I'll start putting some ideas together with a view to a planning meeting at five sharp this afternoon. Tell everyone to be ready and waiting in the conference room by five too. The quicker we progress the investigation, the happier I'll be. The bastard will kill again. It's just a matter of when and how.'

'I'll see you later, boss. Can you give the missus a bell for me and tell her not to expect me back until tonight? For some reason the signal's packed in.'

Grav grinned before turning and walking away. 'That woman's got you pussy-whipped to within an inch of your life.'

'So, you'll give her a ring for me?'

The DI continued walking and shouted out without looking back. 'Yeah, once I build up the courage.' Mrs Mary Rankin was one formidable woman.

Chapter 11

The man downed the dregs of his lukewarm Heinz tomato soup, wiped his mouth with a white cotton napkin, and switched on the monitor on the countertop in front of him.

He leant forwards as if drawn by a powerful magnet, eyes wide with his nose almost touching the screen, and broke into short spasmodic laughter as he witnessed the scene unfolding before him. She was exercising in the darkness again: up, down, up, down, up, down, muscles taut, focussed intently and totally oblivious to his presence. What a stupid bitch! If she thought she was outwitting him, she was very sadly mistaken. Maybe he should punish her for her subterfuge. Maybe she should pay a heavy price for her illicit activities… or maybe not. Perhaps he should let her continue undisturbed. It did at least provide some stimulating entertainment on a regular basis. But, what a pity she wasn't wearing the shoes.

He clenched and unclenched his fists repeatedly and spat at the screen. The bitch, the absolute bitch! Why the hell wasn't she wearing the shoes? He'd made his expectations perfectly clear right from the very start. She was goading him. The bitch was goading him!

His anger peaked with a loud visceral scream heard only by him, and then slowly dissipated as he continued watching, fascinated by her repetitive rhythmic movements. That's it girl: one press-up, two press-ups, three press-ups, four, keep going, keep going. Hers was hardly the correct form. It was more downward dog than plank, to use the eastern yoga parlance seemingly so popular with the new age alternative crowd. But it was all the better for it, all the more stimulating, and that's what mattered. She looked good enough to eat.

He adjusted the resolution and edged still closer to the glass screen after wiping off the spittle with a paper hankie. That's it, Venus Six, that's it, push that tight little bum of yours high in the air, my lovely. Point it towards the ceiling. Lovely, absolutely lovely! The human body had an undoubted beauty both inside and out: the taut skin over muscle and sinew, the soft juicy flesh, the hard white bone and the dark warm blood, with its unique and enticing aroma and taste. Wonderful, truly wonderful! Experience had taught him that.

He moved his face a few inches away from the screen and sighed as Emma sat on the carpeted floor and rested, her chest heaving with the effort of it all. He'd made a good choice. But then he always did. No surprises there. What was the point in keeping a captive if they didn't enhance your experience in one way or another? Yet another triumph for an accomplished man. He was at the very top of the evolutionary tree, the arbiter of life and death, a god! If she was the one, he'd have his fun along with her. And if she wasn't, he'd kill her. It really was as obvious as that. He'd take the lump hammer and smash her skull to smithereens. Bang! She'd die in an explosion of skin, brain tissue and bone. What a satisfying sight! What a satisfying sound! It was a win-win situation. He shouldn't concern himself. There was absolutely nothing to worry about.

He leant forwards again, poked out his tongue greedily, and licked the screen repeatedly like a puppy lapping milk, as tiny beads of sweat began forming on his heated brow. Maybe he should pay her another recreational visit after her next doctored meal. Rohypnol seemed by far the most effective and desirable option open to him. The forget-me drug. Yes, Flunitrazepam suited his purpose very well. Not only was it fast acting, but it had the definite advantages of leaving her dizzy, drowsy, disorientated and confused when she eventually came around. Hilarious! It never failed to amuse him. And maybe he should wear the clown's mask and perform for the camera. He could lick the sweat from her sleeping body if he acted quickly enough. It would be something to look back on, something to cherish, an important addition to his much-valued collection of films. One day he may even make them available to inspired visionaries like himself who could fully appreciate his work and applaud him for his genius. But, such things were for the future. He should focus on the now. Venus Six was worthy of his undiluted attention. There was little purpose in delaying a decision any longer than necessary.

He rose from his seat, took one of several alphabetically ordered and indexed videotapes from a varnished pine cupboard designed for the purpose and inserted it into the VCR. The bitch could wait. It wasn't as if she was going anywhere. It was essential to evaluate and celebrate his prior performance and learn from experience if he were to maximise his infinite potential. As good as he was, there were always things to learn. His techniques could always be tweaked. Even the best could get better.

As the film began, the man turned up the volume, unfastened his navy-blue tailored trousers and remained in his seat until it ended about twenty minutes later. Maybe he shouldn't rush it next time. Maybe a less frenzied approach was worth considering. It was so very hard to control oneself when in the throes of ecstasy.

He stood, wiped himself, pulled up his zip and refastened the clasp of his trousers before placing the tape back in its correct allocated place. He took a step back and admired his collection with a smile, before returning to the monitor. She'd been working out for almost half an hour. What the hell was that about? He flicked a switch and laughed uproariously, as Emma's cell burst into light. She reacted quickly, leaping from the floor and onto the bed in an instant, which he found even more amusing. She didn't have a clue, not the slightest clue. It was an opportune time to test her commitment to his cause.

'Are you awake, Venus? You look a little red in the face. I hope you're not going in for something, my lovely. There is a rather unpleasant bug doing the rounds. Some of my workmates are in an awful state.' And then a loud guffaw that made her tremble. 'Perhaps I should call you a doctor.'

She struggled to control her breathing as her raised heart rate gradually fell. Perhaps it was best to delay her response and say nothing at all, or maybe not. What on earth should she do? It was another no-win situation, one of so many.

Please don't play the tape. Please not the wailing woman. Please not again!

'You appear to be a little out of breath, Venus. What have you been doing to yourself, my lovely? I thought you were sleeping the sleep of the just and lost in your dreams.'

She had to respond. She had to say something. Silence was no longer an option. He'd lose it any second now. 'I haven't been doing anything, master. I've just been resting here on the bed and waiting for you patiently. We haven't talked for quite some time.'

What a ridiculous thing to say! Was the bitch trying to change the subject? Would she dare? 'It's been a matter of hours, my lovely. I know you miss me, but the bills have to be paid. I don't have a money tree in the garden, as much as I'd like to. I can't spend my entire time focussed on your many needs. That would be too much to ask for. Now, tell me the truth before I lose patience.'

'The truth?'

Was the bitch really that stupid? She was walking a metaphorical tightrope and in very serious danger of falling to her death. 'I asked you what you'd been doing. You would be well-advised to consider your answer extremely carefully this time. It could well be your last if I'm not satisfied with your reply.'

Her heart rate soared again as her fight-or-flight reaction kicked in and epinephrine flooded her system. He knew, somehow, he knew. But, how? She was always so careful. She had to come up with something to appease him and fast. Think Emma, think! 'I've been exercising for you, on a regular basis, master. I've done it for you, all for you. I want to look my very best. You stressed its importance when I first arrived.'

Okay, so far so good. She was saying the right things. 'So why in the dark?'

'Could you see me?'

He repeated his question with a harder edge this time, before adding, 'I require an adequate explanation, my lovely. Don't confuse my kindness for weakness. That would be a fatal error.'

Come on, Emma, say something, you have to say something. 'I really wanted to surprise you, master. I thought you'd be pleased.'

'Surprise me how?'

'I want to look beautiful for you.'

She was mouthing the words, but was she sincere? That was the real question. Was she sincere? 'Why? Tell me why and make it convincing.'

Come on Emma, you can do it. She had to say the right things, use the right words. 'I have to look my best, master. You said that yourself. I'm just following your instructions to the letter. You do want me to do that, don't you?'

Silence reverberated around the room.

Had the bastard gone? Please let him be gone. Perhaps he'd left for work, whatever the hell that entailed. 'Are you still listening, master?'

'So, you're trying to say that you're doing it for me?'

Damn, damn, damn! He was still there watching and listening, like a vulture hovering above the decaying corpse of the life she'd lost. What she wouldn't give for some privacy. 'It's important to look my best. All I can do is repeat myself. That's all I can say. I have to look my best.'

'I want you to lay on the bed perfectly still and not move in the slightest until I've prepared you a meal.'

'What about a shower, master?'

'You can shower after you've eaten, not before. Is that clear? I may contact my employers and tell them I've been unavoidably delayed.'

Oh, God, please no. 'Yes, master, I'll do exactly as you say.'

'Is there anything you need?'

Should she ask? Was it worth the risk? Yes, it could prove useful, a potential weapon of sorts if she ever got the chance to use it. 'I need a razor, master. For my legs, you understand. It's an essential part of my grooming routine.'

'I hope you don't plan to cut yourself, Venus? You wouldn't be the first and I feel sure you won't be the last. But, it's a far from reliable form of self-destruction.'

What did the bastard want to hear, yes or no, yes or no? Make your choice, Emma, make your choice and be done with it. 'No, master, I just want to look my best for you, as I've explained.'

He placed his mouth only inches from the microphone and yelled, louder, louder and louder, until she surmised the room itself may be trembling, 'Disobey me even once and I'll show you what cutting's all about! You'll suffer, my lovely. I'll take a shiny scalpel and cut your pretty face off, one small morsel of flesh at a time... Your nose, your ears, your lips and your cheeks, until you're a living and screaming skull.' And then quieter, in gentler tones, clearly expressing each word. 'Now lay there in silence, my lovely, until I tell you otherwise.'

Chapter 12

DI Gravel checked the wall clock above his desk, gathered his notes together at exactly 4:58 P.M. and headed in the direction of the police HQ conference room, located on the ground floor. Time keeping was important to him. Lateness wasn't an option in his professional world. He had to be on top of his game and lead by example. It was how he'd always operated and he had no intention of changing at this late stage of his career. Like it or not, this case would define it for good or bad. Here was hoping the team came up with something useful and soon. So far they had fuck all.

The loud animated chatter came to a sudden halt as Grav pushed open the door with the sole of his black leather shoe and stood at the front of the room. A long day was about to get longer.

He glanced around the room, pleased that everyone required was in attendance, but frustrated by the limited resources at his disposal. The curse of small rural forces had come back to haunt him, as it had once before when faced with an organised abuse enquiry, ultimately leading to several convictions and long prison sentences.

'Right, let's make a start. We'll get the practicalities out of the way first. We all know what we're dealing with. Five girls have died in horrible circumstances and a sixth is missing and presumed alive until proved otherwise. We need to find that particular young lady and fast if we're to have any chance of saving her life.' And then a pregnant pause to emphasise the significance of his statement. 'Room three on the second floor is currently being cleared of all the training crap and the like and will act as an operations room from tomorrow morning and for as long as this investigation continues. I'll base myself there and will fulfil the role of the senior investigating officer as per usual. I'll make the key decisions, I'll give the orders and you'll all be crystal clear what your job is from one day to the next. You all know how it works by now.'

He paused for a second time, allowing the attendees to contemplate the intense police work to come. 'And now for the bit you don't want to hear: all leave is cancelled for the foreseeable future.'

Grav waited for the discontented murmuring to slowly dissipate before saying, 'Okay, you can stop the complaints. Like I said, five young women are dead. That's five mutilated young women with their heads caved in, five young women whose lives were snuffed out by some vicious demented bastard who'll kill again and again if we don't stop the fucker. Achieving that end is now my main priority in life and the same applies to you lot. I know some of you had holidays planned. I know you were looking forward to spending some quality time with your loved ones. But, if you wanted an easy life, you shouldn't have joined the police service.'

Everyone sat in complete silence and waited for their boss to continue, as they knew he inevitably would. 'Thank you for today. You all put a lot of effort in and I know this stuff isn't easy. For some of you, it's a first murder case. Others have prior experience, but it's important to recognise that every case is different. This case is unlike anything the force has dealt with before. With that said, we will operate as a close-knit team as we always do. We'll make no assumptions, we'll investigate every angle methodically and leave no stone unturned. Predictable clichés I know, but they work. If any of you come up with anything, anything at all, I want to know about it immediately. You'll be glad to hear that all aspects of the investigation will be coordinated, monitored and evaluated by yours truly, with DS Rankin's able assistance. You talk to DS Rankin and he talks to me. If we all do our jobs, we'll achieve the right results.'

The DI masked a grin and allowed time for a well-intentioned ironic cheer to dissipate before continuing. Banter and dark humour played essential roles in relieving the inevitable pressures of the job. Within reason, they were to be encouraged. 'All right, all right, I know you're all fans of the DS. Now, let's move on. You can ask for his autograph when I'm finished.'

A young detective, newly seconded from the uniform service as part of his two-year probationary training, raised his hand in the air and awaited a response.

'Put your hand down, son, this is a police station, not a fucking classroom.'

The young constable's face reddened and he wished the floor would open up and swallow him whole. 'Sorry, sir!'

'Come on son, spit it out, we're all on the same side here. I've got a pint with my name on it.'

As the young constable shuffled uneasily in his seat, everyone laughed, glad not to be in the firing line themselves. 'I was just wondering if Emma Jones could be one of the girls found in the wood, sir. I was in primary school with her. She's a great girl. My mum and dad know her parents.'

Grav glanced around the room and silenced it without the need for words. 'I was just coming to that, son, thanks for asking; it's a fair question in the circumstances. I thought much the same thing myself. I'm still waiting on the results of the DNA test, but the dental records don't match the only body that fits with the timescale. In truth, we have no idea who the girl is at this stage, but she's not Emma. We can say that much with certainty. I've already informed the parents by phone and I'll be paying them a second visit just as soon as this meeting is over, to confirm it in person.'

A long-serving detective constable sitting at the back of the room rose to his feet. 'Just so I'm clear, sir. Are we treating Emma's disappearance and the murders of the five girls as parts of the same case?'

'Yes, we are, Mike, until proved otherwise.' And then another joke to lighten the tension. 'Have you been reading my notes? I was just coming to that.'

The constable lowered himself to his seat. 'Just asking.'

'In truth, we can't say with any certainty if Emma was taken by the same individual who brutally killed the five young women we found in Caerystwyth Wood. But, with that said, I think it's likely. There are very good reasons in this case to think that Emma was taken by the same man.

117

She meets the victim profile. That should be crystal clear to all of us. She's the right age and height and she has the same hairstyle and colour. As of now, I strongly suspect that we have a killer who originates from this area, or at least knows it well, but who hunts for his victims in other parts of the country, before dumping the bodies on our patch. Mike will be contacting all the other force areas, in Wales initially, and then further afield, to establish if they have missing persons meeting our victims' descriptions. We've already established that none of the missing persons originating from our area, Emma Jones excluded, fit the bill.'

Grav glanced in DC Rees' direction. 'Mike, I want you to make a start on that tonight and crack on with it first thing. Communicate any relevant results to DS Rankin or myself as soon as you get them, yeah?'

'Will do, sir.'

'I've asked the South Wales force to examine the CCTV records of the relevant night as a matter of priority. They've dragged their feet a bit up to this point, but today's developments will change that pronto. They won't want to come in for any criticism if and when the shit hits the fan.'

DS Rankin met Grav's eyes. 'What are the chances of identifying the car allegedly seen by Price?'

'We're only talking about cameras in the city centre at this point. Their installation was well-publicised in the Welsh papers and on the TV and radio news, so I suspect any informed perpetrator will have avoided them like the plague. You don't kill five girls and still be on the loose without knowing what you're doing. With that said, you never know

118

your luck, but I'm not holding my breath. I'd like you to pay another visit to Cardiff in the morning, Clive. Find out how things are progressing and have another chat with our Mr Price. See what you can get out of him.'

'Will do, boss.'

'Right, let's move on. Three of you, DCs Wilkins, Green and Sheridan, will be making house-to-house enquiries. I've spoken to the new uniform chief super and she's making fifteen additional uniform officers available to support us. This is now a no-expense-spared enquiry.'

Grav turned and pointed at the map on the wall behind him, marked with three large Xs in black felt pen. 'The way I see it, there are three viable access points to Caerystwyth Wood.' He tapped the map with a jumbo marker pen taken from the desktop in front of him. 'Here, on the Gwyn estate, here, in Jobe's Well Road and here, at the far side of Trinity Fields near the rugby pitches. From what I can see, the Trinity Fields option is the most likely.'

He paused again, allowing the attendees to note and digest his hypothesis. 'The killer could potentially drive through the estate, lift a body from the car, possibly in the early hours of the morning before dawn, and carry it along the path and into the wood. It's certainly possible, but I'd say the chances of being seen are high. Risking it once would be one hell of a gamble, five times almost unthinkable.'

He turned stiffly and pointed to the second X. 'Jobe's Well Road has both significant advantages and disadvantages. As you all know, it's a relatively quiet road dominated by half-empty industrial units and a few private houses. The chances of being seen would be very much lower than option one, particularly after dark, but the road is a good distance from the burial ground. The killer would have to carry the bodies up a steep slope, through thick foliage and then at least a thousand yards or more across uneven ground. Again, it's theoretically possible, assuming the killer's built like a brick shithouse, but I wouldn't bet any money on it. He'd have to be Superman to pull it off.

Trinity Fields, in contrast, would be my entry point of choice. We're talking about several sports pitches, rugby and the like, unlit after dark, with a narrow, well-maintained, single-track tarmacadam track that leads directly through the fields and to a single detached house at the very edge of the wood. I'd have thought the chances of being seen and caught out are relatively low. There's zero through traffic and the burial ground is no more than fifty yards from the road at its nearest point. In my opinion, it's got to be the most likely option.'

Rankin nodded his agreement. 'I've taken the dog up there a few times for a bit of exercise. The house belongs to an elderly woman who's been on her own since her husband died a few years back. I'm pretty sure he was a local GP. I can call on the old dear on the way to Cardiff, if that helps? You never know, she may have seen something.'

Grav smiled fleetingly without parting his lips. 'Thanks Clive, it's appreciated. The old dear's probably blind as a bat knowing our luck, but she may have seen or heard something.'

He lifted the side of a clenched fist to his mouth and coughed, clearing his phlegm-laden, tobacco-irritated throat. He really should give up the cigars again before they killed him. 'With all that said, we can't make any assumptions. That's how things are missed and in cases like this, missing things can cost lives. When we form a theory, we test it against the evidence. Understood?'

There was a chorus of, 'Yes, sir!'

'DC Wilkins, you'll be focussing on the estate along with three woodentops. DC Green, you'll be visiting Jobe's Well Road along with another two uniform officers and DC Sheridan, you'll be covering the sports fields and the surrounding area along with four able assistants. I want the three of you to talk to DS Rankin after the planning meeting for your specific orders. Let's see if we can come up with something that points us in the right direction quickly.'

'Julie, I want you to compile a list of all offenders in the force area with a history of violence and or sexual offences against women. Establish their current addresses, if they've been in and out of the nick in recent years and speak to the DVLA in Swansea to see what they're driving now and in the past five years. Clear?'

'Yes, sir? What about contacts' vehicles? He could be using someone else's car.'

'Good point, keep it in mind. The computer system should help you make the links, if those links exist.'

'Will do, sir.'

'I'm going to be in Caerystwyth Wood from first light, together with the remaining allocated uniform officers and a mountain rescue team from Snowdonia, who have a dog specially trained to sniff out bodies. We may not have found them all. There could be other victims. I plan to cover every inch of the place before we finish. I'll be back at the station from about one o'clock onwards, if you need to see me. I'm trying to sort out a press release later today, sharing what information we can, and appealing for information. We will be keeping the details of the victims' injuries on a confidential need-to-know basis. Keep your frigging mouths shut. I will personally kick you in the arse if any of you break confidence… Any questions? No, then I'll crack on. I've already spoken to the three officers who'll be manning the phones following the press release. No doubt we'll have a few nutters ringing in as per usual, wanting to confess to being Jack the Ripper and the like, but we may get something we can use. It's got to be worth a try. The right witness could break this thing wide open.'

He paused for breath and then continued with a fag packet rattle. 'Those of you who are allocated tasks in the community will no doubt be glad to hear that transport has been arranged for you lucky people at 6:30 A.M sharp. Be here by 6:15 at the latest. I do not want any delays.'

Grav chose to ignore the evening's second half-hearted ironic cheer.

'We want to know about anything suspicious: footprints, tyre marks, sightings of any unrecognised individuals, vehicles parked near to the entrance to the wood, anyone carrying anything into the wood, anyone digging in the wood, anything that could have been a body or a shovel, anyone seen with blood on their clothes, etcetera, etcetera. Understood?'

'Yes, sir!'

'You all need to be on top of your game, people. This is as high profile as it gets. The press are going to be all over it like a rash from day one. Let's make sure we dot the Is and cross the Ts. Let's nail the bastard for Emma, let's nail him for all those girls lying cold in the morgue and let's nail him before he kills someone else.'

Chapter 13

DS Rankin checked the Mondeo's rear-view mirror, signalled right, and turned into Trinity Fields just as the sun was breaking through the white marble clouds at 8:10 A.M. the next morning. He was pleased to see several other officers spread out and diligently examining the area of ground between the road and the first line of trees. He beeped the horn twice and waved his acknowledgement as he drove past and into the grounds of Hillfield House.

As he left the car, treading carefully to avoid the many muddy puddles still in situ after the night's intermittent rain, Rankin noted that the house looked more run-down than when he'd last seen it, only months before. The extensive grounds appeared windblown and bedraggled; with overgrown bushes, untrimmed hedges and a large circular, once-immaculate lawn that was slowly but surely transforming itself into a field.

Rankin surveyed the scene as he approached the once-shiny, black front door with its tarnished brass furniture. He observed that the house itself wasn't so very different to the garden, with peeling yellowed gloss paint on the fast-deteriorating wooden window frames, overflowing and overburdened metal gutters and window panes badly in need of cleaning. Maybe the old lady had passed on, or maybe she just couldn't manage the maintenance any more. That could be it. It wouldn't be surprising either way. She was getting on a bit, to say the least.

Rankin knocked and kept knocking with gradually increasing force. He could hear Radio 4 somewhere in the building. She was at least alive. He hadn't had a wasted trip. Come on lady, get a bloody move on. She had to be in there somewhere.

He strolled around the building, intending to peer through one filthy window or another and draw her attention with a tap on the glass and a smile. But, all were shielded by internal dark wooden shutters that kept out the light. He returned to the door and knocked again, harder this time to compensate for her poor hearing. Come on woman, get a bloody move on. He had places to go, things to do, people to see.

The old lady made her weary way down the long steep staircase leading from her first-floor granny flat with the aid of a hospital-issued silver metal walking stick, adjusted to her height. It took her a lot longer than it once had to negotiate each and every step, and Rankin was about to give up on his visit and walk away, when she finally unlocked and opened the door. 'Hello, dear, I thought I heard someone knocking. Can I help you?'

The DS smiled his best smile, hoping to put the old lady at her ease. 'My name's Detective Sergeant Clive Rankin from the local police. I don't know if you remember, but we had a brief chat around Christmastime when I had my golden retriever puppy with me.'

The old lady visibly relaxed, the tension seemingly melting away instantaneously. 'Ah yes, Polly, lovely dog! I had two black flat-coated retrievers myself many years ago before marrying the man who changed everything.'

Rankin nodded. 'I remember you telling me. You showed me a photograph of them playing at the beach on the Pembrokeshire coast.'

She laughed and looked suddenly younger. 'Yes, yes, I did, didn't I. It was Amroth. Good of you to remember our meeting. My memory isn't what it was, I'm afraid. Would you like to come in for a nice cup of tea, young man? I'd enjoy the company. I don't get many visitors these days.'

Young man, eh. He hadn't been called that in quite some time. He checked the stylish Omega Seamaster wristwatch, received from his wife as an overly generous fortieth-birthday gift the previous summer. 'That would be lovely.'

The old lady beamed and began to slowly ascend the stairs, holding her stick in one hand and gripping the white-painted bannister with the other. 'I'm living upstairs these days, dear. I don't use the rest of the house any more.'

'Really, why's that?'

Should she explain or not bother? He was only making polite conversation. Perhaps, she should let him get on with his day. 'Oh, you don't want to hear about all that, dear.'

Well, she had that spot on. 'No, really I'd like to know.'

So, it seemed he was interested after all. 'The main house is far too large for me, dear. My pension just isn't sufficient to keep up with the bills. Everything's so very expensive these days. Do you know that this house was less than three thousand pounds when we bought it?'

Shame they weren't that price now. 'Aren't the stairs difficult for you?'

She shouldn't have answered the door. And, why did she ask him in? What was she thinking? Why, oh why did her infrequent visitors always expect her to explain herself to the nth degree? Ageing was a natural process, not an illness. 'Oh, the exercise is good for me. I'll stiffen up completely if I don't keep moving.'

To Rankin's relief, she finally stepped onto the landing and added, 'There, I've made it! The lounge is the first door on the left. In we go, in we go. Let's make ourselves comfortable.'

She led Rankin into an adequately furnished room that much like herself had been at its best in a different long gone era. 'Take a seat, dear, and I'll make that nice cup of tea you wanted.'

Rankin pushed up his sleeve and looked at his wristwatch again, but regretted it immediately.

'Are you in a hurry, dear? I hope you're not in a rush to get on your way. I was planning to show you some more photographs.'

'Not at all, a cup of tea will be lovely, thank you.'

The old lady left the room for a time, and called out from the adjoining kitchen a few minutes later, 'Everything's on the tray, dear, come and get it. I can't manage it myself, as much as I'd like to.'

Rankin joined her in the kitchen and carried the tray of tea and biscuits into the lounge as instructed.

'That's it, dear, put it on the coffee table. You can be mother.'

He acceded to her request willingly, sipped his tea from a fine bone china cup decorated with multicoloured roses, nibbled a flavoursome Rich Tea biscuit and pointed to a silver-framed colour photograph on the stylish Art Deco sideboard. 'Is that your husband?'

The old lady nodded. 'Yes, that's George; he was a GP in the area right up to the time of his death. We were married for over forty years. I was just a slip of a girl when we first met.'

'You must miss him terribly.'

She stared at the photo, lost in the past, before suddenly looking away and refocussing on the present. 'Not really, dear, he wasn't a particularly nice man. He was cruel to me, and a terrible father. He found fault in everything my son said or did. I hate to admit it, but his death was something of a relief.'

Rankin placed his cup back on its saucer. Occasionally, just occasionally, despite all his experience in the job, people could still surprise him. This was one of those rare occasions.

He pointed to a second photograph of a boy of nine or ten years, wearing grey knee-length shorts and a sky-blue buttoned shirt with an open collar. 'Is that your son?'

She smiled, and said, 'Yes, that's my Mark, such a handsome boy.'

'Does he live locally?'

She shook her head. 'Oh, no, dear, he's an important academic in Cardiff these days, but he still visits occasionally when his busy schedule allows.'

Rankin tilted his head back and finished his tea gratefully. Surely, it was too much of a coincidence, or maybe not. Wales wasn't a big country. There were cities with larger populations all over the world. 'What does your son do?'

She broke into a smile that glowed. 'Oh, he's a science professor at Cardiff University. Such a talented boy! I'm so very proud of him.'

'Are we talking about Professor Mark Goddard?'

'Yes, that's right, dear. Don't tell me you know each other?'

'We met recently at the university.'

She smiled again, less convincingly this time. 'Oh that's marvellous, he'll be so pleased to know you called on me.'

Like it or not, he had to ask. 'This may seem like a strange question, Mrs Goddard, but what car does your son drive?'

She was puzzled by the question, but answered anyway. 'Oh, now let me think, it's one of those ridiculous two-seater things with a canvas roof you can take down in the sunshine if you're so inclined. Boys and their toys! I have absolutely no idea what make it is, I'm afraid. Why do you ask?'

'That's fine, don't worry about it, Mrs Goddard. It's really not important.'

He checked his watch again, more obviously this time. 'I need to ask you a few questions before I head off. Is that okay with you?'

She grinned mischievously. 'I hope you're not going to arrest me, young man.'

Rankin had heard the joke more times than he cared to recall, but he smiled anyway, before adopting a more serious persona suitable to the subject matter. 'We're investigating the murders of several young women. You may have seen something about it on the local news.'

She appeared surprisingly relaxed as she sat back in her seat, but Rankin noted that her hand was quivering when she picked up her cup. 'I did, dear, all those poor girls. What a terrible world we live in! Is that what those bright lights in the wood were all about? I have been wondering.'

So, she was still observant and inquisitive despite her apparent age. It had to be worth pursuing. 'Do you mind me asking how old you are, Mrs Goddard?'

'I'm eighty-nine years old, dear. Life passes so very quickly. Make the most of it whilst you can, that's my advice.'

Rankin feigned surprise less than convincingly. 'Well, you don't look a day over seventy.'

She smiled. 'If only that were true, young man. Our bodies age and invariably let us down at some point or other, but we feel the same as we always did inside. Our spirits don't age. Does that make sense to you?'

He nodded, surprised by the direction of their conversation. 'Yes, I know exactly what you mean.' Time to get back to business. He couldn't spend all morning chatting. 'This may seem like another strange question, Mrs Goddard, but do you know what an estate car is?'

The old lady frowned. 'Yes, dear, I'm old, not incompetent. I know exactly what an estate car is.'

He had to be more careful with his choice of words. 'I'm sorry, no offence was meant. I didn't mean to imply…'

'I'd stop digging if I were you, dear, the hole's getting bigger by the second. I wouldn't want you to fall in… Now, what else do you want to ask me?'

'Have you seen an estate car, or any other vehicle for that matter, driven or parked anywhere near to the wood anytime in the last five years?'

She paused before replying, seemingly considering her response carefully. 'People bring their cars to various matches, of course, but they park at the far end of the field on the concreted area near to the pitches, rather than by the wood itself. It's more convenient, so why wouldn't they?'

'I'm only interested in vehicles driven right to the wood's edge.'

She nodded her understanding and gave the matter further thought. 'Well, people like yourself do sometimes park along the edge of the wood to walk their dogs. I watch them from my bedroom window on occasions, as an alternative to getting out and about myself. And, there was that one occasion when a car came in the early hours.'

Rankin sat bolt upright in his seat. This could be interesting. 'When was this? Please try to be as specific as possible.'

The old woman looked crestfallen. 'It was in recent weeks I think, but I can't put a date on it, I'm afraid. My memory isn't what it was. The distant past tends to be a lot clearer than the present these days. I get mixed up and get a lot of things wrong. It's a price of living into old age.'

'One week, two weeks, three weeks, more?'

She looked close to tears, her lower lip trembling slightly as she searched for an answer. 'A little longer, I think. I want to help, I really do, but I can't be sure.'

Rankin silently admonished himself. Too much pressure. Far too much pressure. She was a potential witness, not a suspect, and doing the best she could, given her limitations. 'That's great, Mrs Goddard, you're being really helpful. Now, this could be important. Can you remember what time it was?'

Now, that was one she could answer with some degree of confidence. 'Sometimes, in the early hours, I sit at my bedroom window wrapped in a warming quilt and look out for wildlife: badgers, foxes and the occasional red deer.'

Here we go again. 'You can't be more specific?'

She lifted her cup to her mouth, sipped her tea and shook her head. 'Not really, dear, but it was late, I'm certain of that.'

This was going nowhere fast, but he had to persevere. 'But, you definitely saw a car?'

'I'm sorry if I'm not answering your questions to your satisfaction, dear. I'm doing my best, really I am.'

Time for some reassurance and encouragement. 'You're doing just fine, Mrs Goddard. Please continue.'

'I heard it before I saw it. My hearing is still reasonably efficient, if I've chosen to wear my hearing aid.'

Was it worth asking? Yes, why not? He had nothing to lose. 'Can you describe the car for me? Any details would be helpful.'

'Oh yes, it was a red Audi estate car… And, before you ask, I know it was an Audi because my sister Beryl had one for years. They have those attractive chrome circles on the grill. Much like the Olympic symbol, as I recall.'

Well, that seemed convincing. Was it too much to ask for? 'Did you see the driver?'

'Oh, I'm afraid not, dear. I closed the shutters and went back to bed as soon as the silly driver began revving the car's engine to free its wheels from the muddy ground. I wasn't going to spot any animals after that, I can tell you. They like a bit of peace and quiet, just like I do. Extremely inconsiderate, wouldn't you agree?'

He nodded, keen to keep her onside and continue his line of questioning. 'That's extremely helpful, Mrs Goddard; can you remember exactly where the car was located when you saw it?'

She rose stiffly from her chair and led him to a generously proportioned bedroom at the back of the house. 'Open the shutters, dear… That's it, that's it, open them nice and wide.'

She raised her arm and pointed. 'Can you see that clump of gorse bushes with the lovely yellow flowers by the path? They come into flower at the most surprising times and I love them for it. Nature never fails to surprise me, even after all these years.'

133

What a strange thing to say, but maybe she was right. You could write what he knew about flowering plants on the back of a postage stamp.

Rankin peered through the unwashed window, straining his eyes for want of a decent pair of prescription glasses. 'Yeah, I can see the bushes.'

She walked away from the window and rested herself on the edge the bed. 'The car was immediately in front of those bushes and close to the path when I went back to bed. I heard it drive off a few minutes later.'

Just a few minutes? The driver would never have had enough time to dump a body. 'Do you think it could have been longer?'

'Well, I suppose so, dear. I get lost in my thoughts and lose track of time sometimes. And I'd taken a sleeping tablet, which certainly doesn't help.'

Rankin felt his facial muscles tighten as he wondered how reliable the information could possibly be. 'But, you're sure it was an Audi?'

Hadn't she made herself perfectly clear already? 'Yes, dear, I'm certain. I couldn't be more certain. I've already mentioned Beryl's car to you. She could tell you herself, were she still alive. Now, is that all, or do you have any final questions?'

'I'm sorry if...'

'Let's not go down that particular road again, Sergeant; I'm tired and have things to get on with. Now, is there anything else I can help you with before you're on your way?'

'Do you want me to take the tray back to the kitchen for you?'

'No, just leave it where it is please. I can sort it out later in the day when I've had time to rest.'

She'd had enough. She looked close to exhaustion. 'Just one last question, Mrs Goddard. Are you happy to make a written statement?'

'Now?'

'I'm actually en route to Cardiff. Tomorrow morning would be better for me, if that's convenient for you?'

What a relief! It would at least give her time to prepare. 'What time are you likely to call? I don't sleep a great deal these days, medication or not.'

'Would nine o'clock be convenient for you?'

She picked up her walking aid and slowly approached the bedroom door. 'Oh that will be lovely, dear. I'm always up and about well before nine to feed the cat. I'll look forward to seeing you then. I'll have a nice cuppa waiting for you. Don't be late.'

Rankin called back at Caerystwyth Police Station to use the toilet and do a bit of paperwork before making his way south to Cardiff, and it was 3:10 P.M on an unusually hot and sweaty late spring afternoon by the time he pulled up outside South Wales Police HQ in Newport Road. He locked the unmarked Ford in the interests of security and strolled slowly across the large but busy car park, taking time to appreciate the pleasantly warming sun on his face.

The overly officious, young and inexperienced constable at the front desk dropped the macho act he felt obliged to present to the public and became instantly courteous the second the DS introduced himself with a quick flash of his warrant card.

'Relax, son, it may never happen… Inspector Stevenson should be expecting me.'

'Sorry Sarge, I didn't recognise you.'

Rankin smiled, recalling the pressures and stresses of his own early months in the job. 'Why would you, son? We haven't met before. Now pick up the phone and contact the inspector before I get rooted to the spot.'

When the probationary constable received a reply, his relief was almost palpable. 'Hello, Ma'am, it's PC Charles on the front desk. I've got a DS Rankin here to see you.'

'She'll be down in a minute or two, Sergeant. She said to take a seat and make yourself comfortable.'

'That's great, son, now tell me, how long have you been in the job?'

'Only six months. I was in teacher training college before that.'

Rankin nodded, feeling some sympathy for the youngster and wanting to put him at his ease. 'You didn't fancy being a teacher.'

'It just wasn't for me.'

'It will get easier, son, I promise. Just hang on in there and get your probation finished.'

PC Charles smiled nervously. 'Thanks, Sarge. I'll take your word for it.'

'You're welcome.'

Only seconds later, a strikingly attractive uniform inspector in her early forties, with an hourglass figure and auburn hair tied in a bun, opened the door and approached Rankin, who silently acknowledged that she was some distance from what he'd been expecting. Grav wouldn't believe it unless he saw her for himself: a ray of sunshine to brighten the darkest day.

She held out a hand in friendly greeting as Rankin rose to his feet. 'Good to meet you, Clive. I don't think it's going to be a wasted trip.'

That sounded hopeful, more than hopeful. 'Likewise, Ma'am, and I'm glad to hear it.'

She entered the four-digit security code and pushed open the double doors leading into a long brightly lit corridor lined with various offices on each side. 'Follow me, Clive, and you can drop the ma'am bullshit; it makes me feel about a hundred and ten.'

Rankin walked immediately behind her, attempting to focus on anything other than her shapely backside and to concentrate on the task in hand. 'So, what should I call you?'

'Pat is just fine with me.'

She stopped and opened a door with her name and rank emblazoned in black letters on its white-painted surface, about halfway along the corridor. 'Take a seat, Clive, and it wouldn't be a bad idea to stop staring at my tits, if that's all right with you.'

She left Rankin hanging for a second or two, as he stumbled for a response he couldn't find. Had he really been that obvious? Or did all women have some sort of sixth sense where men were concerned? 'What? I...'

'Just marking your card for you, Sergeant. Let's start as we mean to go on... Fancy a coffee?'

Rankin had never felt more uncomfortable in his entire life, and for the first time in his career he began to appreciate what some of the young female constables put up with on a daily basis. Maybe he should tell the lads to ease up a bit on the sexual banter. 'Nothing for me, ta, I stopped at Sainsbury's for a drink and a bite to eat on the way here.'

'Nice to hear that you're living it large. Now, what do you want to know?'

Rankin took a deep breath and gathered his thoughts, acutely aware that he was sweating profusely. It felt good to get back to business. Thank God for small mercies. 'I'm hoping you've finished going through the CCTV for the night of May the first and the early hours of the second.'

'We have, Clive. One of the team's been checking out the results for you. Do you think Emma's abduction could be linked to the bodies found on your patch? It's been all over the news.'

'That's my bet. It's one hell of a coincidence if it isn't. All the bodies were remarkably similar. The killer chooses his victims with care and forethought. Obviously I'm hoping I'm wrong, but she fits the bill perfectly.'

'Are any of the victims from our force area?'

He shook his head. 'We've only managed to identify three of the girls up to this point, all from up north.'

'DNA?'

'Yeah, the results came in this morning. Three of the victims are on the national database. They've got a long history of prostitution and drug abuse in the Manchester area. Same old story really.'

'Some things never change… So, how did they die?'

Rankin leant forwards in his chair and rested his elbows on her veneered desktop in front of him. 'All five victims had multiple fractures and other injuries to various parts of their bodies, which were inflicted before death according to the pathologist. But in short, the bastard caved their skulls in with a blunt instrument, much like the Yorkshire Ripper in the eighties.'

She blew the air from her mouth slowly and deliberately. 'Grav mentioned something about missing digits.'

Oh, so the boss knew her. He'd kept that one quiet. 'Yeah, all the fingers and toes were missing. Trophies, I'm guessing.'

'You're probably right, unless it's a form of torture.'

'Could be both.'

'There are some evil bastards out there.'

He nodded his accord. 'You won't hear me arguing. Any joy with the tapes?'

She smiled before speaking. 'This is where it gets interesting. There were only five potentially significant cars caught on tape at the relevant time: two were families travelling home from Cardiff airport after a holiday in the sun, one was a young woman who'd been visiting her sick mother in your part of the world, another one contained two local fishermen and the last car…' She paused for effect. 'You're not going to believe this. The fifth and final car was a dark blue MK2 Ford Escort estate registered to and driven by our Mr Lee Price.'

Rankin shook his head. 'What? The same Lee Price who claimed to have witnessed the potential abduction?'

She swivelled in her seat and turned on a stainless steel kettle on the floor to her left. 'I could do with a coffee. Are you going to join me?'

Rankin said, 'Yes' this time, thinking that saying no for a second time would seem a tad unfriendly. Maybe sharing a coffee would oil the conversational wheels after his disastrous start.

She added milk and sugar before stirring and handed him the mug without asking how he took it.

'That's great, ta.'

'No probs.'

He held the mug in his right hand and savoured the rising aromatic vapour filling his nostrils and igniting his taste buds. 'So, what time was he caught on film?'

The inspector smiled, showing off white cosmetically enhanced teeth that had cost a small fortune. 'At 2:26 A.M. precisely.'

'And, it was definitely him?'

'Oh, yeah, without a doubt! I've seen it for myself. I'd know the useless lump anywhere.'

'The devious git! Have you had him in yet?'

'No, I thought I'd leave that particular pleasure to you. We only completed our enquiries late last night. We had trouble getting hold of one of the drivers.'

'Laura mentioned that Price doesn't have a relevant record.'

She retrieved a half-empty packet of Penguin chocolate biscuits from her desk drawer, took one herself and offered one to Rankin.

He patted his expanding midriff and politely declined, as she unwrapped her biscuit, dipped it in her coffee twice and took a bite, leaving a residue of creamy milk chocolate on her full lips. 'No, we've known him for years, but there's nothing to suggest he'd do something like this.'

'Never say never.'

She wiped her mouth with a paper tissue. 'I'd be surprised if he's your man, but he's got some questions to answer. I'll give you that much.'

Rankin smiled. 'I think I'll have one of those biscuits after all.'

'Come on, answer the fucking door, you obstructive tosser!' Rankin banged the door again, harder this time with the side of his right fist.

Price switched off the television, swore loudly and peeped out through the half-open curtains. Shit, shit, shit! The bitch pig has sent the drug squad despite his cooperation. The shirt, the tie, the miserable face, he had pig written all over him.

He rushed from the room, sprinted upstairs and into the back bedroom, before rummaging in a drawer for a clear plastic bag packed with poor quality cocaine cut with goodness knows what. What a waste, what a terrible and shocking waste!

He opened the packet with trembling fingers and took a pinch, sniffing it urgently into his inflamed nostrils on the way to the toilet.

Price was very close to tears as he lifted the wooden lid, poured the toxic white powder into the bowl and flushed. The packaging, what the hell was he going to do with the packaging?

He opened the bathroom window, flung it out and watched as the bag floated into the unkempt back garden, as Rankin kicked the door mule style with the heel of his shoe. 'Open up Price, I can kick it in if that suits you better.'

Lee Price opened the door, bristling with contrived indignation, but his bravado melted away immediately when Rankin took a single step forward, pushed him hard on the chest with the palm of his hand and yelled, 'Police. Get in the fucking house and sit down quietly until you're told otherwise.'

Price stumbled backwards, turned awkwardly and headed for the lounge whilst thinking that he had at least got rid of the drugs. 'What the hell's this about?'

The DS loomed above him, staring with unblinking eyes until his suspect eventually lowered his gaze. 'How well do you know the three girls living opposite?'

Price held his head in his hands as the cocaine kicked in and heightened his senses, in that oh so familiar way he'd come to love above almost all else. Had he wasted the drugs? It was beginning to look that way. Oh, no! Almost a grand's worth down the fucking drain. 'I've already spoken to some female copper about all that.'

Rankin leant forwards and placed his face only inches from Price's. His pupils were the size of pinpricks. The scumbag was as high as a kite. 'And now you're going to talk to *me*, Lee. I'll ask you again. How well do you know the girls?'

'Well, I've seen them about, but that's about it. I haven't taken much notice of them, to be honest.'

Why did lying bastards like Price always feel the need to refer to their honesty? He was as transparent as polished glass. They all were. 'So, let's see if I've got this right. You, a fit and muscular red-blooded bloke, live opposite three cracking-looking young women and you haven't taken much notice of them. Is that what you're saying?'

Price shifted uneasily in his seat. 'Okay, I've looked, who wouldn't? But that's it!'

Rankin shook his head and grinned. 'So, you're trying to tell me you haven't spoken to any of them? You haven't tried to get into their knickers. Like fuck you haven't. You're going to have to do a lot better than that, son.'

'Okay, so I've tried to chat them up a couple of times, but the snooty cows aren't interested. They seriously rack me off.'

'Does that make you angry, Lee? You seem pretty angry to me.'

'Well, yeah, I was a bit pissed off about it at the time, but I didn't touch the bitch, if that's what you're wondering.'

'Are you talking about Emma, the blonde girl who's missing? Is that who you're talking about?'

Price shook his head vigorously, muscles taut, bristling with resentment. 'Look, let's get one thing straight. I haven't touched her, I haven't touched any of them. That's not my style. You can ask anyone you like, they'll tell you the same thing.'

'You claim to have seen an elderly looking man carrying something from the girls' lodgings and into an estate car you couldn't identify. Is that right?'

Claim? Claim? You helped the pigs and they still didn't believe you. Maybe he should have kept his mouth shut in the first place. 'I saw what I saw.'

'Sounds pretty unlikely to me.'

'Look, I told you what I fucking saw, what more do you want?'

'Do you drive, Lee?'

Where the hell was this going? The pig was onto something. He may be asking questions he already knew the answer to. Shit, shit, shit! 'Why are you asking?'

'Just answer the question.'

Price took a deep breath and struggled to regain his composure. 'I think I've said enough.'

'Did I hear you right? You don't want to talk to your uncle Clive any more? And, just when we were getting on so well.'

'That's what I said, you sarky bastard.'

Rankin jumped up, grabbed Price by the front of his vest and jerked him forwards. 'You've got a bit of a temper, Lee. Handy with your fists, are you? Do you like hitting girls who don't fight back?'

'No, I fucking well don't.'

Rankin released his grip and allowed Price to fall back into his seat. 'So, do you drive?'

'I'm saying nothing.'

'Look, I'm not going to piss about. You can answer my questions here or at the station.'

'I want a solicitor.'

'So, now you want a lawyer?'

'Yeah! I know my rights.'

TV detective shows had a lot to answer for. Rankin reached down, gripped Price's right wrist tightly and pulled him roughly to his feet, before pushing him face first against the wall with both hands forced high behind his back.

'Is there really a need for the fucking cuffs? You're hurting me, man. You're hurting me!'

Price struggled to free himself half-heartedly, as Rankin advised him of his rights and pushed him out of the house and towards the waiting car. 'You're under arrest on suspicion of kidnapping and murder. It might be an idea to start cooperating.'

'Murder? What the fuck are you talking about?'

Rankin unlocked the car and threw his prisoner into the backseat, before opening the driver's door and getting in himself. 'You'll be formally interviewed at Caerystwyth police station. Unless you've got something useful to say, I suggest you shut your stupid mouth until then.'

Chapter 14

The old woman sat upright in her seat and listened intently as the familiar mechanical growl of her only son's Porsche 911 Cabriolet gradually increased in volume on approaching her solitary detached Victorian house in Trinity Fields. About time, what a day to be late of all days.

She was already ready and waiting in the hall when Professor Goddard turned his key in the Yale lock and opened the door.

'What do you want, Mother? I can tell there's something. I hope you haven't been sticking your nose in where it's not wanted again. Feed the girl, that's all I said, just feed her, say nothing and get out of there as fast as possible.'

The old lady frowned, resigned to her son's invariably antagonistic nature. He was so like his father. So very like his father. 'I followed your instructions to the letter. You should be glad of that.'

He appeared less than convinced. 'And you wore the mask?'

'Yes, Mark, I wore the mask. I always wear the mask.'

'And you didn't speak to her?'

Why did he always feel the need to ask such ridiculous questions? It felt more like an interrogation than a conversation with her son. He had such an unfortunate personality. 'No, Mark, I didn't speak to her. I never speak to her. You told me not to. Why would I want to speak to her? They're usually gone within a few weeks at most. What would be the point?'

'So, what's the problem? There's obviously something. Come on, woman, tell me. I can read you like a book.'

She supported her weight on her stick and turned to start slowly ascending the staircase, one challenging step at a time. 'The police have been here.'

He felt suddenly faint and gripped the doorframe. 'The police! What? When?'

'Calm down, Mark, you'll have a heart attack like your father, at this rate. If you can't handle the pressure, don't break the law. I've told you that before, but will you listen? You can choose to take a different path if it's all too much for you.'

He followed her into her first-floor lounge, all the time clawing at his scalp with frantic fingers. 'Just tell me, Mother, just tell me what happened.'

'A Detective called here this morning. I ignored his insistent knocking initially, but he wasn't a man who was inclined to give up easily. He just kept knocking until I answered.'

Did she really have his best interests at heart? She claimed to. She always claimed to. 'You could have pretended to be out, Mother. Why didn't you just pretend to be out?'

She lifted the black cat from the floor and began gently stroking its head on her lap. 'He'd have come back. I discovered that when your father was accused of indecent assault by that ridiculous patient. They always come back.'

She was right. She appeared to have done the correct thing for once in her miserable life. 'Did you get a name?'

She smiled unconvincingly as the cat began purring loudly. If humans were as likeable as animals her world would be a better place. 'DS Rankin, DS Clive Rankin, not one of the great detectives of this world from what I could see.'

'Rankin? Really? I know the pleb. He called to see me at the university. That's bad news; he's searching for Venus.'

'Well, he didn't find her here.'

He lifted a hand to his head again and began tugging at his short neat hair. 'And, he didn't go into any of the downstairs rooms?'

This was becoming exceedingly tedious. Why ask the obvious? The men in her life had always been such a burden. She should have poisoned her errant husband long before she did. Mark was a cross to bear, who may well have turned out differently if she had. 'No, Mark, I think you'd have heard about it long before now if he had, don't you?'

He nodded and began blinking repeatedly as a bead of sweat ran down his forehead and stung his eye. 'Yes, yes, I suppose you're right... So, what did he ask you?'

Questions, questions, always questions. Maybe she should have poisoned him as well and been done with it. Life would be a great deal easier if she had. 'He wanted to know what you drive.'

Why the hell? 'And you told him?'

'Yes, Mark, I told him. It seemed best in the circumstances. He could have checked the official records anyway. What would be the point in lying?'

She had a point. 'I suppose you did the right thing.'

She frowned. 'I don't appreciate you bringing the police to my door. I had enough of that with your father thirty years ago.'

'Did Rankin look in the garage?'

She shoved the cat from her lap and yelped as it sank its sharp claws into the soft tissue of her thigh. 'If he did, he didn't tell me about it. He'll be back tomorrow morning to take a statement from me.'

His left eye began to twitch. 'But, why? About what? Why a statement from you, of all people?'

Why her? Why not her? That's what he should ask himself. 'I told him I saw a car approaching the wood some weeks ago.'

'You didn't say it was black, did you?'

Yet another ridiculous question. Why did he always underestimate her? 'I'm not an idiot, Mark. Red, I said the damned thing was red. Is that good enough for you?'

'Do you think he believed you? He didn't seem the brightest bulb in the box to me.'

She shook her head and sighed. 'I really don't know. Mark, I'm not a mind reader. Now, can we leave it there, please? I'm tired and ready for my nap. Why don't you go and play with that friend of yours whilst you still have the opportunity?'

His breathing became more laboured as he peered into the unseen distance. It was time to consider all the options. Time to think the unthinkable. 'Do you think I need to get rid of her, Mother?'

Why, oh why was he such a weak-willed and indecisive individual? And just when it mattered most. Surely he could appreciate the potential consequences of getting caught. He'd almost certainly never see the light of day again.

'What's your answer, Mother?'

She paused for a further moment or two, making him wait for her reply. 'Maybe you should and maybe you shouldn't. That's one decision you're going to have to make for yourself, young man… But, if you do decide to dispose of her, please ensure you use plenty of the plastic sheeting. Don't expect me to help clean up the sort of mess you made last time.'

'Yes, Mother, I hear you.'

'And for goodness' sake make sure you eat something. You're looking thinner by the day.'

Chapter 15

Lee Price had drifted into drug-addled intermittent sleep by
the time Rankin brought the Mondeo to a halt and parked as
close to the building's entrance as possible, in Caerystwyth
Police HQ's half-empty car park. The DS stretched
expansively with his arms high above his head on exiting the
car, banged hard on the roof three times with an open palm
and pulled his orally obstructive prisoner from the backseat.
As he walked Price towards reception, he instinctively
decided that it made absolute sense to leave the manipulative
git sweating in a cell, whilst he had a quick word with the
boss.

Grav was sitting alone at his desk in the newly equipped
operations room and glad of the excuse to finally look up
from his computer screen when Rankin pushed open the
door. The newfangled H.O.L.M.E.S system for coordinating
and linking intelligence in complex cases was useful, he had
to acknowledge that, but old-school paperwork and an
experienced local collator would still be his preferred option,
were they available and acceptable in the eyes of the top
brass. Old dogs and all that; things were changing a lot
faster than he was.

'What do you think of the new software, boss?'

The DI rubbed his tired eyes and yawned. 'Could be worse
I suppose.'

'Glad to hear it. It's the way everything's going. We've just got to get used to it.'

Grav handed his old friend two empty mugs. 'Strong, a splash of milk and plenty of sugar. You know how I like it.'

'There you go, boss. And in your favourite mug too. What a service!'

'Thanks Clive, it's appreciated as always. I'm spitting feathers here. The heating's come on for some inexplicable reason. It was bloody freezing in the winter.'

'Do you want me to fetch you a sandwich or something from the canteen?'

Grav shook his head and placed his mug on a Buckleys Best Bitter beer mat liberated from a local pub on a rowdy night out. 'No, you're all right, mate, I'm going to head off in an hour or so. How did it go in the big city?'

Rankin reached up and removed his tie before rolling it up tightly and stuffing it in a trouser pocket. 'Pretty good, all considered. Lee Price is banged up in the cells as we speak.'

The DI took off his recently acquired gold metal-rimmed reading glasses and scowled. 'Isn't he the witness? What the hell's that about?'

DS Rankin summarised the day's events succinctly in words of one syllable. There was no point in complicating matters unnecessarily.

'So, I guess I'm not going to be clocking off early after all. Perhaps a quick pint or two at the club on the way home is advisable.'

153

'I can handle the interview if you like, boss? You're looking knackered.'

'No, we'll do this one together. If he's got something to tell us, I want to hear it first-hand.'

Lee price was sweating profusely and experiencing numerous other unpleasant symptoms of acute drug withdrawal by the time Rankin led him into interview room one and sat him at the small Formica-topped table. He needed a hit more than he could express and the quicker he was out of there the happier he'd be. He should have kept his mouth well and truly shut when he had the chance.

Both Grav and Rankin sat opposite him in silence for a few seconds, increasing the psychological pressure before the DI finally took the lead. 'My name's DI Gravel; you're not going to like me very much.'

'I want a brief. I've already told your pet monkey. I'm saying fuck all until I get a solicitor.'

Grav relaxed back in his chair with his large fingers linked behind his nape and grinned. 'Have you got any particular legal genius in mind?'

If the pigs thought this was the first time he'd been banged up and questioned, they were kidding themselves big time. 'Dave Perkins, he's with Gavin and Proctor in St Mary Street.'

Grav laughed dismissively. 'Have you got this Mr Perkins on speed dial?'

'What are you talking about?'

The DI rose to his feet, walked slowly behind his prisoner and placed a firm hand on each of his shoulders. 'I'd be very careful what I wished for if I were you, Lee my boy.'

'What the fuck are you talking about?'

Grav massaged Price's shoulders as he spoke. 'You look like shit, Lee. I can see the needle marks on those popping veins of yours. I'm guessing the craving's kicking in right about now. What do you say?'

'I know my rights.'

The DI dug his thumbs into Price's shoulder muscles. 'Oh, I'm sure you do, Lee, what with your record and all. I bet you understand your rights better than I do. But, it could take me at least an hour or two to finally get hold of this solicitor of yours, then he'd have to drive here all the way from Cardiff. That'll take some time. And that's if he's available tonight at all. It could well be late tomorrow morning before we can begin the interview.'

'Tomorrow morning? You've got to be kidding me.'

Grav squeezed harder, kneading the muscles and making Price wince, before eventually releasing his grip and returning to his seat. 'Could be longer, maybe tomorrow afternoon is more likely.'

Price sat in brooding silence, contemplating his limited options. The bastards had him by the balls and they knew it full well.

'What do you say, Lee? Shall we knock this on the head until tomorrow? It doesn't bother me either way. I could do with a bit of shut-eye.'

Price was increasingly close to panic as his stomach began to twist and spasm. He badly needed to get out of there and find a dealer before things got even worse. 'What about an on-call solicitor? Just get hold of someone local for me. Someone must be available.'

Grav leant forwards, clipped Price hard to the left side of his head with an open hand and stood to leave the room. 'Throw the tosser back in the cell, Clive. We'll do this sometime tomorrow. He's wasted enough of our fucking time already.'

Price was very close to tears as his anxiety levels escalated and the tremors, shakiness and body aches began to fully kick in. The intense craving was the worst he'd ever experienced. Anything had to preferable to a night without class As of one kind or another. 'All right, all right, let's get on with it.'

'You're sure? You're declining your right to a solicitor?'

'Yes, I fucking well am!'

Grav met Price's eyes and grinned. 'Then, that's exactly what we'll do. We'll get on with it. Anything to please such an esteemed guest. Perhaps you'd like to switch the tape on, Sergeant.'

'Will do, boss.'

'It's 8:26 P.M. on Wednesday, 13 May 1998. I'm Detective Inspector Gareth Gravel. Also present are Detective Sergeant Clive Rankin and the interviewee, Mr Lee Price. I need to advise you, Mr Price, that you are still subject to caution. Anything you say could be used in evidence against you if the case comes to court at some future date. Do you understand?'

Price clutched his stomach and nodded his reluctant confirmation.

'For the tape please, Mr Price.'

He stared at Grav with beads of salty sweat forming on his brow. 'Yes, I understand. Now, can we just get this shit over with?'

Grav held his gaze. 'And can you confirm that you have been offered and refused legal representation?'

'I don't want a fucking solicitor. Is that clear enough for you, or do you want me to carve it in stone?'

'That won't be necessary, but thanks for the offer, it's appreciated.'

'Look, I want to help. I'm willing to help. Can we just get this done?'

Grav pushed up his sleeve and checked his Casio. 'Okay, let's make a start.'

For the next twenty-five minutes Price reluctantly repeated the same outline of events he'd previously told both PC Williams and the DS.

Rankin looked at him and shook his head. 'That's very helpful as far as it goes, Mr Price. We've established what you claim you saw, we've established that you can't identify the make or colour of the car with any certainty, but what we haven't established is what you were doing in Cardiff City centre when you said you were tucked up in bed with a young lady you've failed to name. You've been lying to us,

Lee. You're hiding something and I've got a good idea what it is.'

Price rested his forearms on the table and banged his head against its surface three times. 'So that's why I'm here. It was those fucking cameras, wasn't it?'

Rankin reached across the table and shook him. 'Do you need to take a break, Lee? We can continue this interview sometime tomorrow, if you're having trouble concentrating. Maybe you'll recall events more accurately when you've had some kip.'

Price lifted his head. If he didn't tell the whole truth he'd never get out of there. 'I was buying drugs. Okay, I've fucking well said it. I shagged the tart, left her asleep in the house and drove into town to buy fucking drugs. Everything else I told you was true. Every single word of it.'

Grav shook his head incredulously. 'And you can prove that?'

'I don't want to give names, but I will if it's my only way to get out of here before morning.'

'Let me get this right. You're telling us you can give us the names of a witness or witnesses who will confirm you were in Cardiff and buying drugs on the night Emma Jones went missing, correct?'

'Yeah, I can give you two names if needs must. But, only on the condition you don't tell them where you got the information. I'd get a serious kicking if they thought I'd grassed them up. They're not nice people.'

'And just when I thought I couldn't like you any less.'

'Look, I've told you the truth. What more can I do?'

Grav raised a hand to his face and rubbed his brow. 'Switch the tape off, Clive. This is going nowhere.'

'Will do, boss.'

The DI returned his attention to his prisoner, who attempted to avoid his eyes for fear of what was to come. 'Do you know what you've done, you moronic muscle-bound twat?'

Price closed his eyes against the world and resisted the impulse to weep, as the pressure of the interview combined with his ever-escalating need for a chemical hit became too much for him. 'I just didn't want to get nicked. That's all it was. I told you what I saw and I thought you'd leave it there. I thought you'd just track down the old bloke, find out what happened to the girl and that would be that. Do you want the names, or what?'

Grav leant across the table, gripped the front of Price's vest with both hands as Rankin had only hours earlier and shook him violently until he opened his eyes. 'Oh, you did, did you, you fucking idiot? You just thought you'd feed us a crock of shit and hope for the best. This is a murder investigation, you selfish prat. Five girls are dead at the hands of some maniac who's still on the loose, another's still missing fuck knows where, and I'm sitting on my fat arse wasting my valuable time talking to the likes of you! There's some nutter out there who likes smashing girls' heads in with a blunt instrument and you've wasted our time because you were buying fucking drugs!'

'I'm sorry, I didn't think it mattered.'

The DI raised his right fist, but held himself back. 'I'd like to stick this right down your throat.'

Price was shaking uncontrollably now. As much from drug withdrawal as the fear of it all. He was looking at a charge if he wasn't careful, maybe even a hiding. He could be in there for hours. Wasting police time was never a good idea at the best of times. He had to come up with something to calm the pig down, and fast. 'I'm sorry, I didn't think, I'm really sorry. I don't know what else I can say.'

'You didn't think! You're sorry! Is that the best you've got?'

It was now or never. 'There is one thing I haven't told you.'

Grav released him and fell back in his own seat, panting hard. This had better be good. 'Let's hear it.'

'If I tell you, you'll let me go, right?'

'If you've got something worthwhile to say, now would be a good time to share it.'

'But, I'll be free to go, yeah?'

'I'm fast losing patience, Price. You are seriously pissing me off at this precise moment in time.'

It had to be worth a try. What was there to lose? 'There was something about the old guy I saw that night. You know, the one leaving the three students' place.'

'So, what about him?'

'He was moving too easily, standing too straight, carrying whatever it was with too little effort. This is probably going to sound stupid to you, but the more I think about it now, he may be younger than he looked. You know, like a young guy pretending to be an old bloke to avoid being recognised. It makes sense when you think about it. I don't know why I haven't tried it myself.'

The two officers stared at each other as reality dawned. The abductor was wearing a disguise. Emma had seen him. He'd talked to her: that stooping and seemingly aged individual she'd mimicked so effectively for her two friends' amusement. She'd seen him in Cardiff and she'd seen him in Caerystwyth. He'd been watching her for weeks or even months prior to taking her. He'd watched and he'd waited and planned every cautious move, like a leopard stalking its prey before finally pouncing. The devious bastard could be anyone: almost any age, almost any description. He was male, white, of slim build and of average height. That's all they had. There were many thousands of men meeting that description in every city in the UK. The investigation had stalled again.

Grav said what they were both thinking, 'And you didn't think to say any of this stuff before now? You didn't think it would help? You didn't think it could be important to our investigation?'

'I didn't think you'd want to hear it. It's a theory, just a theory.'

The DI shook his head and chose to ignore the pleading expression on Price's anaemic face. 'That's it for now, Clive, I'll see you in the morning. I've had enough of this tosser for one lifetime.'

Rankin pushed back his chair, rose to his feet and took Price's arm with a steely grip. 'I'm taking a statement from

Mrs Goddard first thing, boss, so I'll see you at about ten if that's all right with you?'

Grav looked back on exiting the room. 'Yeah, no probs, get the on-call doctor to take a look at that idiot before setting him loose. He looks ready to keel over and die on us. I could do without the paperwork.'

'Are we going to charge him, boss?'

'Na, what the hell's the point? Give him a second-class train ticket back to Cardiff once the doc gives you the all-clear, point him in the direction of the station and tell him to piss off home. Let the South Wales force worry about him. He's wasted more than enough of our time already.'

Chapter 16

Rankin was beginning to question the wisdom of taking a statement from Mrs Goddard at all as he slowly approached Hillfield House. Perhaps the old woman was more mixed up than she'd seemed on first meeting. Maybe she'd seen a red Audi sometime in the distant past, rather than recently as she claimed. Or maybe she'd seen it in a different place entirely. She'd said herself that the past was much clearer in her mind than the present. She wasn't exactly the most reliable witness he'd ever come across. Nothing she said would ever stand up in court, true or not. Any remotely competent barrister would tear her evidence to shreds. And now that he thought about it, the old lady could well be suffering from Alzheimer's disease like his poor old maternal gran. What a tragedy that was; she couldn't even remember her own name by the end. What if his witness was gradually going the same way? It was a distinct possibility.

He paused on getting out of the Mondeo and approached the house, deciding to take a quick stroll around the overgrown grounds on the off chance of finding something the search officers had missed. He wasn't particularly hopeful, far from it in fact. They'd done an admirably comprehensive job of things from what he'd seen, but it would at least give him more time to consider if taking a statement from the old dear was really such a good idea after all. On the one hand, there was a serious danger of misleading the investigation with false or inaccurate information, and on the other, of ignoring potentially crucial evidence, however elderly and seemingly unreliable the source. Why was police work never easy? Like it or not, he'd have to use his judgement and make a decision one way or the other. That's what he was paid for, after all.

As he walked around the neglected building, Rankin came across an old concrete block-built double garage with blistered sky-blue-painted wooden doors at the back of the house and decided to take a quick look inside for no particular reason he bothered to quantify. Sometimes the instincts born of experience outshone reasoned argument and forethought and he'd often acted on them with good results in the past. He'd once opened a cupboard door when investigating the assault of a seven-year-old local boy and found a four-week-old baby sibling's body wrapped in a large purple bath towel. It was an experience he'd never forget, however much he wanted to. Such was life for a country policeman.

The DS tried the garage's side door, which had the distinct advantage of being well out of sight of the house, but to his frustration he found it locked. It was the main doors or nothing. Why not give them a try? It was either that or walk away.

At first he thought that the ageing wooden double doors at the front of the ramshackle structure were locked, but after a good deal of prising, with the aid of a stainless steel multitool knife he invariably kept in his pocket for just such a purpose, one of the two doors eventually opened an inch or two. He placed the fingers of one hand through the resulting gap and pulled with gradually increasing force, using all of his fourteen-plus-stone frame to lever the door open sufficiently to enter the dark cobweb-furnished space.

Rankin stood just inside the doors and blinked repeatedly as his eyes slowly adjusted to the dim interior. He walked forwards and scanned the room with keen eyes, quickly identifying various rusting, half-full tins of Dulux paint, an extending ladder, a hosepipe, a large single roll of clear plastic sheeting and numerous items of seemingly redundant gardening equipment and machinery. There was also what appeared to be a large vehicle, parked at an approximate forty-five-degree angle and covered in a heavy-duty, oil-stained and dusty, unbleached canvas tarpaulin.

Rankin approached the vehicle quizzically, took the driver's side edge of the heavy tarpaulin in both hands and gradually pulled it aside, revealing the front grill and number plate of a large and impressive black 1971 Mercedes-Benz 230 Automatic estate car. He made a note of the car's index number, manoeuvred his way to the side of the vehicle and used the fingers of his right hand to wipe the dirt from a small area of the front driver's side window. Why didn't the old dear mention the car?… But then, why would she? It didn't look as if it had been driven for years.

He bent at the waist and peered into the car's leather interior, straining to see with the aid of the limited sunlight entering via the half-open door. A torch, if only he had a torch. Maybe it would be worth heading back to the Mondeo to fetch his from the boot.

He tried the driver's door and found it locked, as was the rear driver's side door. He peered into the car again, contemplating if it were worth the effort to continue, but ultimately decided to try the passenger side. Hang on, wasn't that a newspaper on the rear seat? No doubt, that could tell him something. He pushed back the tarpaulin still further, and dusted off his hands before trying the passenger's side rear door, which to his surprise opened at the first attempt. Unsurprisingly, the interior of the car was significantly cleaner than the exterior and Rankin was more than happy to slide into the generously proportioned cabin. He swivelled in his seat, reached over to retrieve the paper and held it up in front of him at close distance to accommodate his eyesight: The Daily Mail, 14th November 1973, an IRA gang had been convicted of the London bombings. What the hell did violence ever achieve?

Rankin put the paper back where he'd found it, leant forwards between the front seats and opened the empty glove box. He'd seen enough. There was nothing of significance, nothing worthwhile to find. It looked as if the car had been idle for years. He'd run a PNC check to confirm it, of course, when safely back in the Mondeo, but the car appeared to be of zero interest to anyone other than a classic collector or scrapyard. It was a relic of the past, much like its owner. It was time to leave the garage as he'd found it and get on with his day.

The old lady opened the front door on the first knock, and tapped her watch in silent admonishment.

Rankin had expected a wait and was taken aback by her sudden and immediate appearance. 'Sorry I'm late, Mrs Goddard. I was having a quick look at the Mercedes. I hope that's okay with you.'

She remained facing him as she had on his previous visit, but this time she didn't invite him in. 'Oh, you were, were you, young man? And you didn't think of asking permission first? My husband wouldn't like it. He wouldn't like it at all.'

What on earth could he say to that? The man was dead. He was beginning to regret visiting. 'Do you remember that I said I was calling here this morning to take a statement from you, Mrs Goddard?'

The old lady lifted her stick in the air and shook it above her head. 'Of course I remember. Don't start that nonsense again! Why do you think I was waiting for you in the hallway?'

Would he never learn? Time for yet another apology. 'I haven't made a very good impression so far, have I?'

She smiled as her mood softened. 'Not really, dear, why don't you come in and start again? I think that's best. I can forgive most things, what with everything I've experienced over the years. People come with their flaws and idiosyncrasies. It's a reality we all have to accept if we're going to get along. We're all God's creatures.'

Rankin followed her to the top of the stairs for a second time and noted that she appeared to be moving a little easier than on his previous visit. 'You seem a lot stronger today, Mrs Goddard, if you don't mind me saying.'

She turned her head towards him and smiled. 'I get good days and bad days, and today's one of the good ones.'

'Glad to hear it. Shall I take a seat in the lounge?'

'Fetch the tray from the kitchen, dear. I've baked some rather nice cupcakes especially for you. My treat. They're all waiting on the worktop next to the kettle. You know where it is by now.'

How could he say no to that? What a thoughtful lady! 'Tea or coffee?'

She opened the lounge door, lowered herself into her favourite armchair and called out loudly, clearly expressing each word, 'Why don't you make a nice pot of tea for us both, dear? There's a teapot and a strainer in the cupboard to the right of the cooker. I can't abide those awful modern teabags. The tea just doesn't taste the same. Why is everyone in such a hurry these days?'

Rankin dropped a tablespoonful of loose and aromatic Indian tea leaves into the pot and added boiling water from the kettle. 'Nearly done!'

'Now don't you go rushing things, dear. Treat the tea with the respect it deserves. It'll taste all the better for it.'

The DS joined the old lady in the lounge, placed the tray of refreshments on the coffee table as instructed and took a neatly folded West Wales Police statement form from his pocket, having decided to abandon the briefcase.

'There you are, dear. You can add your own milk and sugar.'

He accepted the cup and saucer. 'Thanks, it's appreciated.'

'You're very welcome, dear, and if you were wondering, the car was my husband's.'

'Sorry?'

'The Mercedes, it belonged to my husband. It hasn't been driven since his death.'

Rankin's face reddened. 'I really should have asked before looking at it, I can only apologise.'

She leant forwards and tapped his knee gently with her stick. 'Well, let's forget about that for now and get stuck in. It hardly matters and those cakes aren't going to eat themselves now, are they?'

Rankin poured the tea and helped himself to a cupcake covered in sweet white icing. 'Are you still happy to make a brief statement to the effect that you saw the Audi?'

She smiled warmly. 'I certainly am, dear. Now finish your cake, I've got some very good news for you. You may be catching that killer you're looking for a lot sooner than you anticipated.'

The DS devoured the entire cake in two bites. Where was this going? 'That was delicious, Mrs Goddard.'

'Glad to hear it, dear, now do you want me to complete that statement right away, or shall I tell you my good news first?'

This was probably going to be a complete waste of time. Best to get it over with. 'What have you got to tell me?'

She sat forward again, appearing more animated this time. 'I spoke to my Mark after seeing you yesterday. I told him all about your visit and he thinks he can help.'

Okay, so maybe it wasn't a waste of time after all. 'Help in what way?'

'He's sure he saw the same red Audi as I did. He said as much only last night on the phone.'

All of a sudden Rankin's interest was genuinely piqued. There was no longer any need to feign curiosity. Maybe he really was onto something this time. 'When was this?'

She looked flustered, lost in her thoughts. 'Oh dear, I wrote it down somewhere… Now, let me think… Ah, yes, yes, that's it, on the piece of paper by the telephone. Why don't you fetch it for me, dear? It's on the small table over there under the windowsill.'

Rankin masked his excitement as best he could as he crossed the room and picked it up. 'This one?'

'Yes, that's it, dear, bring it to me and all will become clear.'

He handed it to her as requested rather than give in to the inclination to examine it, and returned to his seat, waiting for her to speak with bated breath.

She looked at it, looked away, and then looked at it for a second and final time. 'Yes, that's it, dear, it was on Christmas Eve just gone. I wrote it down here in shorthand. Mark was visiting me from Cardiff with a gift, when he heard a car just outside the house. He thought it may be unexpected visitors, or someone who'd lost their way possibly, and so he went outside to investigate.' She took a sip of tea, placed her cup back on its saucer and continued, 'The driver drove off at speed when he saw him. Mark thought it was rather strange at the time.'

'And he thinks it was the same car you saw parked near to the wood?'

170

'Well, it was a red Audi, he seemed certain of that much.'

This was getting more interesting by the second. 'Did your son tell you anything about the driver?'

She nodded, pleased as Punch to be able to answer in the affirmative. 'Oh yes, dear! It was a beautiful, bright, moonlit winter night and the car passed within a few feet of him as it rushed off in the direction of the road.'

'And the driver? Can you describe him for me?'

'Oh, yes, dear, Mark was quite unequivocal on the matter. That's the sort of man he is. I'm so very proud of him.'

Come on, spit it out woman, for Pete's sake, spit it out. 'So, what exactly did he say?'

'Hold your horses, young man, give me a chance to check my notes… Ah yes, that's it. He described an elderly gentleman with long grey hair and an unkempt beard. Mark thought he looked as if he was at least in his late seventies, or possibly more.' She laughed. 'Not that you'd think seventy is old when you get to my age.'

Rankin's heart rate increased on hearing the familiar description. It was the same man, surely it had to be the same man. 'That really is extremely helpful, Mrs Goddard, but I'd like to hear it from your son face to face as soon as possible. Can you give me his home address please? I'd like to call on him this evening.'

Think, Margaret, think, she'd walked straight into that one. How would Mark explain that he didn't own a property in Cardiff after all? She took another cake from the plate and took a generous bite, with the intention of buying time.

'Give me a m-minute, dear, I think I c-can save you a trip.

Why don't you have another cake w-whilst you're waiting? You enjoyed the last one.'

Come on, lady, get on with it. Swallow the damn thing. 'Oh, one's enough for me, thanks. I've got to watch my weight, or so my wife tells me.'

She feigned disappointment surprisingly effectively for an amateur actress, frowning and focussing on the floor despondently before looking up and smiling a plastic smile in response to Rankin's throw-away humour. 'Oh, don't you like them, dear? I have to admit I don't cook as well as I once did. My husband told me that more times than I care to remember before he died.'

Was she really that emotionally fragile? God only knew what she'd been through at the hands of that man. 'Not at all, they're delicious. You've talked me into it.'

She ate up the last of her cake, washed it down with a slurp of tea and smiled again, more spontaneously this time. 'You'll no doubt be glad to hear that Mark is attending a meeting in Caerystwyth College this very afternoon. He said he'd call in to say hello before heading home. I can ask him to visit you at the police station, if that helps?'

Rankin put down his cup and placed the creased statement form on the coffee table before holding it still with one hand and smoothing it out with the palm of the other. 'That would be marvellous. I could do without another trip to Cardiff, to be honest. What sort of time is he free?'

'Well, he told me that his meeting finished at about four o'clock, so I think any time after that would be just fine for him. I know he's keen to offer you any assistance he can.

He's been worried sick about that poor girl from the university who went missing. Emma, wasn't that her name?'

Rankin nodded. 'Any time after four is good with me. Tell him to ask for me at the front desk. Perhaps he could give me a ring if the time goes on a bit.' He took a business card from his pocket and handed it to her with an outstretched hand. 'My direct number is on the back. And don't hesitate to use it yourself if you need to get hold of me for any reason at all.'

'Oh, thank you, dear, I'll keep it safe with the one you gave me last time. I'm certain he won't keep you waiting unnecessarily. Mark's an extremely courteous and considerate young man. I'm so very proud of him, as I may have told you before.'

'He's a credit to you.'

If only it were true. Maybe in another life, in a parallel universe, he was the perfect son. But instead, he was her cross to bear for however long she lived. 'Thank you, dear. You're only too kind.'

'I really appreciate your help, Mrs Goddard. The information you've provided could prove extremely useful.'

She smiled contentedly. He was falling for every deceptive word she chose to utter. 'I'm always happy to help if I can, dear.' She wiped a tear from her eye with a Kleenex tissue taken from the inner sleeve of her primrose-yellow hand-knitted cardigan. 'I really can't imagine what all those poor girls went through… It just doesn't bear consideration. It makes my stomach curdle just thinking about it. If heaven can be a place on earth, then so can hell.'

173

She had that particular assessment spot on. He pictured the bodies lying in the cold dark earth and frowned. What a place to end your life and what a way to die. 'He's one sick individual. There's no doubting that.'

'Mark stays at his Cardiff home in normal circumstances, but he's very kindly offered to stay here as often as he can until the maniac's caught and locked up for good. He's such a thoughtful boy. I don't feel safe in my own home these days when I'm alone. Do you think you'll catch him soon, dear?'

Rankin sighed. 'Let's hope so.'

Calls himself a police officer. He couldn't find his backside with both hands. Hopefully the local force wouldn't seek more experienced help from elsewhere. 'You've got to catch him, Sergeant, before he kills again. Because he will, you know, these people always do.'

She had that right. But some things were easier said than done. 'Let's get a brief statement down on paper, Mrs Goddard, and I'll leave you in peace.'

Eighty-nine-year-old Mrs Margaret Goddard held the phone to her ear and listened without reply. Five minutes passed, then ten, and she still held on, waiting and worrying, with her stress levels reaching potentially dangerous heights for the second time that day.

'Hello, Professor Goddard's office.'

The old lady issued a deep sigh of relief. Finally, and not before time! But, at least it wasn't too late to act on her concerns. 'Can I speak to the professor please?'

Professor Goddard's diligent and dedicated admin support officer checked the wall clock, followed by the handwritten lecture schedule pasted on the back of the office door. 'He's in the middle of a lecture at the moment. Can I take a message?'

The old lady tightened her grip on the phone. 'Is that you Jacqueline?'

'Yes, speaking.'

'It's Mrs Goddard, Mark's mother. I need to speak to him, please.'

'Oh, hello, long time no see, I thought I recognised your voice.'

What on earth was the silly mare talking about? They'd never met. Perhaps she should encourage Mark to add her name to his list and put her out of her misery. 'Just fetch him please, it's urgent.'

'You sound a little out of breath, Mrs Goddard. Are you sure you're okay?'

'Just get him, dear, I've said it's urgent. I don't know what else I can do to make it any clearer for you. Perhaps if I screamed into the receiver loudly enough, you'd understand the importance and get on with it.'

She swore silently under her breath. The apple hadn't fallen far from the tree in that particular case. So that's where he'd got it from. 'Message received loud and clear, Mrs Goddard. I'll ask him to ring you back as soon as possible.'

Oh, not again! 'Now, dear, I'll hold on until you fetch him.'

Mark Goddard made his apologies to the attending students, left his lecture prematurely and rushed down the long corridor towards his office, filled to the brim with indignation and resentment.

'Hello, Mother, what is it?'

The old lady closed her eyes briefly and then opened them slowly, focussing on nothing in particular. Thank goodness for that. It was good to hear the silly boy's voice. 'I need you to listen to me very carefully, Mark. This is important. It couldn't be more important.'

It had better be. 'Give me a second, Mother. I'll close the door.'

'Right, Mother, what's this about?'

'Detective Sergeant Rankin left the house about twenty minutes ago. He was snooping around in the garage before interviewing me and taking a statement.'

176

The professor felt as if his heart were pounding in his throat, louder, louder and louder. He'd avoided even the slightest hint of police attention for years. Why, oh why was that changing now? He felt inclined to tear at his face and hair in a destructive frenzy, but instead he calmed himself and focussed on the task at hand.

'Are you still listening, Mark?'

'Of course I am. What the hell else would I be doing? Do you think he's onto something?'

She snorted indignantly. 'The man's an incompetent fool, but even a man of his limited ability is bound to catch on in the end if given sufficient opportunity. A demented chimpanzee with half a brain could manage as much.'

The professor closed his eyes tight shut and frowned. She was good in a crisis. He had to acknowledge that and take full advantage. 'So, what are you suggesting?'

'I paid your guest a brief visit after Sergeant Rankin's departure. I can only assume that you've decided to keep her despite my concerns?'

He paused for a second or two before responding, considering his limited options. 'I really think she may be the one I've been searching for. I'm not ready to give her up just yet.'

She shook her head, resigned to his determined and stubborn nature. He'd always been such a naughty boy. 'I feared you might say that. Is there nothing I can say to persuade you otherwise? She's not the only young blue-eyed blonde in this world of ours. You could always dispose of her now and find another suitable candidate when the police finally lose interest.'

He rose to his feet and pounded the wall violently with the clenched side of his free hand. 'No, no, no, it's totally out of the question.'

She lifted her walking stick high above her head and brought it down with as much force as her aged body could muster, smashing an inherited pink Dalton vase to pieces. He always was such a stubborn boy. Infuriating, absolutely infuriating! 'Well, have you thought of moving her? That may be worth considering.'

'Move her where, Mother? Can you answer me that? Where the hell should I take her?'

This was getting more exasperating by the second. He was so like his father. 'Well, will you at least agree to get rid of that damned car before the police examine it properly? Surely, that's not too much to ask?'

Pressure, pressure, too much pressure. Why didn't she hurry up and die? 'Oh, I don't know, Mother. It's been an extremely useful resource over the years. A body fits in the back perfectly and the Porsche would be useless for the purpose.' He laughed hysterically as he pictured the scene. 'I'd have to prop them up in the front seat and let them flop about as I drove. Can you imagine the mess?'

'Then for goodness' sake, buy something more suitable before it's too late. You're earning reasonably good money at that university. I sometimes wonder if you're as tight-fisted as that mean-spirited father of yours.'

He resisted the impulse to scream a stream of heartfelt insults. Why did she always insist on bringing that damned man's name into the conversation? 'I guess I could consider it.'

She really should have slapped him more as a child. 'Think, boy, think! What if Rankin had brought the car out into the daylight? What if he'd examined it more carefully and found signs of blood? What if I hadn't managed to convince him that it hadn't been driven for years? Where would you and your plans for the future be then?'

'But, he didn't, did he.'

'Now listen to me, and think clearly this time. All it would take would be for some nosey do-gooder to inform the police they'd seen a black Mercedes driven up to the house. Picture it, Mark, and consider the implications. The police would be here long before you could dispose of the girl. And if you think I've got the physical strength to drag her into the wood, you're very sadly mistaken.'

Why did she always feel the need to overdramatise absolutely everything? 'I always use the false plates.'

'Oh come on, Mark, it's just not enough if you want to remain free to indulge your interests. We've got to get rid of it. We've got to get rid of it today! I've been looking through the yellow pages and there's a scrapyard in Llanelli who'll collect vehicles for breaking. They'll even pay you a small remittance that you can put towards your new car, when you finally get around to it.'

Maybe she was right. Maybe she had a point. 'You really think it's for the best? The Mercedes holds very fond memories.'

'I do, Mark. You need to forget the past and focus on the future. I've already spoken to the owner, a Mr Fisher. He'll be picking the car up this afternoon. I've told him that there are no papers and that I'm only interested in cash. He promised to remove the number plates, leave them on the garage floor and crush the car within a maximum twenty-four hours of collecting it, with no questions asked.'

Oh well, it could be for the best. 'So it's a done deal?'

My God, he'd finally got it. 'Yes, Mark, that's exactly what it is. At least one of us has to be decisive. Start looking for a suitable vehicle this weekend. A nice family car, something that doesn't stand out from the crowd. Do I have your assurances?'

'You do, Mother.'

'Well, make sure you follow through with your plans. This is a time for action.'

He bit the inside of his lower lip hard and tasted blood. 'Are we done, Mother? I have work to do. My lectures aren't going to present themselves.'

The exasperating ingrate, and after all her efforts! 'There's one more thing before you go.'

Oh, what now? As if his day wasn't burdensome enough already. 'I'm waiting.'

'It's essential that you see Detective Sergeant Rankin at Caerystwyth Police Station this afternoon as near to four o'clock as possible.'

Oh, for God's sake, what the hell was that about? 'Why? Why? Why? I was planning to spend some time with Venus as soon as I arrive back from work.'

Why did the foolish boy insist on giving them all the same name? A little imagination wouldn't go amiss, for goodness' sake. 'Your social life is going to have to wait, young man. Sergeant Rankin planned to visit you at your non-existent home in Cardiff this evening. Where would that have got you? Things are in serious danger of unravelling if you're not extremely careful. I told him that you were attending a meeting at Caerystwyth College. You'll stick to the same story, I assume, if you know what's good for you. I've dug you out of enough self-inflicted holes for one lifetime.'

Be patient, Mark, be patient. She wouldn't be around forever. 'Why does he want to see me?'

'He was getting too close. Sending him off on a wild goose chase seemed the wisest option. I told him you'd seen the same car as I described and driven by an elderly gentleman matching your usual disguise of choice.'

Clever, he had to acknowledge it was clever. The woman had her uses as he'd observed previously. 'Very well done, Mother, that's fast thinking, even for you. When exactly did I see it?'

At last, some credit where credit's due. He'd always been such an ungrateful boy. 'You heard the car approaching the house on Christmas Eve. I told him that it was dark but moonlit and that I couldn't recall the precise time.'

Okay, there was some sense in that. 'So, how did I see the driver?'

181

'You left the house on hearing the vehicle.'

'Fair enough, that seems plausible.'

My God, he'd actually got it. 'So you're clear on what's required?'

'Yes, thank you, Mother. I'll say what needs to be said. You can be sure of that… Now, to more important matters. Please ensure you don't feed Venus today. Not a morsel, not a crumb, I want her hungry when I'm finally finished with Rankin. I have some entertainment in mind.'

She shook her head and smiled. Boys and their toys! Did they ever grow up?

Chapter 18

Rankin welcomed Professor Goddard with a firm handshake and guided him towards interview room three at 4:03 P.M. exactly. 'Good of you to come in so promptly, Professor. It's good to see you again. Can I get you a tea or coffee before we make a start?'

Should he say yes? Would it make any difference? No, it was of little, if any, consequence. He was overthinking things again, which was never a good idea. 'Not for me, Sergeant, I don't want to leave Mother alone for any longer than is absolutely necessary.'

'Take a seat, Professor, and we'll get this done as quickly as possible.'

Professor Goddard sat opposite Rankin and repeatedly clenched and relaxed his fists under the table. 'Mother mentioned that you wanted to speak to me regarding the vehicle I saw near to her home.'

Rankin took a statement form from a drawer and nodded twice. 'Yeah, that's right. Your mum's one impressive lady for her age.'

That was one word for her. 'Perhaps we could expedite matters, Sergeant. I really would like to be on my way as soon as feasibly possible.'

Rankin tapped the point of his pen on the tabletop three times. 'Fair enough, Professor, I'll get to the point. Tell me about the car.'

Professor Goddard leant his elbows on the tabletop in front of him and looked Rankin in the eye, before repeating the fictitious outline of events detailed by his mother only hours earlier.

'And you're sure it was an Audi?'

'That's what I said, Sergeant. Perhaps you'd like to write it down on that statement form of yours and let me get out of here before Mother's murdered in her own home.'

Why the impatience? Why the sarcasm? He wasn't the only one with a frigging home to go to. 'I need to be certain of the facts before committing them to paper. This could serve as evidence at some future date. It has to be right.'

'Well, get on with it, man. Is there anything else you want to ask me before you make a start?'

'Was the car definitely red?'

He paused for a second or two before responding, as if carefully considering his response. Maybe it didn't serve his purpose to be too specific. 'I feel fairly confident in saying it may have been red, but you have to remember that it was dark.'

He sounded less than certain. 'Your mother seemed sure enough.'

He smiled dismissively and shook his head slowly. 'Her eyesight isn't what it once was, Sergeant. It's important to remember that. And then there's her memory, of course. She sometimes confuses the present with the distant past. It's happening with increasing frequency, regrettably. I fear she may well be showing signs of some form of dementia. You certainly couldn't rely on her observations. Her sister had a red Audi approximately fifteen years ago. Mother's recollections may well be influenced by that fact.'

Shit, shit, shit! Rankin felt his facial muscles tighten and masked his disappointment as best he could. They may have seen the same car on different dates, or maybe not. 'Okay, so let's focus on the car you saw. It could have been a different colour. Is that what you're saying?'

The professor stifled a laugh before it had the opportunity to materialise. The man was in total free fall. He was back in control and pulling the strings. 'I hate to disappoint you, Sergeant, but I have to acknowledge that it's a very significant possibility. The last thing I'd want to do is to potentially provide you with inaccurate information.'

'Can you put a figure on it for me?'

The professor tilted his head quizzically and paused for a moment or two, as if considering his response carefully. 'I'd say there's a sixty to seventy per cent certainty, but possibly less than that. I'm sorry, I really am, but I can't be any more sure than that.'

Oh, bollocks, that was next to useless. But, why the uncertainty? Why the doubt? 'I don't get it. The car passed near to you, you've both said it was a moonlit night and the houselights must have illuminated the area to some degree. How come you're only sixty to seventy per cent sure? It doesn't make a lot of sense.'

Think man, think, this had to be convincing this time. The pleb was suspicious, he was definitely suspicious. 'My colour vision is somewhat defective, I'm afraid. Most regrettably, I have very real problems differentiating

185

between certain colours with complete confidence in daylight, let alone in comparative darkness. It's something I've had to get used to from an early age. I appreciate that it's not what you want to hear given the potential significance of my information, but that's the way it is. I can only apologise. I only wish I could be of more help.'

Rankin recalled his own test for colour blindness on joining the force. All those dots, all those numbers. 'Is it something you've been tested for? You've had a diagnosis?'

'Yes, as a child initially, although it was confirmed some years ago at my request. There's absolutely no doubt in the matter.'

'So, if not red, what colour? Is that something you can tell me?'

The professor adopted a thoughtful expression and waited a second or two before answering, 'Green, or possibly blue. Yes, I think that's fair to say.'

'So, just to be clear, you're now saying that the Audi you saw could have been red, green or blue?'

He nodded his accord and smiled thinly. 'That's exactly what I'm saying. As I said, I only wish I could be more helpful.'

'Look, I want you to think very carefully before answering my next question, because this matters... Can you tell me if any of the three colours is more likely than the others?'

'I'm afraid not. I only wish I could.'

Rankin bit the inside of his lower lip hard. 'And you're sure of that?'

'I couldn't be more certain.'

Rankin was almost afraid to ask his next question, but it had to be asked. 'But, you're still certain it was an Audi, right?'

The moronic plebeian was squirming like a worm on a fishing hook. Why not drive home his undoubted advantage whilst he had the opportunity? 'I'm no expert in these matters you understand; I wish to make that entirely clear. I'm not a car enthusiast, but I'd say so, yes.'

Okay, so that was a lost cause. Any half-decent defence barrister would render the evidence useless without breaking sweat. Time to move on. Time to look for a positive. It was a case of fingers crossed. 'How certain are you of the driver's description?'

'Ah, now, you'll no doubt be glad to hear that that is something I can help you with… I had a clear view of him as the car passed by the house. I was only a matter of feet away from the driver's side window.'

'Okay, so what did he look like?'

'Yes, yes, of course, I was just coming to that. You may be surprised to hear that the car was driven by an elderly gentleman with shoulder-length grey hair and an unkempt scraggy beard. I'd happily swear to that in any court in the land if required.'

Was it worth asking? Yeah, what the hell, things couldn't get any worse than they already were. 'This may sound like a strange question, but could the man you saw have been a younger man wearing a wig and false beard?'

No need to panic, it was far too soon for that. The man was on a fishing exercise, nothing more. He had nothing. That was blatantly obvious to anyone. 'Why would you ask me such a ludicrous question? I've told you what I saw.'

'Just answer the question please, Professor.'

'Very well, if you insist. That certainly wasn't my impression. I'm assuming you want to know the truth. It would be ill-advised to manufacture evidence or make it fit some ill-considered hypothesis, I'm sure you'd agree.'

The cheeky bastard! 'So, you think he was an old man?'

Professor Goddard forced a less than convincing laugh before speaking again. He seemed less than persuaded. Maybe the pleb wasn't quite as stupid as he seemed. 'I'm not sure I can make myself any clearer than I already have, Sergeant, but it seems I must try nonetheless. The car was driven by a man in his late seventies or eighties. I'm certain of the fact… now, is there anything else you want me to clarify before you begin writing that statement you mentioned and let me get back to see my mother? She'll be expecting me.'

'You've got no doubts?'

He pushed up the sleeve of his summer-weight Savile Row linen shirt and made a show of checking his gold-plated automatic wristwatch. He was nothing if not determined. Would the fool ever get the message? 'None whatsoever! He was elderly. That's my answer and it's not going to change on the basis of your implied insistence. If you ask me the same question a thousand times, I'll give you the exact same reply. I don't know how I can make it any clearer for you.'

Grav was going to love this… He'd best get the statement written, for what it was worth. 'Okay, enough said, let's get on with it.'

The professor perused and signed the statement with an exuberant flourish of an impressive Montblanc fountain pen when prompted, and stood as if to leave. He strode slowly towards the door, but paused momentarily before exiting and looked back, meeting Rankin's increasingly tired and dejected eyes. 'There is one thing I should probably mention before I leave you in peace.'

What the hell would he say next? The man's evidence was close to useless. 'Tell me more.'

'I was in two minds about sharing this with you at all, but what with the circumstances… you know what I'm saying.'

'Yes, of course, there's a killer out there. If you've got information, you've got a legal and moral duty to share it with me.'

'Very well, when you put it that way. There are some rather unpleasant rumours relating to young Peter Mosely circulating on the university campus. Most regrettable, he's always seemed a pleasant enough individual to me.'

Rankin rose to his feet and approached the professor purposefully. Maybe the interview wasn't going to be a complete waste of time after all. 'What sort of rumours? What are we talking about?'

Were spur-of-the-moment revelations really such a good idea? He had to think fast and come up with something plausible to take full advantage of his initiative. 'I'm not usually one to cast aspersions without good reason, you understand. I really don't want to do poor Peter a disservice. That's the last thing I'd want.'

Oh come on, spit it out man, for fuck's sake. He didn't have all day. 'Just say what you have to say and let me decide if it's important.'

He was falling for it. The pleb was swallowing every single word. 'An anonymous female student left a brief letter on my desk yesterday morning whilst I was presenting a lecture, alleging that young Peter had touched her breast and tried to kiss her against her wishes when she was studying in the university's library.'

'He tried to force himself on her?'

The professor took a single step backward and focussed on the blue linoleum flooring fleetingly, before lifting his head again and meeting Rankin's inquisitive eyes. 'Well, I think that's probably overstating the case somewhat, but it seems so. I'd be extremely surprised if there's too much to worry about.'

Mosely! How about that? First impressions could prove surprisingly unreliable. 'And you've still got this letter?'

The idiot was as malleable as warm putty. 'Oh, yes, but not on me, naturally; it's not something I'd remove from the university campus without the Dean's prior consent.'

The self-important pompous prat! 'So where is it?'

'I locked it in a desk drawer in my study for safekeeping. It seemed advisable. I thought it may be required at some point or other if disciplinary proceedings are initiated by the university authorities. It may well come to that, I'm afraid.

190

These things can't be ignored in today's world. So much has changed in recent years. The days of having a quiet advisory word with the wrongdoer in such circumstances are long gone. I'm not entirely sure that such changes are for the best, but that's the way it is.'

'I'm assuming you haven't spoken to Mosely, right?'

Professor Goddard shook his head repeatedly and said, 'No, not as yet. I was planning to at some point out of basic courtesy. It seems the least I can do.'

Don't even think about it, Professor. Don't you bloody well dare. 'Have you told anyone else? Anyone at all?'

'No, no, I haven't as yet. I thought it advisable to consider the matter very carefully before acting on what, at the end of the day, is an anonymous letter. With the wisdom of hindsight, given our conversation, I would accept that I was simply delaying the inevitable.'

So, Mosely knew nothing of the letter. That was a positive. At least something was going the right way for a change. 'That's good, but you need to keep it that way. This is a criminal matter now. There'll be plenty of time for any necessary disciplinary action when we've finished with him.'

'Really? A criminal matter? Is that absolutely necessary? I feel sure young Peter didn't mean to upset the student concerned, whoever she is. I'm beginning to regret opening my mouth at all.'

'I'm telling you to leave it to us.'

'Surely young Peter should be made aware of what's happening. It seems blatantly unfair to…'

Rankin visibly tensed, his nerves taut. 'If anyone warns Mosely of what's coming, you included, I'll charge them with attempting to pervert the course of justice.'

The professor frowned and took a backward step. 'I do not appreciate your attitude, Sergeant. I'm here at my own volition and doing my utmost to assist you. I fail to understand your aggression.'

'Did you recognise the handwriting?'

'If you require my cooperation, I suggest a less hostile approach would be advisable.'

'Just answer the frigging question.'

Careful Mark, now wasn't the time for slip-ups. There were forensic handwriting experts available to the police. There was little point in taking unnecessary risks. 'It's a typed letter, I'm afraid. Such a shame in the circumstances, I'm sure you'd agree.'

DS Rankin swore crudely under his breath. 'I need to see it.'

Oh, you'll see it, pleb, you'll see it. Don't concern yourself on that accord. 'I'll be at the university in the morning, if that helps you?'

'Please take a seat, Professor, we have a second statement to write.'

Professor Goddard returned to his seat and smirked, inwardly relishing what he interpreted as his Machiavellian genius. If the fool thought he was making progress, he was delusional. Dance to my tune, you gullible pleb. Whirl and prance as I pull your strings.

Chapter 19

Professor Goddard's earlier meeting with Rankin was still playing on his mind when he parked his two-door Porsche 911 in a pleasingly quiet Llanelli side street, about half a mile or so from Wayne Fisher's disorganised scrapyard at 2.22 A.M. on Friday, 15 May. It seemed the pleb detective sergeant wasn't quite as unintelligent as he'd first appeared. He was stupid, there was no denying that, he wouldn't be joining Mensa anytime soon, but he'd displayed a spark of simplistic intellect, despite his gullible and over-trusting nature. It made sense to take suitable precautions where he could. There was little, if anything, to lose and everything to gain. He was in control now, just like he'd always been. That was the only logical explanation for the events. What other interpretation was there?

The professor checked the road repeatedly on locking the car, relieved but not surprised by the absence of unwelcome passers-by or early morning curtain-twitchers. Llanelli was asleep and lost to its dreams for good or bad and that suited him just fine.

He made his way through the deserted, early morning Welsh industrial town, with a surprisingly burdensome olive-green plastic receptacle containing a gallon or more of petrol in one hand and his false number plates in the other. It took him approximately seven minutes to reach his destination of choice at a fast-walking pace and he was both cheered and gratified when the scrapyard's large, drab, grey-painted wooden doors came into view in the light of the half-moon in the clear sky. Things were already going his way. Just as he liked it. Just as he'd expected. Fate was on his side.

He found the main gates secured by a formidable steel chain that he immediately decided would be virtually impossible to dislodge, and he hurried around the adjoining walls in an attempt to find an alternative entrance that suited his purpose. Surely there had to be a way into the place without the necessity of climbing. Physical exercise, he pondered, was such a demeaning and unpleasant process. Not at all suitable for a man of his elevated status and impressive intellect and achievements. If only he had a willing assistant to do his bidding. Hopefully, given sufficient time and preparation, Venus Six would meet that bill.

He quickly circumnavigated the entire large rectangular enclosure, examining every inch of the walls, but failing to discover an alternative entrance to meet his needs. As frustrating as it was, if he was going to get into the damned place, there was only one way to do it. It was physical exertion or nothing. It seemed there was no other viable option available to him. Such obstacles were regrettable, but far from insurmountable. For goodness' sake man, get a grip, stop pontificating and get on with it. It was a price worth paying. His guest and the pleasures she brought to his life were well worth a little sacrifice. He just had to accept that reality.

The professor turned slowly in a circle, scanning the street with keen eyes in search of inspiration, before finally settling on a workable plan he considered acceptable. He placed the petrol container and number plates at the base of the approximate six-foot-high, thick stone wall for safekeeping and checked the street again for the umpteenth time, left to right, right to left, and back again on crossing. No one was watching. No one to hinder his plans. There was just him and the moonlit night.

The professor approached a large green wheelie bin located on the fragmented concrete driveway of a modest 1960s semi-detached, two-bedroom bungalow on the opposite side of the road. He lifted the grubby lid gingerly with reluctant fingers, grimaced as the putrid stink filled his nostrils and removed three gradually decomposing black refuse bags. If he was going to climb the damned wall, he was going to need an impromptu ladder of sorts and as disagreeable and revolting as it was, the wheelie bin would at least serve his purpose well enough. It was a case of needs must. It really was as simple as that.

He urgently pushed the now half-empty bin across the road, all the time silently cursing the infuriating noise of its plastic wheels turning on the rough tarmacadam stone-strewn roadway. Too much noise, far too much noise. Surely they'd hear it. Surely some interfering nosey busybodies would hear it and stick their interfering noses into his important and private business. The bastards! The interfering bastards! He'd tear their damned faces off if he got the opportunity.

The professor increased his pace as a startled mongrel dog on full alert barked and howled in the far-off distance, and he said a silent prayer of thanks to a God whose existence he denied when he reached the wall only seconds later. He picked up the number plates from the floor and hurled them into the yard with a flailing arm, before reaching up and placing the heavy petrol container on top of the wall to await him. Next, he turned the wheelie bin carefully on its side, avoiding the putrid, bacteria-infested liquid running from its disturbed contents with fast-moving dancing feet, and supported his entire weight by placing the palms of both hands against the wall's rough surface. Now all he had to do was climb onto the damn thing and get on with his night's work.

The professor silently cursed Rankin as the hard plastic bin gave slightly under his weight, but to his relief it had sufficient strength to support him, enabling him to pull himself on top of the wall, belly first, inch by cautious inch, and pull himself gradually forwards. Come on man, a little more effort, that's all that was required of him. And she was worth it. The bitch was definitely worth it. One day she'd fully appreciate his genius.

He lay face down on top of the wall for a second or two, panting hard, twitching and sweating profusely and acutely conscious of his heart pounding in his chest cavity. It was time to progress matters. Time to do what he was there to achieve and get out of there unseen.

Professor Goddard slowly lowered the petrol container towards the ground with an outstretched arm and allowed it to fall the last two feet or so. It landed on a prominent area of hardy overgrown grass, directly between two rusted and broken cars of indeterminate make, with a barely discernible thud that he observed no one else was likely to have heard. He was well on course as expected. He was a man on top of his game. A man in total control of his destiny. And there was nothing whatsoever anyone could do about it. Not Rankin, not Gravel, not his interfering mother, no-one.

The professor adjusted his position with careful attention to detail and used maximum effort to swivel his entire body a full 180 degrees, so that he was still lying face down directly on top of the wall, but with his legs facing the scrapyard. He paused momentarily, resting his tired muscles and allowing himself time for a self-congratulatory symbolic pat on the back, before lowering his legs triumphantly towards the ground. He was inspired. Nothing, if not inspired. A genius at the height of his considerable powers.

He stilled himself and stood statue-like, confused and incredulous. What the hell was going on? There was something warm running down his leg. There was something seeping into his shoe. Had he lost control of his bladder like those vacuous whimpering girls? What the…?

He turned in the direction of the moonlight, stared down at his right leg and kicked the wall hard with the sole of his shoe when he first saw the large tear in his tailored trousers and the thick dark blood trickling from his torn knee. He cast a keen eye over the rest of his body and discovered a further deep gash high on the thigh of his other leg, close to his groin. Damn, damn, damn! The wall was impregnated with sharp shards of broken glass. Why hadn't he spotted them? Why the hell hadn't he felt them as they cut into his vulnerable flesh? It seemed that adrenalin was a surprisingly effective painkiller. That explained it. Maybe he should attempt to create a calmer atmosphere when torturing his guests in future. It was certainly worth considering. But enough of the future, he had to focus on the task at hand.

He pressed firmly against his wounds to slow the bleeding, before lifting each hand to his mouth in turn and licking them hungrily, smearing his face with blood and savouring its familiar metallic tang. Now the injuries were starting to sting and he could feel the pain. The bastard, the absolute bastard! Fisher would pay for the inconvenience and discomfort he'd caused. Yes, he'd pay a suitably high price, but as unfortunate as it was, now was not that time.

The professor bent down at the waist to avoid placing any unnecessary pressure on his injured knee, took the petrol container in one bloodstained hand and walked slowly between various dilapidated vehicles of every conceivable description piled high in every part of the yard. Where had the bastard dumped the Mercedes? Where was it? Where the hell was it?

He could see without significant difficulty in the light of a spring moon still fortuitously free of clouds and he found the car only minutes later. It was parked to the left side of a tin and rust corrugated building that he surmised must serve as an office of sorts, if a Neanderthal simpleton such as Fisher required such a thing.

He paced around the car, touching it, appreciating its beauty, before stopping and staring at a scribbled handwritten *for sale* sign taped to the inside of the windscreen with parcel tape. The devious conniving bastard, the absolute bastard! Could anyone be trusted to act with integrity? It seemed not in this world. If only he could get his hands on him and tear him apart. If only he could peel the skin from his moronic face and feed it to him one thin slice at a time, as he screamed his heart out.

The professor sat on the car's bonnet, enthusiastically indulging his fantasy for a full minute or two, before taking slow deep breaths and refocussing on the night's work. It was time for action. Time to implement the climax of his plan.

He removed the car's petrol cap, unscrewed the top of his container and poured about twenty-five per cent of the contents over the entire body of the vehicle. And then, for no other reasons than spite and revenge, he used a raised elbow to smash two of the office windows and poured most of the remaining petrol into the run-down ramshackle structure. Once satisfied with his work, he retrieved the number plates, threw them into the building to join the preceding broken glass and walked slowly from the Mercedes to the lowest point of the outside wall, crouching down and pouring a thin trail of petrol as he went.

Everything was ready. Just as he wanted it. Just as he'd pictured. He was a genius. He'd said it before, and he'd say it again. A misunderstood genius in a misguided and judgemental world of fools.

The professor ended his brief self-congratulatory lament, focussed and utilised all his strength and weight to roll an old, empty, battered oil drum up close to the wall, before climbing on top, taking a recently purchased box of Swan Vesta matches from his trouser pocket, striking one and breaking into a broad toothy triumphant Cheshire cat smile, as a bright flame shone out in the semi-darkness. He waited for a moment or two, protecting the flame with his hand and ensuring the match was well lit, before eventually tossing it to the floor, causing the fuel to ignite. A yellow-blue flame travelled quickly across the uneven ground towards the waiting Mercedes estate car just thirty or so feet away. He urgently scrambled on top of the wall, ignoring the numerous shards of razor-sharp glass embedded in the concrete and watched, transfixed, as the flames leapt and danced up the side of the car, feeding acrid smoke into the night sky.

The explosion that erupted only moments later, as soon as the flame found the petrol tank, sent a shock wave of energy in the professor's direction with sufficient force so as to send him upwards and then down, tumbling off the wall and onto the hard pavement beyond, with his ears ringing and his bruised and battered head filled with violent vibrating sounds that made him flinch.

He somehow dragged himself onto all fours, despite the shock and the pain, and glanced up horrified as electric bulbs came on and curtains opened in the various houses and bungalows on the opposite side of the street. A door was opening. Shit, shit, shit! An interfering meddling bastard was leaving his house. No, no, no! The prying swine was walking in his direction. He was gaining pace. He was getting nearer, nearer and nearer.

'Are you all right, mate?'

The professor struggled to his feet with the aid of the wall and stared at the pavement, avoiding the man's gaze. He started to walk away, one small shaky determined step at a time, as quickly as his battered body would allow. Go away, go away, get out of my face you interfering slob. Mind your own business and go away.

The man strode after the professor in the heat of the nearby inferno, catching up with him despite his best efforts to get away and tapping him on the shoulder insistently. 'Are you okay, mate?'

Professor Goddard increased his pace. 'I'm fine, just fine.'

'Fuck me, can you feel that heat? The place went up as if a bomb hit it.'

The professor didn't respond, but kept walking.

'You don't look too clever to me, mate. The back of your head's pissing with blood! Do you want me to call an ambulance?'

He kept stumbling onwards, one lurching step at a time, picking up his pace as best he could on unsteady legs and looking away from the man in the interests of anonymity. Just go away. Please go away! Leave me alone. 'I'm fine, thank you. Now, just leave me in peace, please.'

But the man didn't let up, concerned that the professor may collapse at any moment, and feeling somehow responsible for his safety. 'You're covered in blood, mate. I can ring from the house, it's no bother. I don't want you collapsing on me.'

The professor broke into a desperate loping trot as his fight-or-flight response fully kicked in. If only he had a knife, if only he could stab the meddling swine and shut him up for ever. 'Just leave me alone and piss off, you accursed Neanderthal.'

What the hell was he banging on about? 'What's that, mate? You're not making a lot of sense.'

'Just leave me alone!'

The man suddenly turned away and hurried back in the direction of his house, as a steadily growing group of local residents began to crowd into the brightly illuminated street, his plump, thirty-something, blue-pyjamas-clad wife amongst them. 'Who's that bloke, Dai?'

He took her hand and rushed her back up the path towards their open door and into the narrow hallway. 'I've got no idea, love. Did you see the state he's in? How he's still on his feet is a mystery to me. I asked him twice, but the silly sod said he doesn't want an ambulance.'

'He's probably in shock.'

'Yeah, I'm sure you're right, love.'

'Well, go on, call an ambulance.'

He shook his head. 'He doesn't want one, love.'

She folded her arms and stared at him indignantly. 'Just ring anyway, Dai. Do the right thing for once in your life! He's probably not thinking straight after a bang on the head, or something.'

'Okay, okay, I heard you the first time.' He picked up the phone and urgently dialled 999. 'I'm onto it, love. Now, get back upstairs and make sure the baby's all right. I can hear her bawling from here.'

The professor rushed onwards, one unsteady step at a time, with the mix of dopamine and endorphin in his system acting as an extremely effective painkiller. The sound of loud and lively Welsh-accented chatter gradually decreased and subsided as he turned into a back lane leading off the residential street. He made his weary way back in the direction of the Porsche, without looking back, never looking back, whilst acutely aware of the shadows and light painted on various buildings by the leaping blue-yellow flames behind him.

The journey took him significantly longer than it had in the original direction, as he repeatedly stumbled and fell on weak and traumatised blood-soaked legs. By the time he eventually reached the car, dawn was threatening to fill the world with light and he was more than a little relieved to climb into the driver's seat and start the powerful precision built engine, which roared into mechanical life with a single turn of the key. He performed an efficient U-turn in the traffic-free road as his escalating pain began to draw attention to his injuries and he glanced repeatedly in the rear-view mirror, urging himself onwards as the egg-sized lump on the back of his head began to swell and throb. Focus on the road, Mark. Just focus on the damned road. Venus Six is waiting for you, and you'll be home before you know it. Just keep going. Just keep driving and don't give in to sleep.

The professor drove ever so slowly, ever so cautiously, drifting in and out of semiconsciousness like a punch-drunk fighter throwing blows on virtual autopilot after a severe beating. He slavishly adhered to the speed limits avoiding any ill-considered manoeuvre that could potentially draw unwanted attention to him or his car as he travelled back in the direction of Caerystwyth. He winced and tightened his vice-like grip on the leather steering wheel each and every time a siren sounded loudly in the night or a bright blue light flashed in the darkness. Various emergency vehicles sped down the A40 in the opposite direction, their drivers and passengers concentrating on the crisis at hand and totally oblivious to his presence, despite his car's impressive and comparatively unusual nature.

When the professor reached Trinity Fields, a full hour and twenty minutes later, they were bathed in subtle early morning light and the lightest of mists, that gave his woodland burial ground an eerie, mesmerising, ghostlike quality, that he couldn't appreciate or even notice despite its undoubted majesty.

He pressed his foot down on the accelerator, sped towards the house and pulled up out of sight of any potential prying eyes. It took him three attempts to unfasten his seatbelt with a shaking bloodstained hand. He leant forwards, ran an inquisitive finger over the painful, gradually swelling lump on the back of his bruised head and felt suddenly overcome with an irresistible wish to sleep, as the mental and physical efforts of the night's work finally took their toll. As tempting as she was, Venus Six would have to wait. A few hours' sleep and he'd give her his best.

Chapter 20

Grav was already standing at an unusually quiet Caerystwyth Rugby Club bar, engaged in animated conversation with the regular larger than life dyed blonde barmaid, whose large and prominent breasts seemingly threatened to burst out of her overly tight low-cut top at any moment, when Rankin hung up his bright orange raincoat and entered the room at 8:23 P.M. on Sunday, 17 May.

All right, boss? Of all the bars in all the world…'

The DI laughed, revealing what remained of his natural teeth. 'Has Mary had you watching Casablanca again?'

'It's romantic apparently. I think she may be trying to tell me something. I could recite the entire script by heart if I had to. She just can't get enough of the frigging film.'

'That's women for you!'

'It used to be The Sound of Music, so it could be worse.'

Grav nodded. 'Things can always be worse.'

'Mine's a pint of Buckleys, if you're buying.'

The off-duty DI took a single ten-pound note from his trouser pocket, unfolded it with clumsy fingers and placed it on the bar with a resounding slap of his right hand. 'You're nothing if not predictable, Clive my boy. Fancy some pork scratchings?'

'No, ta, I had a big plate of stodge before coming out.'

'Two pints of best bitter and a packet of scratchings please, love.'

'Two pints of amber nectar coming up, Grav.' Liz bent down and picked up two reasonably clean glasses from a shelf under the bar, unwittingly revealing an impressive attention-grabbing cleavage. 'Are you any nearer to catching that maniac everyone's talking about? I'm scared to go out on my own after dark. Well, it's not surprising is it? I've told our Sharon to keep a kitchen knife hidden in her handbag just in case. Stab the bastard, that's what I told her. Stick it in his eye and twist. That should slow him down a bit.'

'We didn't hear that, Liz, what with all the noise.'

She glanced to the right and left. 'We're the only ones here, you silly sod.'

Grav accepted his pint gratefully and happily slurped the malty head from its top with pursed lips. 'Investigations are ongoing. I think that's the best I can say.'

'Well, get your f-ing fingers out then, no woman's safe until the evil bastard's locked up. What the hell's wrong with you lot? Don't they pay you enough?'

The two men made their weary way towards their usual table in a corner at the far side of the worn-out pool table, with their tails well and truly between their legs. 'Fancy a quick game, boss?'

Grav pulled out a seat and placed his glass on an alcohol-sodden Babysham beermat before replying, 'Not tonight thanks, mate. We need a bit of an informal catch up, if that's all right with you.'

Rankin grabbed a chair and joined him at the table. It was a statement of fact rather than a question. 'Yeah, wouldn't be a bad idea. What do you make of the Mosely letter?'

'I had a quick chat with Pat Stevenson after you mentioned it. She's sending someone around to pick it up from Goddard's secretary in the morning. He rang the station to say he's taking a few days off sick with the flu or something along those lines. It makes sense to see exactly what the letter says before Mosely's pulled in and questioned.'

'Is that down to us or the Cardiff lot? I can pick him up tomorrow afternoon if that helps.'

'I agreed that Pat's team would make the arrest, but that you can sit in on the interview. They'll focus on the one allegation initially, although it's over to you if it seems there's any reason to believe he could be involved in our lot.'

Rankin took a gulp of beer. 'How exactly?'

'Oh, come on, Clive, I don't need to spell it out for you. Let Cardiff do their job focussing on the letter, but if you think he may be a candidate for the murders, ask him a few questions, nick him, and bring him to Caerystwyth for further questioning.'

'He hasn't got a record, nothing at all.'

'Yeah, I'm well aware of that. I saw the result of your PNC check on your desk a few days back. I know he's an unlikely candidate, but we can't ignore the possibility. These things have got a habit of coming back to bite you in the arse.'

'I met the bloke, I talked to him face to face. I can't see it to be honest, boss. A quick grope in the library maybe, but murder? He'd have been little more than a kid when the first girl was killed. He just hasn't got it in him from what I've seen.'

'He's got to be worth a look, Clive. If we do fuck all and it turns out he's involved in any way at all, where does that leave us? Up shit creek without a paddle, that's where. I don't need to tell you that. Do you want to be back in uniform and doing shifts until your retirement?'

'Yeah, I know what you're saying… Any further thoughts on a press conference?'

'I've talked to one or two journalists and we've issued the odd press release as and when, but the new chief super's been against a full-blown press conference up to this point. She finally had a change of heart on Friday afternoon after I made yet another grovelling request on bended knee.'

'What the fuck's that about?'

'Oh, I think she's crapping herself that a decision she makes may provoke our man into killing the Jones girl. You know, in case it screws up her meteoric rise to the top. We wouldn't want that, would we?'

'You don't rate her?'

'Well, she doesn't exactly fill me with confidence, if I'm honest. She's got all the qualifications in the world: MBA this, PHD that, but fuck all real front-line experience from what I can make out. She's a theory merchant. I think that sums her up. She's one of those fast-track people who were promoted before they were out of nappies.'

'Yeah, that's been my impression too; I heard she was heading up the training college in Cwmbran before being foisted on us lot, bless her cotton socks.'

209

'Aren't we the lucky ones! Come back CS Chapman, all is forgiven. At least he knew how to take charge when it mattered. He knew where the buck stopped and stepped up accordingly. The woman's constantly trying to let me know who's boss when it comes to the little things that don't matter a great deal. I feel like curtsying whenever I see her.'

'Yeah, I know what you mean. I've even stopped scratching my balls in public.'

The DI lifted an open hand to the side of his head and held it there for a second or two. 'I actually saluted her like Corporal Jones in Dad's Army when I bumped into her in the corridor a couple of days back… Yes, Ma'am, anything you say, Ma'am. Would you like me to kiss your arse for you, Ma'am?'

Rankin struggled to stifle a laugh. 'You didn't?'

'Of course I fucking didn't, you prat! What do you take me for? I was pounding the beat when she was still wearing her school uniform.'

'But, she's agreed to it now? The press conference, she's given you the go-ahead?'

'Yeah, she actually made a decision for once in her life. It's arranged for Wednesday afternoon at two prompt. I've got various journalists coming and the Welsh TV people. Oh, and I've asked Emma's parents to be there. I want them to feel a part of it. I need them to know we're pulling out all the stops to find their daughter.'

'You'll have them all there, Grav: the BBC, ITV, the national papers. It's been all over the media. Serial killers tend to hit the headlines in our part of the world. This isn't America.'

'Yeah, I know, I know… I had a brief chat with Dave Hardy, the psychology lecturer I know at Swansea University. He's working on some psychological ground rules for us. Making a direct personal appeal to the killer not to harm Emma, trying to get him to see her as a person who's loved and valued, encouraging him to contact us himself, trying to engage with him and gain some clue as to his identity. You know the sort of things I'm talking about.'

'Yeah, I understand. It's got to be worth a try.'

'Yeah, and we can make a high-profile public appeal for information. You never know your luck. House to house enquiries haven't come up with much.'

'They haven't come up with anything at all, boss, that's the truth of it. Have you thought of using the newspapers to our advantage? Some rich git put up the money to fund a comprehensive press campaign in the Yorkshire Ripper case. I watched a documentary about it a couple of weeks back on Channel 4. Interesting idea, not that it got them anywhere. Basic policing and a lucky break by a couple of uniform plods cracked it for them in the end, despite all the money and resources they threw at it for month after month.'

Grav downed the remainder of his pint, head back, in one two-second swallow. 'Let's hope it doesn't get that far. The vicious bastard! Was it twelve or thirteen victims?'

'Thirteen!'

Grav stared into his empty pint glass, contemplating what was to come in the days and weeks ahead. 'Dave mentioned an American mate of his, who's done some profiling work with the FBI. He's actually over here making a few quid on a lecture tour after a second costly divorce. He may be able to offer us something useful.'

Rankin nodded enthusiastically. 'Sounds like a plan. We've got nothing to lose. Have you had the chance to speak to him yet?'

'Na, I've been trying to contact him for a couple of days now, but he's not an easy man to get hold of.'

'No joy?'

'Not as yet. He hasn't got back to me, but I'll keep trying. He's giving a lecture in Bristol on Thursday evening. I'll drive down there myself and approach him directly, if he hasn't phoned me back before then. Dave tells me he's a bit of a piss artist, but knows his stuff. He's helped crack some fairly high-profile cases in the States, apparently.'

'Sounds positive.'

'I thought so.'

'Another pint?'

'Is the Pope catholic?' He had to drown his sorrows somehow.

'There you go, boss.'

'Thanks, Clive, it's appreciated… Any progress with the Audi enquiries?'

Always the same tired questions. And, was it an Audi at all? Maybe sometime soon he'd be able to come up with something worth saying. 'Nothing more than I've already told you, boss. It's all looking a bit shaky. Gary Harris looked interesting initially: right car, a history of domestic violence, an indecent assault conviction on a sixteen-year-old schoolgirl a few years back, but he was banged up in Swansea nick for three of the last five years. He's well out of the frame.'

'I could have told you that myself. He was involved in a pub brawl that went too far. Some poor sod up from the south of England for a Llanelli match at Stradey ended up with one ear and a badly broken nose. Jo Breen handled it for me. GBH. It was about time Harris did a bit of stir.'

'You won't hear me arguing. I bet his wife enjoyed the break.'

Grav laughed. 'She was shacked up with some other poor mug by the time he was released.'

'Who could blame her?'

Rankin downed the remainder of his beer and stared into space, deep in melancholy thought. 'Do you really think there's anyone we know who may fit the bill?'

Grav paused before responding. 'I just can't see it, Clive. My gut feeling is, it's either a local man who's not known to us at this point, someone who's gone off the rails and is hearing voices, that sort of thing, or more likely someone who travels to or through this area on a fairly regular basis and knows it well. I'm talking about some evil demented bastard who kills in other parts of the country, up north for example, and then uses the wood as a convenient dumping ground en route to somewhere else.'

'Who are you thinking about, a lorry driver, a travelling salesman, someone along those lines?'

Grav nodded once and looked suddenly older as his facial muscles tightened and his gut churned. 'There's one hell of a lot of traffic between here and the Irish ferry at Fishguard, for example. Delivery lorries, tankers, the military and all the rest; it could be any of them, when you think about it.'

'Have we talked to the Irish police?'

'Yeah, I gave them a shout a couple of days back and put them in the picture, but they haven't come up with any obvious candidates.'

Should he ask? Yes, he may well get his head bitten off, but so what? It wouldn't be the first time, and it certainly wouldn't be the last. 'Have you thought of asking for help from the Met, boss? They've got a full-time murder squad and more detectives than you can shake a stick at. You have to admit we're not exactly flush with resources in this part of the world.'

Grav tilted his head back and drained his glass. Rankin wasn't wrong. 'You're starting to sound a bit like the new chief super, Clive my boy. We managed to nail Galbraith without outside assistance. Cases don't get much bigger than that perverted cunt and the other paedophile scum he offended with. What makes you think we can't do the same with this bastard?'

'Yeah, but...'

'Just leave it, mate, there's no room for discussion. I just don't want to hear it! We are going to nail this killer, *us*, we're going to do it, not some flash git in a sharp suit from London. There's nothing that the Met could do that we can't do ourselves.'

Rankin held his hands high in the air as if surrendering. 'Okay, okay, I get the message.'

'Got time for another pint?'

Well, at least he'd tried, even if his words had fallen on predictably deaf ears. Hopefully it wouldn't come back to haunt them. 'Yeah, why not, but it'll have to be my last. Mary was in one hell of a mood when I left the house. I thought I wasn't going to get a pass at one point.'

What he wouldn't give for a bit of well-intentioned female nagging. 'Women's problems?'

Rankin laughed as he pictured her standing facing him with her hands resting on her hips in that disapproving way of hers. 'That's one way of putting it! I would say her mood swings are down to the pregnancy, but she hasn't been expecting for the last ten years.'

Grav grinned, the tension melting away. 'That bad, eh?'

'It's been a fucking nightmare recently… And don't quote me on that by the way. I'm quite attached to my balls. I'd like to keep them where they are if at all possible.'

Grav moved his chair back a couple of feet and stood, glad to have both changed the subject and raised the mood. 'Well, at least she keeps you on your toes. Good for her, I say. Someone's got to do it when I'm not around to keep a close eye on you.'

'Thanks a bunch. Who are you, my fucking mother?'

'Oh, come on, you love every bloody minute of it. How long till the baby arrives?'

'About three months and counting!'

'It's going to be one hell of a change of lifestyle for an ancient dog like you. You're old enough to be the kid's grandfather before it's even born.'

'Yeah, thanks for pointing that out. That'll do my self-confidence a power of good.'

'No, seriously, are you looking forward to the new arrival?'

Rankin nodded eagerly, as he pictured his soon-to-be new reality. 'Yeah, I am Grav, it's been a long time coming. I'd almost given up on the idea of ever being a dad. It's been years. We were even talking about adoption for a while. We'd approached the social services. Phillip Beringer came around to explain the process.'

'I'm pleased for you, mate, really I am.'

'As soon as the social approved our application, she was pregnant.'

Grav looked away as poignant memories of long gone happier times closed in and surrounded him mercilessly. 'Let's put it down to the mysteries of the universe... It only seems like yesterday when Dewi was born.'

'How old's he now?'

'He'll be twenty-nine in January.'

'Is he still in the Caribbean?'

'Yeah, Barbados. I may even pay him a visit when this lot's over with. I haven't seen much of him since Heather passed on.'

'Barbados, how about that? He was a kid in college when I last saw him. Doesn't time fly when you're enjoying yourself?'

Grav chuckled to himself. 'You're not wrong, mate. I think I'd better get the beer in before the violins start playing.'

'Cheers, boss. I thought I was in danger of dying of thirst for a second there. What was our lovely Liz banging on about?'

'Her youngest daughter's getting married next month. It seems Liz can't stand the bloke.'

'Anyone we know?'

'Na, I don't think so. It's some Pikey who came to the area to pick cockles in Ferryside and shagged her one night in the car park when they were both seriously pissed. She's only sixteen, for God's sake. Liz is not a happy woman.'

'So I'm guessing we're not invited to the wedding then.'

'I wouldn't hold my breath.'

Rankin stood and slotted a fifty-pence coin into the wall-mounted juke box, before returning to his seat and waiting for the first of three tracks to begin. 'Did you hear about the fire at Fisher's scrapyard? It seems the whole place went up in smoke. There was one hell of a mess apparently.'

Grav nodded his recognition. 'Yeah, Trevor Simpson mentioned it. My money's on an insurance job; I'd be willing to bet our Wayne's claim form will be one impressive work of fiction.'

Rankin tapped his foot along to a Jimmy Hendrix classic, as the soaring electric melody filled the room with sound. 'I don't think Fisher can read or write, as it happens. He never went to school, from what I remember.'

217

'Yeah, you're right now that I think about it, but no doubt some other scrote will help him out for a percentage. He's an ignorant git, but not short on useful criminal contacts.'

'Are we looking into it?'

Grav took the last Hamlet cigar from a packet of five, stuck a match and went to light the tip. 'Bigger fish to fry, Clive my boy, bigger fish to fry. We'll leave Fisher to the woodentops on this happy occasion.'

'You're sure? We've been trying to nail the slippery sod for a good while.'

'Oh, his time will come. It's a case of priorities. You know what I'm saying. I've never been more sure of anything in my life.'

Inspector Pat Stevenson stared into Mosely's ashen face and kept staring until he looked away and focussed on the white-painted wall a few feet behind her. 'Switch the tapes on, Sergeant, I think it's time we began the interview.'

'Will do Ma'am.'

'Before we make a start, Peter, I need to remind you that you're still subject to caution. You do not have to say anything. But it may harm your defence if you do not mention when questioned something which you later rely on in court. Anything you do say may be given in evidence. Do you understand?'

The young man nodded, his dark dyed fringe flopping down and covering one eye as he tilted his head forwards.

'Speak up for the tape please, Mr Mosely.'

'Yes, yes, I understand.'

'This recorded interview is being taped at Cardiff Central police station. I'm Inspector Pat Stevenson of the South Wales Police. Also in attendance is Detective Sergeant Clive Rankin of the West Wales Police and, can I have your full name please, Mr Mosely?'

'Peter John Mosely.'

'According to my watch the time is 11:32 A.M. on Monday, 18 May 1998. Can you confirm that you've declined the offer of a solicitor?'

He nodded again and pushed his hair away from his eyes with long delicate fingers.

'Out loud for the tape, please.'

Mosely sat upright in his seat and stared at her indignantly, but his wavering hands and rapidly blinking eyes betrayed his true state of mind. 'I haven't done anything wrong. Why would I need a lawyer to hold my hand? I'm an innocent man.'

'If you're sure, Peter, but a duty solicitor is always available if you change your mind.'

How many times did one have to say the same damned thing? 'I've never assaulted anyone in my life. That's not the sort of person I am. I'm a pacifist. I despise violence of all kinds. I don't need a solicitor or anyone else for that matter.'

Quite a speech! And it seemed genuinely heartfelt. Time to see how he responded to the specific allegations. Here was betting it wouldn't take very long for his newfound bravado to disappear. 'Why do you think you've been arrested? Why do you think you're here?'

He paused before responding, appearing very close to tears as he faced reality. Saying the words made it more real somehow. 'I was t-told I'd been arrested on suspicion of sexual assault. It's utterly ridiculous. I just can't understand why anyone would say such a thing about me.'

'Would you describe touching a girl's breast as violent?'

He didn't respond, suspecting it was a loaded question intended to catch him out.

'Would you agree that trying to kiss a girl could be considered abusive?'

He narrowed his eyes. Was she trying to trick him? Yes, that was probably it. He has to consider his replies carefully. 'Well, that would depend on the circumstances, wouldn't it?'

'Okay, so you're saying that in some circumstances sexual contact of any kind could be considered violent.'

Mosely gritted his teeth and exhaled as his blood pressure increased and his face reddened. 'Yes, yes, of course it could, but what the hell's that got to do with me?'

Inspector Stevenson opened a blue cardboard file on the desktop in front of her and took out a single-page letter, retrieved from the professor's secretary that morning. 'One of the female students at the university has alleged that you touched her breast and tried to kiss her against her wishes.'

Mosely gripped the table with both hands as his mouth fell open with the shock of it all. 'I haven't been out for weeks. I'm saving for a deposit on a flat.'

'She says it happened in the library. She says it happened whilst you were at work. She says you crept up behind her, reached over her shoulder as she sat reading and stroked her breast. She says you grabbed her by the hair and tried to force your tongue into her mouth when she shouted her objections. I'd call that violent, wouldn't you?'

A single tear trickled down Mosely's prominent cheekbone as he sat in confused silence.

'What have you got to say for yourself, Peter? We require a response.'

A myriad tiny stars floated in front of his eyes, as stress-induced changes in his nervous and circulatory systems restricted the amount of blood reaching his brain.

'Grab him, Clive, I think he's about to keel over!'

Rankin quickly reached across the table and placed a steadying hand on each of Mosely's slight shoulders. 'Take your time, Peter. Deep breaths, son, that's it, no rush. Just answer our questions, and this will be over before you know it.'

Mosely gradually regained his composure and his eyesight cleared as he struggled to relax. 'Who'd say that? I haven't done anything. I swear to God, I haven't done anything to anyone!'

Rankin sat back in his chair. Maybe he had and maybe he hadn't. But either way, the interview was a fishing exercise with very little bait. A more experienced streetwise offender would have spotted it a mile off. 'The student raised her concerns with Professor Goddard in writing.'

He shook his head. Ah, now it was beginning to make sense. Goddard, bloody Goddard! The man had it in for him. 'So, who's this girl? When exactly is it supposed to have happened? I'm guessing the letter's not that specific.'

Pat Stevenson returned the letter to the folder and waited for Mosely to continue. Sometimes saying nothing was best. Interviewees sometimes dug a pretty big hole for themselves when given the time to talk.

'He can't stand me. The man hates my guts.'

'Who are we talking about?'

Wasn't it obvious? Did he really need to spell it out? 'Professor Goddard, who else? The man's a bully! Emma was his pet project. He was always pestering her on some pretext or other. He hated the fact that we were together. He resented it with a burning intensity. The man claimed I wasn't doing my job properly, that I was lazy and couldn't be trusted. He even spoke to my boss and suggested my contract should be terminated. The bastard would say absolutely anything to get me into trouble.'

Rankin shook his head incredulously and took the lead as the uniform inspector sat back in her chair. 'So let me see if I've got this right? You're trying to claim that a respected academic such as Professor Goddard would fabricate evidence because of some unlikely vendetta between the two of you? That's really the best you can do? Have you got any idea how ridiculous that sounds?'

Mosely was beginning to feel a growing confidence born of indignation. This was all down to Goddard. It had his name written all over it. 'I have the right to know who's made these unfounded allegations against me. So, tell me the girl's name. I'm waiting. Come on, you can't, can you? If you could I'd have heard about it long before now.'

Rankin paused, considering his next move carefully before redirecting the line of questioning. 'Your girlfriend goes missing after she dumps you and now a female student alleges an indecent assault in broad daylight. It doesn't exactly look too good, does it?'

Mosely jumped to his feet and pointed at Rankin with a thrusting digit. 'One, Emma didn't dump me, and two, I have not and never have indecently assaulted anyone in my life. Goddard's out to get me! He's fabricated these allegations for his own twisted reasons. How many times do

I have to tell you? It's the truth. Why the hell can't you understand that?'

Rankin fixed him with a steely glower. 'I can see that you've got a temper, Peter. It might be an idea to calm down a bit.'

Mosely slumped back into his seat as his newfound bravado melted away like an ice cube in the hot summer sun. It really was a no-win situation. He was damned if he did and damned if he didn't. 'I really haven't done anything. I don't know what more I can say to convince you.'

'Do you drive, Peter?'

'Drive? You said these fantasy allegations are supposed to have happened in the library. What's driving got to do with anything?'

Rankin moved to the very edge of his seat. 'Just answer the question, Mr Mosely, there's a good lad.'

'I've got a moped... Happy now?'

'So, you don't own a car?'

It was all a matter of official record. Either the police were incompetent or they were asking questions they already knew the answers to. Why would they do that? And why ask about driving in the first place? That was more to the point. 'I've never owned a car. I can't afford to run one on my paltry salary.'

'But you've passed your test. You've got a full driving licence, yes?'

'Yes, but...'

'Do you have access to a car? From a friend or a relative, anyone like that?'

Mosely shifted his weight uneasily from one buttock to the other as his left foot became numb. 'Why the talk of cars?'

Was he buying time? 'It's a simple enough question, Peter. Have you borrowed or rented a car at any time in the last five years?'

'I've only been driving for three years.'

'And?'

'I borrowed my mum's car when I moved into my bedsit, but that's it.'

'When was that exactly?'

Mosely was becoming increasingly confused by every new inexplicable question. 'Last November, but why would you want to know that? She gave me her permission to borrow it. I didn't take it or anything.'

'What type of car was it?'

'It's a Ford Escort diesel, but why…?'

'Saloon or estate?'

'It's an old rusty estate car. Mum's still got it. She's had it for years. What does it matter?'

Surely this ineffectual kid wasn't the man he was looking for. It seemed extremely unlikely as he'd concluded on their first meeting. 'What colour is it?'

'Black, black, what's it matter? Black!'

Rankin looked towards the inspector and met her eyes, before refocussing on Mosely. 'So you're saying she's still got the car?'

Mosely shook his head slowly. They thought he'd taken Emma. Ridiculous as that was, it was the only logical explanation for the line of questioning. 'For God's sake, yes!'

'Does your mother live locally?'

'She lives just outside Caerystwyth. Why would you want to know that?'

That was one hell of a coincidence. 'And, if I talk to her, she's going to confirm your story. Is that what you're claiming?'

'Claiming? What do you mean claiming? Talk to her, talk to my father, talk to my brother, talk to whoever the hell you want. I haven't done anything. I've got absolutely nothing to hide. I didn't touch some unnamed girl at the university, and for the record I'm worried sick about Emma. Is that what this is all about? I still love her with all my heart. I miss her terribly every single second of every single day.'

Rankin took a pen from his pocket. 'What are your parents' full names and address, son?'

'Trevor and Helen Mosely, Rose House, Caerystwyth Road, Castletown.'

'Do you happen to know the postcode?'

'I haven't got a clue.'

'No worries, I know the street.'

The DS closed his book, returned it to his pocket with the required information scribbled inside in blue ink and swivelled in his seat to face the inspector, who nodded her silent agreement. The interview was at an end for what it was worth. It was a case of checking out his story and progressing from there. They had nothing of worth. Nothing that would result in any charges and they both knew it full well. If Mosely had indecently assaulted an anonymous female student he was likely to get away with it, unless additional evidence surfaced in the coming days. If he had anything to do with Emma's disappearance, which seemed highly unlikely, there was zero evidence to support the hypothesis.

As Rankin reached out to switch off the recording equipment, Mosely became increasingly agitated, wringing his hands together repeatedly and breathing heavily, as if he'd taken part in some demanding physical activity. They believed the bastard's lies. They actually believed the crap in that fabricated letter! 'What about Goddard? Surely you're going to talk to Goddard about all this?'

Rankin chose to ignore what he considered Mosely's predictable protestations and stood to leave. 'Can you keep him here until I've spoken to his parents later today, Pat?'

'Yeah, I'm sure I can arrange that for you.'

'Thanks, it's appreciated.'

Inspector Stevenson handed her prisoner an explanatory note detailing what would happen to the tapes, gripped him firmly by the arm and led him towards the door. 'Come on young man, I'm sure the custody sergeant can find you some suitable accommodation for an hour or two.'

Chapter 22

Grav popped a second Trebor Extra Strong Mint into his mouth in a further attempt to mask the lingering smell and tang of the previous night's alcoholic excess, and checked the wall clock above his desk for the third time that morning. 'How am I looking, Clive my boy? Is my tie straight?'

Rankin looked up from his paperwork and grinned. 'Stunning as always, boss, how long have you got before kick off?'

'I'm meeting Emma's parents in reception in about ten minutes.'

'It wouldn't be a bad idea to run an electric shaver over your chin if you've got the time. You don't want to upset the chief super again. Mine's in the top drawer if you want it.'

The DI rose to his feet and glanced at his reflection in the nearby window. 'No thanks, mate, I think I'll do. It's a press conference not a beauty pageant.'

'Well, it's there if you want it.'

'I fucking well hate this high-profile press shit. You know what the arseholes are like. Always looking to criticise anything and everything to sell a few miserable papers to the masses. Do you remember some of the crap they wrote about the Galbraith case? What a bunch of bastards!'

Rankin nodded and pushed his paperwork to one side. 'Yeah, but it's got to be done, boss. Let's just hope it results in something useful this time. We could do with some luck for a change.'

Grav bent down stiffly and polished the front section of each of his black slip-on shoes with a thick woollen sleeve of his increasingly bedraggled jacket. 'Let's hope so, Clive my boy, let's hope so.'

When DI Gravel opened the conference room door with Emma's anxious and fidgeting parents in close attendance, the chief superintendent was already seated behind one of two adjoined light oak, veneered tables, facing a legion of journalists. She was resplendent in a newly dry-cleaned dress uniform with four highly polished shiny buttons that reflected her impressive attention to detail. As he took a single step forward, he was momentarily stopped in his tracks by a barrage of clicking flashing cameras that left him dazzled, and he waited for the sudden frenzy to subside before guiding Mr and Mrs Jones towards their seats and finally sitting himself.

The fresh-faced, recently appointed chief superintendent rose easily to her feet with her carefully prepared notes clutched tightly in one hand and held up an open palm to draw the attention of all those present. 'If you could all take a seat and quieten down, I'll introduce you to the panel and we can progress matters from there.'

Her attempt to introduce some semblance of order to the proceedings was predictably met with a bombardment of barely decipherable, overlapping questions that made little if any sense and left her reeling. She stilled herself, successfully collecting her thoughts despite the cacophony and addressed the gathering in piercing, high-pitched south of England tones, clearly pronouncing each and every word above the gradually receding din. 'There will be plenty of time for questions at the appropriate time later on, but for now, I would ask that you listen to what the police and Mr and Mrs Jones have to say. Emma's parents are going through an extremely difficult time, as I feel sure you can appreciate. I would ask you to respect that fact and to behave accordingly.'

As the room gradually responded to her appeal and the babble reduced to virtual silence, she referred to her handwritten notes for the first time and continued, 'Right, that's better, thank you, we'll make a start… My name is Chief Superintendent Hannah Davies, the operational head of policing for the Caerystwyth division. I'm pleased to introduce you firstly to Mr and Mrs Jones, the missing girl's parents, who will make a brief statement shortly, and secondly to Detective Inspector Gravel, who is the lead detective on the case. DI Gravel will address you now and bring you up to date with the developments in the case, as far as operational matters allow. There are some issues we are unable to address publicly at this point and I apologise for that in advance. As frustrating as it may seem, it's not something that can be avoided.'

As Grav pushed his chair back a few inches and stood, he was cursing his arthritic knee joints and reluctantly acknowledging that CS Davies had done an admirable job of handling what was always going to be a difficult situation.

Wonder of wonders. It seemed she did have her uses after all.

He scanned the room with clouded red eyes and began his note-free and heartfelt presentation, in the usual to-the-point, no-nonsense style admired by his subordinates and equals, but not so much by the force's top brass. 'Right, you're all very well aware that the bodies of five young women have been found in a local wood. They were killed and buried at intermittent periods in the last five years and it won't come as a surprise to you to hear that we have very good reason to believe that they were murdered by the same man. We have identified three of the victims up to this point: a Sarah Breen, who was twenty-one years of age, Gloria Peacock, who was just nineteen and Joanne Gillespie, who was twenty-two when she died. Enquiries have established that all three girls were sex workers in the north of England, with a history of drug abuse. Two of these girls grew up in local authority care. The other two, as yet unidentified women, are of a similar age and height. They all had either natural or dyed shoulder-length blonde hair.'

He glanced at Mr and Mrs Jones, whom he noted were sitting clutching each other's hand, before adding, 'Emma, the missing university student, meets the same physical description. Although, and I want to stress this, there is absolutely no suggestion that she has any history of prostitution or drug use. If the same man took Emma, as we suspect is the case, he has deviated from his usual pattern of offending.'

Grav paused to allow the resulting chatter to abate before continuing, 'Enquiries are ongoing in an attempt to put a name to the two currently unidentified girls and to notify their families accordingly. Various police forces in the north of England are trawling through their missing persons records as we speak, with that aim in mind. As and when we know their identities, we will notify you of that fact via a press release.'

He turned, removed his woollen jacket, hung it on the back of his chair, tugged his rugby club tie loose at the collar, undid the top button of his shirt and faced the room again, as the chief superintendent looked on disapprovingly in that now-familiar indomitable way of hers. 'It goes without saying that the killer poses a very significant risk to females. Arresting him and arresting him quickly is our highest priority. But, like it or not, that's a lot easier said than done. We're going to need the public's help to catch the bastard, and that's where you people fit in.'

The chief super didn't exactly have her head in her hands at that point, but she may as well have had and Grav could sense her undoubted displeasure emanating from her every pore as he cleared his throat loudly and continued, 'We have very good reason to believe that at least one of the victims was transported to the burial ground in an estate car, which may or may not have been an Audi. We are unsure of the car's colour at this point, although red, green or blue are strong possibilities. If any member of the public has seen such a car anywhere in the immediate vicinity of Caerystwyth Wood anytime in the last five years, they are urged to contact the police immediately. Any such information could be crucial to the investigation.'

The chief superintendent took a deep breath, stood for a second time and waited for Grav to take a seat, as her left foot tapped repeatedly against the parquet flooring, in an involuntary subconscious attempt to control her growing anxiety and irritation. The DI was old school. That was the best way of looking at it. He was a dinosaur. The type of officer who would soon be extinct. 'Thank you, Inspector. That was...'

Grav remained standing and looked her in the eye. 'I haven't finished yet.'

Her facial muscles tightened as she resisted a determined frown that appeared on her face despite her best efforts to contain it. She turned back to face the throng of journalists, feeling more than a little embarrassed. 'It seems that the inspector has more information to share with you before I ask Mr and Mrs Jones to address you in person.'

She returned to her seat quickly and self-consciously shuffled her papers, as the DI manoeuvred his considerable bulk around the table and stood directly in front of it, within two or three feet of the first row of media reporters. 'Not only did the killer transport five young women's battered bodies to Caerystwyth Wood, but he then had to get those bodies from wherever he parked to the burial ground. Now, even the closest point where he could potentially have parked whatever vehicle or vehicles he used, is a significant distance from the burial site, and that would have taken a great deal of effort on his part. Dead bodies aren't light.

They're not easily moved. He would have had to carry or drag each body over rough, uneven and sloping ground. That would take some doing, even for the strongest of men.'

He paused again, allowing the information to sink in before continuing, 'Now, I'm assuming the bastard transported the bodies after dark, probably in the early hours of the morning when the chances of detection were minimised. With that said, there's always someone about. Someone *must* have seen something. If anyone saw anything suspicious, anything at all, I want to know about it as soon as possible. Pick up the phone or call at the station in person. Did anyone see a man carrying anything that with hindsight could have been a body? It could have been covered in something, like a sheet or a rug for example, to make it less obvious. Or, did anyone see a man carrying a shovel towards the wood, in the wood, or away from the wood? He must have had one, or something similar. Graves don't dig themselves. I don't give a toss what any potential witness was doing when they saw something. I don't even care if they were out thieving. People can come forward, no questions asked, if required. Even the seemingly most insignificant information could be crucial to catching the man who brutally murdered and mutilated those girls.'

He stopped speaking again for a second or two, catching his breath, conscious of his chest tightening and his heart beating in his throat… 'And I want to make it crystal clear that someone out there knows who this killer is. It could be your husband, your boyfriend, your brother, your neighbour or workmate. Just think about it for a minute. Have you had your suspicions? Have they been acting strangely? Have they taken an overly significant interest in the details of the case on the news or in the daily papers? Has there been blood on their clothes?… I'm appealing to anyone who has any information or suspicions to think about the dead girls and to come forward. If you're protecting this man, consider what he's done. Consider what he may do in the future if he's not caught. If you know something and keep it to yourself, you'll be partly responsible if and when he kills again. It's not something many people could live with. It just doesn't bear thinking about…'

He took a blue Ventolin asthma pump from a trouser pocket and inhaled two urgent puffs before adding, 'And that brings me to Emma Jones… Are there any questions before I move on?'

A long-in-the-tooth, alcohol and tobacco-ravaged journalist representing a popular tabloid, shouted above the resulting commotion to make himself heard, 'Why isn't the chief constable here? Come on, what's your answer?'

Grav scowled and glared at the man before responding. The miserable sods were always looking for an angle. Anything to tear apart, spit on and grind into the dust, whatever the cost to an investigation and the people on the receiving end. 'Look, if you want to talk politics, you're talking to the wrong man. My job's to catch the killer, nothing more, nothing less. That should be clear enough for you. Now, does anyone have any sensible questions that are actually worth answering, before I continue?'

The journalist had heard it all before more times than he cared to remember and wasn't inclined to give up easily. 'What's more important than five murders and a missing girl? Why isn't he here? Maybe he's at the golf club again. I've been told he likes to play around. And that wasn't a slip of the tongue, by the way.'

A quickly vanishing smile left the chief superintendent's face to be replaced by an anxious glower as she reached over and tugged at Grav's sleeve, effectively silencing him before he said something she suspected she'd seriously regret, but that she knew wouldn't bother him in the slightest. A small but vocal part of her admired his attitude. A part of her wished she was more like him. A part of her wanted to tell them all exactly what she thought of the top man's absence. But, that didn't get you up the greasy pole. It didn't get you to the top. It was time to play the game.

She stood, waited with increasing impatience for the inevitable journalistic laughter to subside and noted that Emma's mother was whimpering pitifully, before saying, 'Mr Brown has been called away on urgent business and has asked me to apologise for his unavoidable absence. I will be updating him re developments just as soon as this meeting is over.'

She chose to ignore the resulting jeers, admonishing herself for not allowing Mr and Mrs Jones to speak first and leave the bear pit at an earlier stage of the proceedings, as the psychologist has so insistently advised. That was another lesson learnt. Mark it down to experience.

Grav leaned towards her and spoke directly into her ear virtually at touching distance, causing her to flinch slightly when hit by the toxic, heady mix of stale cigar smoke and minty confectionery on his polluted breath. 'I still haven't finished.'

Oh no, and just when she'd thought things couldn't get any worse. 'You haven't?'

'Na.'

'Is it important?'

Grav nodded once. 'I'd say so.'

Okay, swallow your pride little lady, the investigation has to come first. She rapped hard on the tabletop with her clenched knuckles and spoke up loudly and clearly, insisting on being heard above the prattle. 'Detective Inspector Gravel has further matters to discuss. Can I ask for silence?'

She returned to her seat and listened with a degree of trepidation as Grav rested his substantial weight on the edge of the table. 'Right, people, back to Emma Jones... I've already told you that she matches the physical description of the five dead girls. Read what you want into that, but the potential implications should be obvious to anyone. She was abducted from her student digs in Cardiff in the early hours of the second of May. That's now nearly three weeks ago! Finding her and finding her fast is crucial if we've got any chance at all of finding her alive. She was carried from her digs and placed in the back of an estate car in a city street popular with students. Someone must have seen something, whatever the time of night. And this is where you lot come in again. We need your help. *I* need your help. And more importantly, Emma Jones needs your help. I want her smiling face on the front of every newspaper and on every TV news report until she's found.'

He turned and pointed towards Mr and Mrs Jones, who were looking increasingly shell-shocked with every minute that passed. 'Just look at the parents. Look at the state they're in. Imagine how you'd feel if it were your daughter in the hands of this man. Like I said, we know the bastard used an estate car at the time of the abduction, but little more. I want to know the make, model and colour of that car. Anyone with information should pick up the phone. They shouldn't hesitate. This is far too important for that... Now, is there any sensible questions before I hand over to the chief super?'

'Have you got any key suspects?'

'Have you got a description?'

'How close are you to catching him?'

'What are the chances of Emma being alive after all this time?'

'Are women safe in the Caerystwyth area?'

'Will he kill again?'

'How long until you make an arrest? Our readers want to know the answer. They're demanding an answer! Days, weeks, months? The clock's ticking, Inspector! Can you hear it? How long? Come on, how long?'

The DI looked around the room in silent contemplation as one unanswered question after another was shouted out by what felt like a baying mob calling for his blood. And who could blame them? Why wouldn't they ask? He would, in their place. But, what the hell could he say in response to what were entirely reasonable questions? He had fuck all of worth to offer. That was the truth of it. Nothing to placate them. Come on Grav my boy, say something. You've got to shut the fuckers up somehow. 'Okay people, if you can shut up for long enough for me to answer your questions, I'll tell you what I can.'

This time the chief super really did have her head in her hands for a fraction of a second, before pulling herself together as best she could, focussing on the task at hand, rising to her feet, and checking her Rado ceramic watch pointedly. This was not going as she'd planned. No wonder the chief constable had delegated the task and disappeared to God only knew where just as fast as his size tens could carry him. Best to get it over with and the DI out of there as soon as practically possible. 'I really don't want to keep Mr and Mrs Jones waiting for any longer than is absolutely necessary. Detective Inspector Gravel will make one final brief statement, and then it will be their turn to speak.'

Grav nodded, relieved by the relative silence, as large wet pungent sweat patches developed and expanded under both his fleshy arms and stained his cotton shirt. 'Look, I could stand here and spout some mindless bullshit version of events, but that's just not my style. I'm going to tell it like it is, for good or bad, the same as I always have. We are doing all we can. It's bloody obvious, but I'll tell you anyway. Every single available officer is focussed on, and dedicated to, this investigation. Arresting this man is our number-one priority. But, with that said, I've got no intention of making promises I can't back up with action. This type of investigation poses major challenges to everyone involved. It's high-pressure and complex work that takes time. To sum it up, we are not currently in a position to make an arrest, and I can't put a timescale on when that situation will change, as much as I'd like to. It just isn't possible.'

A young and inexperienced local weekly newspaper female journalist, sitting attentively in the second row, held her right hand in the air like a child in a classroom, and said, 'So what happens now?'

Grav inhaled a further three excessive puffs of his medication deep into his tobacco-ravaged lungs. You tell me, love. I need all the help I can get. 'As I said earlier, investigations are ongoing. I want to take this opportunity to appeal to any member of the public who has any information, however seemingly insignificant it may be, to contact us urgently.' Hadn't he said all that before? Wasn't he repeating himself? Come on Grav, hold it together, man. Get a grip. Maybe a few notes wouldn't have been such a bad idea after all.

He turned and pointed to the whiteboard on the wall behind him. 'There's a dedicated freephone number which has already been well-publicised. Anyone who wants to talk to us can phone that number, or contact their local police station if they'd prefer that option. I don't care how people contact us, as long as they do it....' And then he paused for about five seconds, before looking directly into the lens of the BBC Wales television camera located at the front of the room to his immediate left and speaking again, clearly pronouncing each and every instinctive word in soft breathy West Wales tones. 'This isn't part of the script, but I'd also like to make a direct personal appeal to the killer.'

He took a step or two towards the camera and stared at it with unblinking eyes. 'If you're listening, if you see this, I'm talking to you and only to you. I want you to contact me. I want to speak to you man to man, just you and me. You have my personal cast-iron guarantee that your number won't be traced and that anything you say to me will remain confidential to the two of us, unless you choose otherwise. It won't be used in evidence, or shared with the press without your specific prior consent. You decide the rules. You decide what we talk about and you decide who, if anyone, gets to hear what we've said to each other. If you want our conversation to stay secret, that's fine. If you want the press to announce it to the world, that's fine as well. It's in your hands. You're the man. I won't try to influence you one way or the other. Just pick up the phone, contact Caerystwyth police station and ask for Detective Inspector Gareth Gravel. You can ring whatever the day and whatever the time. I'll leave direct orders ensuring that you're put through to me, whatever I'm doing, whether I'm at work or at my home. Just contact me and we'll talk one man to another, no holds barred. I'm interested to know more about you. I'm interested to discuss your methods. If you think about it, we've got a lot in common. We're both climbing the same mountain, just from different sides. I'll be waiting to talk to you.' The DI had absolutely no intention of keeping his promises.

The chief superintendent reintroduced Emma's parents whilst Grav returned to his seat and sat in thoughtful silence. He glanced in their direction again and noted that Mrs Jones appeared very close to breaking down completely. She looked older, increasingly frail, her face deeply lined underneath the understated make-up. So very different from the somewhat intimidating and admirably determined woman he'd met only weeks before. Stress had a habit of doing that.

Everyone waited as the tension mounted, but neither parent spoke at first. They just sat there gripping each other's hands tightly below the table and staring out into the room as the cameras flashed repeatedly, and unwelcome mental pictures invaded their anxious minds. Grav leant towards them in his seat, and patted Mr Jones on his broad back. 'It's time to say something, Ray. Like we talked about. Do you remember? Just tell them how you feel. Tell them about your little girl.'

The father nodded, said, 'Yeah,' in a faltering voice reverberating with raw emotion and rose unsteadily to his feet with his wife at his side.

'Come on, Ray, tell them about Emma. Tell them what a wonderful person she is.'

He turned his head, smiled at his wife unconvincingly and said, 'I will, love. I can do this.'

She mirrored his smile as her tears began to flow. 'Of course you can, love, Emma's depending on you.'

Raymond Jones took a deep breath, blew the air from his mouth with an audible high-pitched whistle and began, 'Emma is our only child, and she means everything to us.

Our beautiful daughter is just nineteen years of age. Her life has just begun. She has a life to live, and she should be l-looking forward to a bright, happy and successful future. She's a lovely, intelligent and hard-working girl, who wants to be a research scientist when she finally completes her studies at Cardiff University. And, she's doing really well on her course. She's attaining good grades, and wants to go on to achieve a Master's degree, and even a PHD after that, all being well. Her tutor, a Professor Mark Goddard, says she shows great promise, and I've no doubt that, if g-given the ch-chance, she'll go on to achieve great things. She's the sort of girl who wants to help others. She's the sort of person who puts others before herself. She's the sort of girl who puts herself out to raise money for charity. She even works as a volunteer in a Cardiff Oxfam shop when her studies allow her the time. That's the sort of person she is: an ordinary, wonderful, kind and generous young girl, who doesn't deserve to die. Not now, not at such a young age, and not at the hands of a killer.'

Mrs Jones squeezed her husband's hand, and spoke directly into his ear, 'Well done, love, you spoke from the heart; now it's my turn.'

'Are you sure you're up to it?'

She nodded. 'Just try to stop me.'

That was the determined woman he knew. That was the courageous woman he married. 'Okay, I'll be here at your side for as long as you need me.'

Anne Jones dabbed away her tears with a clean white linen handkerchief taken from her patent leather handbag, and looked directly into the lens of the television camera, as DI Gravel had earlier in the proceedings. 'I'm speaking to whoever took Emma from her student bedroom in Cardiff on the second of May this year. Whoever you are, wherever you are, I'm appealing to you as a mother. If my daughter is still alive, I'm begging you to think about who she is and what you've done and to let her go. Please don't harm her in any way. She doesn't deserve that. If you want to kill someone, then kill me. I'd gladly exchange my life for hers. Please free her to be with her family again.'

She stopped speaking for a time, collecting her thoughts and searching for the correct words, words that would have the powerful emotional impact she craved. 'And, if she's dead, if you've already killed my lovely, beautiful, innocent girl; if it's already too late to save her precious life, please have the basic decency to tell the police, or the press, or anybody else, where she is, so that we can bury our daughter properly and mourn her loss together. That's not too much to ask, is it? Either way, alive or dead, whatever you've done, we want our little girl home with us.'

Chapter 23

The room resembled numerous other opulent modern four-
and five-star hotel watering holes, with subtle lighting,
multiple small, smokey-grey glass-topped tables,
comfortable, well-padded black leather seats, an appealing
well-stocked bar and enthusiastic attentive staff in
immaculate livery.

The inspector looked on as Dr Randolph Tremblay the
second downed a third double whisky with a rapid flick of
his wrist and said, 'Just give me the bottle, barman, I'll sign
it to the room,' in a slow Texan drawl as smooth as melted
chocolate.

'And I thought the Welsh could drink.'

The doctor gripped the three-quarters full bottle of
American whisky in one hand and his empty glass in the
other as he headed for a chair in a quiet corner of the bar. 'I
like to think of it as an occupational hazard, Inspector. It
comes with the territory. I find it helps not to think too
clearly for too long these days, if you know what I'm
saying.'

Grav took a seat opposite the doctor and nodded. 'Yeah, I
guess it takes the edge off.'

Dr Tremblay refilled his glass almost to the halfway point,
lifted it to his lips and took a predictably overly generous
swig of the golden liquid, before placing his glass back on
the table and leaning towards Grav, who was sipping a half
pint of weak bitter shandy less than enthusiastically. 'Why

not join me, Inspector? You don't look like a shandy man to me.'

The big Texan seemed as sober as a judge. The man could certainly knock them back a bit. He certainly put Rankin in the shade. Why not book a room and enjoy a few drinks? It might be an idea. He had the taste for it. Na, he had to get back to the patch. Grav held up his glass in full view. 'I'll stick with this stuff, thanks. I'll be heading west as soon as we're done here. Things to do, people to see. You know how it is.'

'So it seems I'm going to be drinking on my own again.'

'It seems so.'

The doctor relaxed back in his seat and placed his feet on the low table, revealing caramel-brown, handcrafted western boots with two-inch cowboy heels, which made him appear even taller than his natural six-foot-four-inch frame. 'So what can I do for you, my friend?'

About bloody time. 'I caught the last half hour or so of your lecture. Impressive! Did you have any direct involvement with any of those cases?'

Dr Tremblay smiled warmly and held out his hands, as if waiting to be handcuffed. 'Now, that depends on what you mean by involvement. I didn't actually kill any of those gals, if that's what you were wondering.'

Another fucking comedian! Just what he needed after a long day. 'Look, I haven't got time for this shit. I've got five dead girls, another one who's missing and very little to go on. I haven't driven halfway across the country to listen to you taking the piss.'

The big Texan broke into a smile that lit up his angular face. 'I like you, inspector. I like you a lot. I'm going to help you, if I can… So, tell me, what can I do for you?'

'You've got real experience, right, it's not all theory?'

'Yes, I have.'

The DI silently acknowledged that he was satisfied with the response. The man exuded a world-weary self-confidence born of experience. The big American didn't feel the need to justify himself and that was good enough for him. Maybe it would prove not to be a wasted trip after all. 'Can you give me some pointers? I need to be sure I'm covering all the bases.'

The doctor tilted his head at an approximate forty-five-degree angle and met Grav's eyes. 'That's one hell of a task without seeing the files!'

'Is it one you can help me with?'

'How long have you got?'

Grav stretched out an arm, poured the remainder of his lemonade shandy into a large nearby terracotta plant pot and picked up the whisky bottle. 'As long as it takes, Doctor, as long as it takes.'

The doctor nodded and smiled engagingly. 'Well, make yourself comfortable, my new friend. It's going to be a bumpy ride.'

'So where do you want me to start?'

'Why don't you run me through the key details of your case from the very beginning and we can see what we're dealing with?'

The DI spent the next hour or so outlining every aspect of the case from beginning to end, leaving nothing out and paying fine attention to detail.

'Is that it?'

'I'm afraid so. That's as good as it gets.'

'So you've only been able to identify three of the victims up to this point?'

'Yeah, all prostitutes from other parts of the country.'

'So, if he has abducted this Cardiff student, this Emma Jones, it seems he's strayed from a well-established modus operandi.'

Grav nodded and picked up his glass. 'It seems likely.'

'And you're sure it's the same man.'

'Yeah, I am. I'd bet my life on it.'

'So, either he's gaining confidence or he's getting sloppy. Either way, it may give you a better chance of catching him.'

'Let's hope so.'

The doctor drained his glass, lowered his feet to the floor, picked up the bottle, and refilled both glasses before responding. 'All right my friend, I think I've got a reasonably clear picture of what you're facing.'

'Okay, so what type of man am I looking for?'

'That's a big question.'

Grav sipped his drink and savoured the familiar malty spirit on his tongue, before placing his glass back on the table. 'You're the expert, what's the answer?'

'First things first, and this is important. You need to drop any misleading Hollywood-driven preconceptions that you're looking for some Hannibal Lecter-like evil genius

248

who plans every move in infinite detail. You may be, of course, they do exist, but probably not. They're in the minority, thank the good Lord in heaven. Reality tends to be far much more complex than the movies make out.'

Grav sighed loudly and shifted his weight in his seat as his ageing knees began to stiffen and complain. 'I was thinking more evil bastard than evil genius, to be honest.'

'Look, you need to understand that there's no generic fits-all profile that's going to help you catch this predator. The bad news is that most of these killers aren't your stereotypical solitary social misfits who live in self-imposed isolation. Neither are they two-headed, salivating, drooling rabid monsters you could spot a mile off. They don't come with *psycho* stamped on their foreheads. They may even appear likeable until you really get to know them, if you get my gist. The only people who actually see the killer's true nature are the unfortunate victims. They hide it well, that's what I'm saying, they hide it well.'

Grav nodded twice. 'Yeah, I know what you're saying.'

'So, you have to appreciate that your man may be hiding in plain sight. He could have a wife and children, a home and a job. He could be the guy next door, or even someone you work with… Look, I guess what I'm trying to say is that despite what he is, despite the heinous things he's done and whatever his motivations, he may well appear to be a surprisingly normal member of your community. And, that's your problem in a nutshell: a lot of these people blend in so well that they're ignored by both the police and their potential victims. That's how they get away with it for as long as they do. They're often the last people you'd suspect: the unremarkable, the seemingly ordinary. If you heard me talking about Gary Ridgeway, the Green River killer, you'll know exactly what I'm talking about.'

'Yeah, I caught the last ten minutes.'

'You look at that man and think, really? Him? That insignificant, goddamn fucking asshole killed at least forty-nine women in a three-year-period? You've got to be kidding me. Even after you know the full facts of the case, it can still be hard to accept. We don't see the monster behind the mask.'

'Forty-nine, that's well over one a month!'

The doctor drained his glass and frowned. 'He killed prostitutes, drug addicts, the homeless, easy targets, just like your man, right up to the abduction of the Jones girl. It was probably even more than forty-nine. Crazy when you think about it. But, it's his apparent ordinariness I want to drive home to you. Those women knew there was a murderer on the loose, they knew he was hunting and killing on their patch, but it didn't stop them getting in Ridgeway's vehicle, because he seemed so damned unthreatening. Do you get my point? The police missed valuable clues for precisely the same reason. Don't make that mistake, Inspector. Don't rule any suspects out without very good reason.'

'I get it. You're preaching to the converted. One of the vilest bastards I ever had the misfortune to meet had everyone conned for years. He was one callous manipulative bastard, dripping with insincere charm and self-importance.

A child killer employed as a consultant child psychiatrist. It's hard to get a man like that out of your head.'

'Okay, that's good. So, you know what I'm talking about. Ted Bundy was a classic example of that type of killer: a serial kidnapper, rapist and necrophile who felt zero remorse and charmed the people around him to meet his own deviant needs with seemingly effortless ease. Women loved him and denied his guilt. They even sent him fan mail in prison. He was a good-looking and intelligent guy, and he used it to his advantage.'

'I read about that. He was one evil bastard.'

'You're not going to hear me arguing with that particular conclusion… Now, there's one guy who's better off dead.'

'So how does it help me?'

The doctor took the first Marlboro cigarette from a packet of twenty, lit the tip and savoured the nicotine hit as the noxious fumes spiralled into the air. 'I don't know that it does, Inspector… Who've you looked at up to this point?'

Grav lifted the whisky to his lips and sipped the warming liquid before responding. 'We've been working our way through a list of sex offenders, in addition to those men with a history of violence towards women.'

'That sounds like a very long list.'

'Yeah, and that's if he's on the list at all.'

'Well, I guess it's a start. Any standout suspects?'

'I only wish there were. Like I said, all we've got is a vague and inconsistent description of a vehicle used by the killer and the report of a potentially heavily disguised individual, who may or mayn't be significantly younger than he appears.'

'So, at least you've got an idea of his ethnic identity, height and build. It's a basic starting point.'

'Yeah, he's white and of average build and height, but that matches most of the male population of the UK.'

'It's got to be better than nothing.'

Grav laughed humourlessly. 'I guess so, but only just.'

The doctor checked the time and shouted out loudly, ordering three packets of salted peanuts without leaving his seat. 'Anything for you, Inspector?'

'I'm all right, thanks. I had a couple of sausage rolls on the way here.'

Dr Tremblay thanked the waitress, ripped open the first packet, poured half its contents into his open mouth and began chewing. 'At l-least you're not assuming that the killer's motivation is s-sexual. I've witnessed that error more than once over the y-years. It could be, of course, but not necessarily. You may not be looking for a sex offender at all.'

Talk about stating the fucking obvious. Na, who was he trying to kid? He'd never felt more out of depth in his life. 'Can you expand on that for me?'

'Give me a second to s-swallow this lot… There you go, that's better… Your man could be motivated by feelings of uncontrollable rage, thrill-seeking, attention-seeking, or a combination of some or all of them. And then there are the guys who hear voices telling them to kill a certain group of individuals. Your Peter Sutcliffe is a good example of that ilk. Do you know the case?'

'It was all over the news for months a few years back.'

'Keep an open mind, that's what I'm saying. Don't make any assumptions and use what you know about the case to both add to and narrow down your list of suspects as and when you can. Basic good police work.'

'I'm just thinking out loud here… The three victims we know of were taken from the north of England, but dumped on our patch, yeah?'

'That's what you told me.'

'So, what are the chances of him being a local man? He obviously knows our patch well enough.'

'It's hard to say with any certainty, to be honest, Inspector. Most serial killers hunt, kill and dispose of their victims within a defined area. It's what the FBI like to refer to as a *zone of comfort*. But, with that said, there are anomalies. From what you've told me, it seems your killer may well be one of those rare exceptions.'

'That's the way I see it.'

'You need to consider itinerant men who move from place to place, homeless individuals who stay in an area for a time and then move on, and those individuals whose employment lends itself to travelling around the country, such as truck drivers or those in military service, as you suggested yourself… You're thinking along the right lines, my friend. Keep doing what you're doing and maybe, just maybe, you'll get a break. Your man's gotten away with killing at least five girls without getting caught. He's likely to be feeling empowered, and that may be a positive in investigative terms. He may well slip up if and when he kills again. It's not that these people want to be caught. It's that they *think* they can't be caught. They get overconfident. Like it or not, that may well be your strongest hand.'

Grav emptied his glass greedily as the blood drained from his face. 'That's the best you've got? Wait till the bastard kills again and hope he leaves some clue? You're supposed to be the expert, the man with all the answers. I'm in danger of drowning here and you can't offer me anything better than that?'

'Yeah, I know it's not what you came here to hear, Inspector, but that's the way it is. False hope is no hope, my friend. You've got to deal with the reality. Maybe next time one of those cigarette butts will give you the DNA evidence you're looking for. Maybe he'll be seen. Maybe you'll find a better witness who's actually got something worthwhile to offer you. Hell, maybe someone will give you his name.'

'I won't hold my breath on that account… Do you think there's any chance of him stopping before being caught?' He was clutching at straws, desperately clutching at straws. And he knew it full well.

Dr Randolph Tremblay the second ran a hand through his neat short brown hair and smiled thinly. 'You're not getting desperate are you, Inspector?'

'Just answer the fucking question.'

'It's not unheard of. I can think of one or two serials who stopped killing before getting caught, but it's a long shot, a rare exception rather than the rule. It's certainly not something you can rely on. If I were a betting man, I'd say your man's enjoying himself rather too much. If you don't put an end to his activities, he's likely to kill again and soon.'

Chapter 24

The professor repeatedly picked at the large crusty scab at
the back of his head with the first two nails of his right hand,
whilst reaching up and switching on the spotlights with his
left. He grinned as Emma opened and shielded her eyes from
the intense glare and yawned. The stupid bitch thought it
was morning again. The poor deluded mare. Some things, he
pondered, never failed to amuse him despite their familiarity.
It was taking pleasure in the little things that gave life colour
and made it worth living. 'Good day, my lovely, I have good
news for you. Did you remember? Did you get me a card?'

She pulled the sky-blue quilt around herself to protect her
modesty within the limits of her situation and sat upright,
already dreading what the new day would bring. What on
earth was the vile bastard talking about this time? What did
the beastly man want her to say? Continued silence wasn't
an option. She'd made that mistake before. Come on Emma,
say something girl, you've got to say something. 'I don't
know what you mean, master.'

'You don't? Really? I thought you'd be as excited as I am.'

Think Emma, think, search your anxious mind. She was
close to panic now, frantically searching for an answer that
would satisfy him to some degree. 'I don't know, I'm sorry,
master, I just don't know what you're talking about.'

The bitch was squirming, just as he liked it. Squirm away,
my lovely, squirm away. 'There's no need to get upset,

Venus Six. Put a smile on your pretty face and let go of the quilt. It's a happy day, a day of celebration... Now, do you know? Shall I tell you, or would you like more time to think? I've had to take a few days off work after that unfortunate accident I mentioned, and so there's no rush. We've got all the time in the world.'

That wasn't good, it wasn't good at all. What to say? How to play it? What response was he looking for this time? 'I'm really sorry, master, I just can't figure out what you're talking about, however hard I try. Perhaps you could help me. Perhaps you could give me a clue. I'm not as clever as you are.'

He laughed, amused and gratified by her response. 'Well, at least you've come to understand that, my lovely. It would be a potentially fatal error to underestimate me, even for a moment.'

The deluded bastard had an ego the size of the room. 'I would never do that, master. You're a truly great man.'

Yes, he was, yes he was! None of the others had realised that. She was inspired in her assessment. She was special, just as he'd suspected, just like he was. 'Then I'd better tell you about our special day and allow you to join the celebrations.'

She clutched the small razor blade tightly under the quilt and pictured herself slashing his throat again and again and again. 'Thank you, master.'

'It's our four-week anniversary, my lovely. I marked it on my calendar in blood-red ink for posterity. It's four weeks to the day since you arrived in your new home. Isn't that marvellous? That's something to remember for as long as you live, wouldn't you agree?'

Oh God, four whole weeks! Four weeks in a concrete box. Four weeks without a breath of fresh air in her lungs. Four weeks without sight of the sky… But, at least she was alive. That was something to hold on to. And, they had to be looking for her. Surely, they were looking for her. 'Happy anniversary to you, master. It's good of you to spend time with me.'

'Well, thank you, Venus. That's very good to hear. I was hoping you'd be as pleased as I am. I thought I'd prepare you a very special meal with a few surprises to brighten your day. I'll see what I can find in the freezer.'

She lifted the quilt to allow the light to illuminate her lower body and confirm her suspicions. The numerous fresh scratch and bite marks on her skin told their own undeniable story. He'd done it again. The vicious demented bastard had done it again. She tightened her grip on the blade and decided to act on her inclinations at the first opportunity. 'You made love to me again last night, didn't you, master?'

He was taken aback, genuinely surprised by her use of the L word. 'You've no complaints, I presume?'

It had to be worth a try. What was there to lose? 'No, of course not, master. Why would I complain? It's just that I think I could be a much better lover were I conscious when you visit me. You could explain your needs and I could do my utmost to meet them. That's something we could both enjoy together, isn't it?'

He thought for a moment, before dismissing the suggestion out of hand. 'Oh, I don't think so, Venus. You do want me to be honest with you, don't you?'

Don't give up Emma, don't give up quite yet. If she were to gain the chance to attack and escape, she had to create the opportunity. 'I want to show you how much I've come to care for you, master. You're the only important person in my life.'

Was she being sincere? Were her words a true reflection of her feelings? Yes, they probably were. 'I rather enjoy the lack of interaction, Venus. I love the way you lie there silent and unmoving. The repeated rise and fall of your chest and the warmth of your body are perhaps a little off-putting at times, but I'll soldier on with the current arrangements, if that's all right with you?'

A wave of hopeless depression rolled over her as a potentially viable escape route closed in an instant. 'Please think about it, master. It would mean so much to me.'

All was silent for a minute or two before he said, 'I have an idea I want to sound out with you before I prepare your breakfast.'

She counted to five inside her head and sighed. What now? How much more of this crap could she stand before losing the will to live completely? 'What is it, master?'

'I neglected to mention that I saw your needy parents on the BBC Wales six o'clock early evening news, in the company of an evolutionary throwback who referred to himself as Detective Inspector Gravel.' He chortled to himself. 'I think I may have finally discovered the missing link. If he's in charge of the investigation, I've got nothing to worry about. The man's a complete oaf!'

So, the police were looking for her. She'd featured on the news. Her case was high profile. That was hopeful. It had to be hopeful. 'What did my mum and dad say, master?'

He moved an inch or two closer to the monitor and studied her reaction closely on the screen. 'It seems that your unfortunate mother is somewhat distraught, my lovely. She even offered to take your place, although that's not an option worth considering. She doesn't come close to meeting the criteria and so you're here to stay. She looked old, broken, a woman in rapid decline. Such a sad thing to witness. I hope that's not too distressing for you to hear.'

That wasn't the mother she knew. She was brave, courageous, stoical. 'She'll be missing me, master.'

'Oh, I wouldn't worry too much about that, Venus. I got the distinct impression that she thinks you're already dead. She even asked me to tell her where your body is.'

Emma slowed her breathing and resisted the impulse to weep. 'Will you let her know that I'm still alive, master?'

He remained silent for a full thirty seconds or more before eventually responding to her heartfelt question, focussing on and enjoying her obvious discomfort. 'Well, I did consider it. I really did… but I've had a much better idea that I feel sure you'll find amusing.'

Oh, God, no! What was the raving maniac thinking now? 'What is it, master?'

'Move a little closer to the camera, my lovely. I want to watch your eyes closely as you listen to my plan. I can see into your soul and read your every thought. I see everything and I know everything. Your life is in my hands.'

Was there any point in asking again? He was toying with her, that was obvious, but she had to know the answer, however depraved, however terrifying. 'What's your idea, master?'

'Ah, so you really do want to know. I'm glad you're taking an interest in my activities. It's good to share.'

'Does it involve my mother? I'll do whatever you want if you leave her alone. Please tell me.'

He laughed as she became more and more desperate and resorted to pleading, as others had before her. 'Well, make yourself comfortable, pin your ears back, and I'll tell you in a moment or two. Are you ready?'

She pulled the quilt even more tightly around herself than before and nodded once. 'Yes, master, I'm listening.'

'I thought it may be rather amusing for you to write your mother a letter telling her not to expect you home. We could include a lock of your yellow hair as proof. That would get the police scratching their heads. I'll give it some thought and let you know if I decide to proceed.'

Oh, God, he was ready to murder her. Be brave Emma. There'd be no begging for her life, no pleading for mercy. Her words would fall on deaf ears anyway. Why give the bastard the satisfaction he so obviously craved? 'Are you going to kill me?'

'Oh, there's no need for tears, my lovely. Don't go upsetting yourself on my account. I've no plans to kill you, or at least not yet. I may kill you or I may keep you. It's not an easy decision to make. Now, is there anything else you want to ask me?'

She felt a mixture of relief and revulsion. 'What about my father?'

'You're forgetting your manners, Venus. Once more and all will be darkness.'

Play his game Emma, play his ludicrous game and buy more time whilst you still can. 'What about my father, master?'

He reached out and adjusted the volume. 'What about him?'

'How did he seem? Did he say anything?'

He chose to ignore the questions. 'You may be surprised to know that I've considered allowing you into my personal lounge for an hour or two after you've eaten today's meal. It's a mark of my developing trust. You would be ill-advised to abuse the privilege.'

She looked away and masked her excitement as best she could. At last, at last, things were changing. There may be the opportunity for escape. 'Thank you, master. That would be wonderful. I get lonely in here on my own.'

Be careful what you wish for, my lovely. Things aren't always as they seem. Don't get your hopes up. 'I want you to eat your meal as soon as I serve it. Ensure you devour every delicious mouthful and then sleep the sleep of the just. Enjoy your dreams as best you can and when you wake up, we'll spend some time together. Now, that's something to look forward to. I may even film our meeting for posterity.'

'Thank you, master.'

'I'm glad you're pleased, Venus. Think of it as a reward. Now, put on your shoes, brush your hair and dance for me.'

Emma grimaced as she awoke some hours later, the searing pain in her ankles dominating every aspect of her anxious existence. She attempted to roll over in an automated sleep-laden attempt to take the pressure off her screaming heels before opening her eyes, but her wrists jarred in the shiny stainless-steel shackles securing her hands to the room's only, aged, black-painted Victorian cast-iron radiator. She opened her eyes slowly and witnessed her new reality with a sinking feeling that enveloped her like dark impenetrable fog. She'd thought that things couldn't possibly get any worse, but it seemed she'd been wrong.

'Ah, I can see that you're finally back with me in the land of the living, my lovely. I hope you appreciate your new surroundings. It's my favourite room of all those in the house, with the exception of yours. They tell me that variety is the spice of life, although old habits die hard in my experience.'

She stared down at her bloody bandaged feet in the semi-darkness and then peered out into the gloom, as he suddenly cackled like a demented hyena and walked slowly towards her, in silhouette-form initially, as on that first night, but then gradually materialising and becoming more detailed for the first time as he drew near. She narrowed her eyes and focussed on the garishly designed clown mask, with its white face, blood-red nose and dark blue patches around small, circular, emotionless eyes, all topped by a course jet-black nylon wig. She stared at the dehumanising features with their threatening persona and associations, and tried to picture the ordinary, unremarkable human face below the rubber. She studied that mask for a long moment as he stood there in silence, allowing her to drink in his image. She then lowered her eyes, taking in the smart dark single-breasted business suit with its waistcoat and three fastened buttons, that she was certain she'd seen somewhere before in the world beyond the walls. But where?... Who was the man behind the mask?... If only she could think clearly... If only she could remember.

She winced painfully as he raised a reddish-brown leather brogue-clad foot and agitated her right heel, causing her to pull away as far as her chains would allow and attempt to scream. But all was silence as she struggled forlornly to open her mouth and fight for breath as if drowning in endless thick and suffocating treacle. The professor had wrapped her head with almost half a roll of strong grey plastic carpet tape as she lay drugged and unconscious. He had taken his time, luxuriating in the task, applying the tape precisely with the utmost care and covering her face from an inch below her delicate rounded chin, to just below her increasingly sunken, once bright and full of life, piercing blue eyes.

And then he broke the silence and spoke again, whilst slowly revealing a razor-sharp ten-inch bread knife from behind his back that glinted menacingly as a spray of bright afternoon sunlight broke through the translucent clouds and invaded the room through a small gap between the blistering wooden shutters to his left. 'Oh, please try to control yourself, my lovely. Weren't you taught good manners as a child? Surely you could hold on, rather than make a spectacle of yourself again. It's not exactly lady-like. I've provided you with more than adequate facilities to meet your girlish needs. Mother won't appreciate you staining her carpet one little bit.'

And then he knelt at her side at touching distance, avoiding the wet patch of the carpet, and ran the sharp edge of the blade slowly over her body: up, down, left to right and back again, repeating the process again and again and again, before unexpectedly clutching her hair with one hand to steady her head and thrusting the knife's sharpened tip into each of her delicate nostrils in turn. He smiled as she groaned in pain and he began lapping at the blood dripping from her nose with a keen probing pink tongue, which he poked through a conveniently located opening in the mask.

When he'd drunk his fill, he stopped, stilled himself, turned away and returned to his feet with a single athletic adrenalin-fuelled jump. 'I think you'll now find it's somewhat easier to breathe through those pretty nostrils of yours, my lovely. I had the foresight and generosity of spirit to pierce holes in the tape as you slept to allow you to draw breath, if you make a little effort. I've just made those holes a little larger for you. Breathing shouldn't be too demanding, despite the blood flow. I'm sure you'd indicate your approval and gratitude, were you in a position to speak. I do so appreciate courtesy.'

He took a single step towards her and held the knife at her throat as she wept silent tears, and looked away without moving her head for fear of further punishment and injury. 'Now, let me think, let me think. How did my last guest communicate her appreciation when in similar limiting circumstances? Ah, yes, yes, that was it, now I remember. She was a surprisingly ingenious creature given her many limitations, even when in extreme agony with her nerve endings jangling like a tambourine on a spin cycle. It was quite a turn on. I still regret killing her sometimes in my weaker moments. Perhaps you could learn from her experience and nod your head to indicate your appreciation of my efforts. I really do think that's the least you can do in the circumstances, wouldn't you agree? I've gone to a lot of effort on your behalf. I hope you're finding your new circumstances as entertaining as I am.'

As the blood began to congeal and mix with the mucous, she attempted to blow her nose hard to clear her restricted nostrils as far as possible. She sucked in the oxygen greedily before nodding once and loathing her reluctant enforced compliance with every fragment of her anguished being. What the hell was wrong with the man? He was a monster, evil personified, a godless creature devoid of basic humanity. One day he'd pay for his crimes. One day he'd be locked up for the rest of his miserable life. One day he'd truly understand custody. The bastard, the absolute bastard!

'Are you in pain, my lovely? It seems so obvious, now that my eyes have adjusted to the light and I can see you properly, sitting next to the radiator, helpless, vulnerable,

266

with blood seeping onto your body and extenuating your alluring pale white skin like nothing else could. I would offer you some analgesics or something similar to relieve your burden somewhat if I could, but sadly I'm all out of them. Mother suffers arthritis, or at least she claims to. It may be some sort of attention-seeking behaviour on her part now that I think about it, but either way, she's become rather reliant on various drugs of one kind or another these days, the aspirins included. She's not as young as she once was and so I make allowances for her weaknesses and failings in a way I never would for you or your kind. She is my mother after all.' He laughed. 'The poor dear craves death sometimes, when it all becomes too much for her. She's even talked of suicide. "I'm ready to die. I've had enough of this life." You know the sort of thing I'm talking about. I feel sure you can relate to that and empathise with her feelings a lot better than I can. It seems it's not a skill I possess. I feel nothing for others. I see such emotions as unhelpful weaknesses to be avoided. I think sympathy comes a lot more naturally to females than to males such as myself for reasons I don't fully comprehend. Wouldn't you agree? It seems rather obvious from my point of view.'

She strove to adjust her position an inch or two as her arms began to ache alarmingly and the soft skin of her wrists grated against the rough metal, becoming increasingly raw with every seemingly endless second that passed. It was crap, total utter crap, but she decided to nod again anyway. What else could she do? What real choice was there? Why bring further suffering on herself? Her situation appeared hopeless, absolutely hopeless. Maybe the monster's mother had the right idea after all. Maybe holding on to life was futile despite the stoic inner voice urging her on. Perhaps death was the best option left to her. Perhaps it would be a victory of sorts in itself.

She closed her eyes tight shut and began to pray, whilst all the time questioning if she'd receive an answer from a God who's existence she'd come to occasionally doubt in her seemingly endless suffering. Please God, if you're out there somewhere, help me. Have mercy. I'm waiting for guidance. Tell me what to do. Should I give up, or should I continue to endure this living hell for as long as I can? Either get me out of here or let me die. I just can't take any more of this. I want it to end. I need it to end one way or the other… Or was she dead and in hell already? It seemed like hell. It felt like hell. It could be hell, couldn't it? Perhaps there was a demon under that mask. Maybe she'd already breathed her last… No, no, that made no sense. Hold it together, Emma, hold it together.

He looked down at her, dropped the knife to the floor, unzipped his trousers and inserted one fumbling hand through the gaping opening. 'Pain excites me, Venus… No, no, that's not specific enough for my purpose. I understated the case. I want to explain this to you properly, if I'm to tell you at all. I need you to understand exactly where I'm coming from, what I do and why I do it.'

His eyes lit up and shone through the small round holes as he continued talking and his levels of arousal soared more and more rapidly. 'Inflicting pain excites me more than I can say. That's the best way of explaining it! Not the odd punch and kick and slap, or similar. I'm talking about real pain. The sort of excruciating pain that's impossible for the subject to bear. The tearing out of fingernails and hair, the drilling and pulling of teeth, the amputation of fingers and toes. The types of extreme pain that leave the recipient begging for compassion that never comes. It just takes a bit of imagination on my part: cutting, burning, electrocution, suffocation, drowning. The options are almost endless when you think about it. And, the greater the pain, the greater the suffering, the louder the screams and the more desperate the victim, the more I enjoy it and the higher the rush. I love the terror in their eyes. I adore the cursing, the pleading, the begging and their final despairing confused acceptance when they come to believe the end is near. There's nothing like it, nothing that even comes close. I learnt that at a surprisingly young age.'

He laughed, head back, Adam's apple protruding below the white rubber edge of the mask. 'I didn't actually abduct my first guest until about five years ago. I regret that now. I don't know why I didn't think of it before. I missed out on so many glorious opportunities. The five girls pictured on your walls gave me infinitely more pleasure than the many who died before them.'

He rubbed his penis repeatedly with rapidly moving fingers and smiled contentedly as it engorged with blood and poked through his open zip. 'And, at the end of the day, when I'm alone in bed with my merry musings, I like to think that all those girls served a useful purpose. They didn't die in vain.

My attentions justified their existence in a way our misguided society fails to appreciate. Do you understand? I've abandoned any semblance of a conscience, if I ever possessed one. I've chosen to fully accept and embrace my true nature and to satisfy my longings to the maximum degree at every available opportunity. How many people can claim that? It's what I live for.'

He paused to catch his breath as she raised her head and looked on. 'What do you think, Venus? Does my chosen path make any sense to you from your very different world? All that's missing in my life as of now, is someone who's like-minded to share my interests. I'm looking for a Bonnie to my Clyde, a Myra to my Ian, a Rose to my Fred. They had the right idea and indulged their desires without inhibition. Can you do likewise? That's what I'm asking myself. Are you the woman I'm looking for? I'm hoping you can abandon society's self-imposed limitations as I have and that we can follow in their illustrious shadows together.'

He waited with increasing impatience for a response that didn't transpire. 'Now would be an opportune time to nod your agreement, my lovely. I need to know that you're paying full attention to my lecture. I need to know that you're listening carefully and taking it all in. I need to know that you are at least considering my proposal. Do you partner me or die? That's what we need to decide between us. It's one or the other, you see. There's no other path on which to travel. And, in case you were wondering, I'll make a final decision in the coming days. I can't tell you precisely when, but you won't have long to wait. Think of your current circumstances as an extended job interview. I think that's the best way of looking at it. Give your best and we'll soon know where we both stand.'

Lecture? Come on Emma, think girl, think! The way he pronounced the word, the educated soft Welsh accent, the inappropriate heavy emphasis he placed on the C. She'd heard it somewhere before, she'd definitely heard it somewhere before, but where?... At the university! Yes, that was it, at the university... No, surely not, it couldn't be, could it?... Hold on, didn't he have a gold signet ring like that worn by the demonic clown?... Oh God, of course he did. It was Goddard. It had to be Goddard!... Really? The man she'd trusted, the man she'd admired, the man she'd looked up to?... He'd seemed so nice, so caring, so thoughtful, so interested in her academic progress, so very different from the salivating, cackling, drooling jester from the netherworld now standing before her.

He suddenly drew his arm back behind him and brought it forward forcibly with his fist clenched tightly, breaking the delicate bridge of her nose for the second time in a matter of weeks. 'Yes, the suffering of others excites me, Venus. It excites me like nothing else in this big, bad and indifferent world of ours. It's the foreplay before the climax of death, when the light finally leaves my victim's eyes forever. I like to take my guests as close to death as possible, without them actually breathing their last breath. It's a way of ensuring both that my pleasure lasts for as long as possible and that their wretched hardship is maximised. It's exciting me now, just thinking about it. I've even successfully resuscitated one or two, before continuing their imprisonment and torture and eventually killing them. I delay the climax for as long as possible to heighten my anticipation of the endgame. I'm a god in that instant. I'm the leading man, naturally, but it's a dance in which they also play their own crucial part. Like a cat playing with a mouse, or a cobra that's about to strike its prey. It's a wonderful release for both killer and victim, that one day I hope you'll come to fully appreciate and embrace as I do.'

She snorted once, then twice, to aid her breathing to some degree and shook her head incredulously, without considering the potential implications.

'You're shaking your head, my lovely. I hope that doesn't indicate your disapproval.'

She began to tremble and regretted her brief defiance immediately, as he sniggered like a naughty over-indulged child, lifted his right leg high up to his chest, stamped down hard on her left ankle with the heel of his shoe and ejaculated simultaneously, spraying globules of white sticky semen into her hair and sighing at the top of his voice as endorphins flooded his system. 'Ah, now that's much better! I've had a terrific time. It was a pleasure to spend time with you, my lovely. I had my doubts initially, but I'm glad you suggested it. Our face-to-face meeting was well worth the additional effort on my part. What do you say, Venus? Did you enjoy yourself as much as I did? I feel sure you did.'

She was frozen in indecision and didn't move, but he chose to ignore it this time, mistakenly concluding that she was very probably semiconscious due to her restricted breathing.

He leant towards her and tore the tape from her head and face. 'There you go. That should make breathing a little easier for you. I'll return you to your room in due course when you may wish to take a shower to freshen up. But, rest assured, we will do this again sometime soon, when I feel so inclined, I promise. I may even allow you to roam free around the room next time, as a very special treat. That's something to look forward to. I had the inspired foresight to sever your Achilles tendons whilst you slept. I don't think I need worry about you leaving me at this stage. I suspect walking would be an impossibility.'

She opened her mouth and sucked in the air greedily.

'Say thank you, Venus. Where are your manners? I thought I'd trained you so much better than that. You're not going to disappoint me again, are you?'

She breathed deep, filling her lungs. 'Th-an-k y-ou, m-a-st-er.'

'Pardon, did you say something? You must try to express yourself more clearly.'

'T-thank you, m-master.'

'Again!'

'Thank you, m-master.'

'Louder!'

'Thank y-you, master!'

'Very well done, Venus, that's a greatly improved performance. Shout it out and announce it to the world. I'm your master, your god, your reason for existence!'

He knelt down next to her again a couple of minutes later, took a small metal key from his trouser pocket, unlocked her shackles and returned to his feet. 'I think it's probably advisable for you to crawl as far as the bathroom, where you can sit in the shower tray before turning on the water. You'll be able to reach the tap. None of my previous guests experienced any significant difficulties in that regard when unable to stand, as I recall… Oh, and one last thing before you toddle off on all fours. I've disposed of that razor blade you kept hidden under your mattress. I wouldn't want you cutting yourself and bleeding all over the quilt or anything as awful as that. If I don't look after you properly, who's going to do it?'

Chapter 25

DS Clive Rankin sipped the warm and aromatic camomile tea recommended by his wife less than enthusiastically, hurled his half-empty box of organic herbal stress-management tablets into the grey metal wastepaper bin to the side of his desk with such force that the resulting clang reverberated around the room, and picked up his office phone on the fourth insistent ring. 'Hello, CID.'

'Is that you, Sarge?'

He sipped the fast-cooling liquid again and grimaced. What did she see in the damned stuff? 'Of course it is, you silly mare. Who else were you expecting?'

'It's Sandra on reception. There's some bloke called Edward Heywood here to see you. He asked for the DI, but he's out and about and I thought you were the next best thing.'

Rankin smiled despite his all too familiar lower backache. 'Oh, you did, did you? Thanks for the vote of confidence.'

'Glad to be of service, Sarge. If the organ grinder isn't available… How does that old saying go now? Can you remind me?'

Rankin grinned, appreciating the cheeky but well-intentioned morale-boosting banter. 'So, what does our Mr Heywood want with us?'

'He says he's got some information pertaining to the murder inquiry. He reckons it could be important.'

Rankin jumped to his feet, suddenly on full alert and paying attention. 'Keep him talking, Sandra, don't take your eyes off him and make sure he doesn't leave the building under any circumstances. I'll be with you in two minutes maximum.'

'No problem, Sarge, I can put him in interview room one, if that helps? I think it's free.'

'Sounds like a plan. You do that and make sure he stays there. I'm on my way as soon as I put the phone down.'

Rankin pushed open the door with the worn soft rubber sole of his suede Hush Puppy shoe, and entered the small interview room with its ageing white peeling paint, to be met by an unremarkable-looking, slightly built middle-aged man with short receding, once bright red hair, who rose from his chair and held out an open hand in friendly greeting. 'Eddie Heywood, nice to meet you.'

The DS took Heywood's hand in his and shook it firmly before releasing it and smiling. 'Detective Sergeant Rankin, good of you to come in. Take a seat and we'll proceed from there.'

'Thanks, I could do with taking the weight off.'

Rankin tapped the table three times with the first two fingers of his right hand. 'Right, what have you got for me?'

'Are you in charge of this murder case that's all over the news?'

Rankin shook his head and grinned. 'No, I can't say I'm in charge, but I am part of the investigation. Why do you ask?'

'I think I may be able to help you.'

'Are you local?'

'Yeah, we've got a smallholding in the wilds halfway between Caerystwyth and Llanelli.'

'Near Llwyncelyn?'

'Yeah, that's it, about a quarter of a mile from the new wind turbines.'

Rankin slid a single sheet of A4 paper and a clear plastic biro across the table and said, 'I think I know the place you're talking about. A mate of mine lives nearby. Mel Nicholson, he's a child protection social work manager. Do you know him?'

'Yeah, we were in the same class in school together.'

'Small world… If you can write your full name, date of birth, address and contact details on there for me, that'll save us a bit of time.'

Heywood picked up the pen and began writing slowly, printing each word in bold capitals with stiff movements of his left hand. 'Yeah, no probs… There you go.'

Rankin took it from him, folded it and placed it in an inside pocket of his jacket for safekeeping. 'Right then, you said you may be able to help us.'

He nodded assuredly. 'The missus told me that you've been asking if anyone's seen an estate car anywhere near to Caerystwyth Wood.'

The DS edged forwards in his seat and rested his folded arms on the table in front of him. This could be it. This could be important. Maybe here was the man to come up with the goods. 'And, you've seen something?'

'Yeah, a few months back. I'd been doing a bit of night fishing on the Towy and was walking past the entrance to Trinity Fields at about two in the morning, when a big black Mercedes swerved in front of me and nearly knocked me over. I don't think the old git driving even saw me at first.'

'When was this exactly?'

He nodded his head slowly and smiled. 'I can put an exact date on it for you. I can remember buying a box of fireworks for the kids earlier in the day. It was bonfire night.'

'Did you pay by card or cash?'

He thought for a second or two before answering. 'Cash, I think, in the new supermarket in King Street. I couldn't believe how expensive the bloody things were. They cost me over a tenner and they were all over in about twenty minutes.'

'I don't suppose there's any chance you've still got the receipt?'

He shook his head and frowned. 'No chance at all.'

'Okay, no problem. Are you sure it was a Mercedes?'

'Yeah, one hundred per cent, no doubt at all.'

'And, it was black?'

'Yeah, as black as the ace of spades.'

'Saloon or estate?'

Bloody hell, this was a bit like being on Mastermind. 'It was definitely a five-door estate car.'

Rankin's breathing quickened, as the possible significance of the information played on his mind. 'You're sure?'

'Yeah, yeah, I couldn't be more sure. I remember it as if it were yesterday. The fool could have killed me. It's the sort of thing that sticks in your mind.'

Okay, so the man was unequivocal. At last a witness who knew what he'd seen. 'About how old was it? The Merc, how old are we talking?'

'I'm not really sure. Pretty new, I guess, maybe five years maximum. I wouldn't mind one myself. You could get a lot of stuff in the back.'

'You don't think it was an old classic?'

'Oh, now you're asking… No, I wouldn't say so.'

It could be a coincidence. The old lady's car wasn't the only black Mercedes in the world. 'So, where exactly did it go after nearly hitting you? Be precise please as this matters. I need you to get it right.'

'Yeah, no bother. He drove up through Trinity Fields and towards the big house at the top. You know, the old detached place near the first band of trees.'

Oh, yes, he knew. He knew only too well. He should have looked at the Goddard's car more carefully when he had the opportunity. He should have called in the SOCO boys to check it out properly, whatever the old woman said. 'Did you see the driver?'

Heywood laughed. 'Yeah, in the orange glow of the street lamps. It was some old fart who should have given up driving years back. He came within inches of me. I don't think he even knew I was there at all, until I yelled some abuse at the top of my voice and gave him the V sign.'

'Was he an old man with long grey hair and an unkempt scraggy beard?'

Eddie Heywood looked puzzled. 'Yeah, an ageing hippy, how do you know that?'

'Give me a minute, I'll fetch a statement form and we can get this lot down on paper.'

Rankin considered heading upstairs to leave the statement and accompanying contact details in the incident room after saying his grateful goodbyes to his witness, but after a moment or two pondering his limited options, he ultimately decided that he just didn't have the time to spare. If he'd missed something, if he'd cocked up despite his years of experience, it was time to put that right. And, maybe it was a coincidence anyway. Stranger things had happened. It was too soon to call out the cavalry. He'd look a right prat if the car proved to be an irrelevance. Yeah, check it out first and proceed from there.

The DS stopped in reception for long enough to tell Sandra that he'd be out for at least a couple of hours and wished her a good day, before heading to the police garages located directly behind the main building to pick up and sign out one of the force's unmarked communal CID cars.

It was a pleasant, temperate spring morning and the small Welsh market town with its surrounding green rolling hills and hedgerows looked resplendent in the bright sunshine, but the DS didn't have the time or inclination to appreciate the glorious vista. He jumped into the Mondeo's driver's seat, started the diesel engine on the second turn of the key, manoeuvred expertly into the road, pushed his foot down hard on the accelerator and headed in the direction of Trinity Fields. He drove a lot faster than advisable, overtaking when the opportunity arose and losing patience with any driver who impeded his progress in any way at all.

Rankin arrived at his destination within fifteen minutes of leaving the police station and parked on an area of rough gravel about fifty feet or so from the house. He pondered recent developments as he approached the front door with its misleading persona of gentile respectability. The old dear was confused. The car could be a complete red herring. Or maybe not, maybe the car had been used in commission of the crimes. The possibility certainly couldn't be ruled out completely. He had to know the truth one way or the other.

The DS knocked and kept knocking with gradually increasing force until Mrs Goddard finally opened the door reticently a couple of minutes later. 'Oh, hello dear, I thought I heard someone knocking. It's lovely to see you again. Come on in.'

'Is your son in, Mrs Goddard?'

'No, he's back at work, dear. Can I help?'

Rankin got straight to the point, silently admonishing himself for losing patience with the old woman again, as he said, 'I need the keys for the Mercedes.'

She feigned confused surprise, buying time and searching for an adequate response that may satisfy him. 'Really, dear? I wasn't expecting that. Come in, come in, they must be upstairs somewhere. I seem to remember seeing them in one drawer or another.'

The DS was tempted to push past her and rush up the stairs, but instead he walked slowly behind her as she gradually ascended the staircase towards her first-floor accommodation. The old woman stopped briefly on reaching the landing, looked back and smiled warmly. 'Ah, it's always a relief to get to the top these days. My legs aren't what they were. Now, I could do with a nice cup of coffee before finding those keys you want. Will you join me?'

Rankin wanted to say no, he wanted to *shout* no, but Mrs Goddard reminded him of his long since deceased paternal grandmother and he loathed disappointing or upsetting her. 'Why don't you take a seat and put your feet up and I'll make the drinks for us? I know where the kitchen is.'

Think Margaret, think. How could she explain the car's absence? If she said she couldn't find the keys, he'd look in the garage anyway. He wasn't a complete fool. Why wouldn't he? She could feign shock and claim it must have been stolen or claim bewildered ignorance, but that was never going to satisfy the interfering busybody. 'I wouldn't hear of it, young man. When I'm too old and decrepit to make refreshments for a guest, I'll know it's time to give up and go to my grave.'

That was a bit full on. 'I'm a bit pushed for time to be honest, Mrs Goddard.'

She just stood there, swaying slowly from left to right and back again, whilst supporting her weight on her stick, with a sorrowful expression on her heavily wrinkled face. 'Why do the young always assume that people of my generation are useless? Don't you think I'm capable of making a simple cup of coffee in my own home? I'm old, not demented.'

She looked close to tears. Perhaps he'll let her make it and cheer her up a bit. The car was safely in the garage. It wasn't going anywhere. Why upset the old love any more than he had already? He was very probably on a wild goose chase anyway. 'I'm sorry, Mrs Goddard, I thought you might welcome the help. It was stupid of me. I'll sit down here and you can make us some refreshments.'

She beamed. 'And a nice bowl of bread and butter pudding? My late husband sometimes used to say it was the best he'd ever tasted.'

'Oh, go on, why not? It's not long until lunchtime.'

'That's the spirit, dear, we'll have a marvellous time together. I enjoy the company. It makes a welcome change. I'll be back with you before you know it.'

Rankin relaxed back in the armchair and waited with increasing impatience as she disappeared into the kitchen. 'Two sugars for me please, Mrs Goddard.'

She pushed open the serving hatch and smiled. 'And I thought you were sweet enough already.'

The old lady closed the hatch tightly, and spooned three heaped teaspoonfuls of instant coffee into a bone china cup before adding four teaspoonfuls of sugar and turning away to approach the medicine cupboard located on the wall at the opposite end of the room above the washing machine.

She rested her walking stick against the rounded edge of the worktop, reached up stiffly and took a clear plastic bottle three-quarters full of Temazepam syrup from the middle shelf. She unscrewed the white plastic top, hurried back across the room with the open bottle clutched in one hand and added approximately triple the recommended adult dose of the fast-acting hypnotic tranquilliser to Rankin's drink. She poured in the thick and sticky green liquid carefully, stirring vigorously for about thirty seconds until satisfied with the mixture. That should do the trick. He should be out of it and lost in his dreams within minutes of emptying the cup. Or, at least he would, if she could persuade him to drink the concoction in the first place.

She lifted the cup to her lips and sipped it inquisitively. Not bad, not bad at all! All she could taste was the excessively sweet strong coffee, just as she'd hoped, just as she'd planned. Her ungrateful son had a lot to be grateful for.

The DS consulted his watch eagerly and called out from his seat, 'Can I give you a hand with anything, Mrs Goddard?'

She pushed open the serving hatch for a second time and poked her head through. 'Oh, that's very kind of you, dear; it was coffee you wanted, wasn't it?'

Oh, come on woman, get on with it. If she found the car keys it would be a frigging miracle. 'Coffee will be just fine, thanks.'

Her face suddenly vanished from the open hatch, but she continued talking animatedly as she approached the large larder fridge. 'I'll just get the pudding from the fridge and heat it up a bit. Would you like some cream with it?'

Oh shit, not more delays. 'I prefer my bread and butter pudding cold, thanks, and without cream.'

She smiled. He was rushing. That was to her advantage. And he didn't suspect a damn thing. That was likely to serve her purpose very well indeed. 'Oh, if you're sure, dear. Perhaps you could fetch the bowls for me and carry the tray. It'll be rather heavy, all considered.'

Rankin hurried into the well-appointed kitchen, keen to progress matters as fast as feasibly possible, without upsetting the old woman any more than he already had. 'Let me take that from you.'

'Oh, thank you, dear, you're too kind. I've put two bowls ready for us on the counter and the dessert spoons are in the drawer next to the sink. I like to do things properly if I'm going to do them at all. People can be so very slovenly these days… That's it, that's it, dear, put everything on the tray and carry it into the lounge for me. Put the tray on the coffee table. Are you sure you don't want cream? I'm intending to have some.'

Rankin picked up the fully laden tray and headed for the lounge. 'Not for me, ta, it looks delicious as it is.'

'Well, I hope you enjoy it… I'll just fetch my walking stick before joining you. I'm not too steady on my feet these days, as I may have mentioned. Make yourself comfortable and enjoy your coffee. Mine's the one with milk. You did want yours black, didn't you?'

The DS sipped his drink and really didn't fancy it at all. It was too strong and too sweet. All in all pretty revolting. Perhaps best let it cool down a bit and drink it quickly without letting it touch the sides. She must have added enough coffee and sugar for six mugs, let alone one cup.

'It's great, ta, but I'll add a drop of cold water to cool it down a bit if that's okay?'

She reappeared at the door leading from the kitchen to the lounge, and made her way towards the settee. 'Oh, all right, dear. I didn't make it too strong for you, did I? I seem to make a great many mistakes these days.'

'Not at all, Mrs Goddard, it's lovely, couldn't be nicer.'

She slumped in her seat, exhausted by her efforts, leant forwards and began spooning generous portions of the homemade pudding into the two bowls, adding fresh single cream from the carton for herself, whilst awaiting Rankin's return. 'Oh, I'm glad you like it, dear. I'm grateful for the company. I don't receive many visitors these days as I may have told you before. So many of my friends and relatives have passed on to a better place. I sometimes think that it would be rather nice to join them.'

Rankin sat in his comfortable armchair to the right of the settee and began eating his pudding with genuine gusto. Okay, so the coffee was awful, but the pudding wasn't bad at all.

'What's it like, dear?'

He answered whilst eating, increasingly frustrated by the delays. 'It's lovely, just like my old mum used to make.'

She smiled again, pleased that things were continuing to go her way. Such a pleasant man. Such a sensitive man. Such a naïve fool. He appeared to have no comprehension whatsoever of the danger he faced. 'Why don't you wash it down with some nice coffee? You added the cold water. It must have cooled down enough by now.'

Rankin nodded. Best get it over with. He raised the cup to his mouth and emptied half its contents down his throat, struggling to ignore the pungent taste and keep it down.

'That's it, dear, one more swig and it'll be gone. You just sit there, drink up and enjoy your pudding and let me see if I can find those keys for you. I'm sure I'll find them in no time.'

She struggled upright with the aid of her stick and focussed on Rankin, watching him closely as he emptied his cup down his throat. He was breathing more deeply. He appeared more relaxed than he had been since his arrival. The medication was working its magic just as she'd hoped. It wouldn't be long now and she had to time it just right.

The old woman walked slowly across the room and glanced back with a subtle turn of her head, just as Rankin yawned and shook himself vigorously, keen to shake off the sudden and irresistible desire to sleep. She approached the French eighteenth-century walnut escritoire desk, stopped, glanced back again with less subtlety this time and made a show of opening the top drawer. She rested her stick against the wall to the desk's immediate right and shuffled through the contents in a fake attempt to find the non-existent keys and continue the charade. At that moment Rankin closed his eyes for the first time.

Margaret Goddard closed the drawer quietly, picked up her stick and made her way back across the room on tired legs until she reached Rankin's side. She reached down, placed an open hand on his shoulder and shook him gently. 'Wake up, dear, you look ready to go to bed for the night.'

Rankin opened his eyes, the room becoming an impressionist blur of bland colours. 'Sorry, I think I must have drifted off for a minute there. I've not been sleeping very well recently. I've never felt...'

'You mustn't overdo it, dear, there'll be someone else to do your job long after you're gone. My husband made the mistake of believing he was indispensable, but now he's dead and gone and my world's a better place. None of us are essential in reality. None of us matter a great deal. We come, we go and the world carries on without us.'

Rankin rubbed his tired eyes with the back of one hand, forced himself upright in his seat and yawned loudly. What the hell was she banging on about? 'I'm sorry about this, Mrs Goddard, I must be going in for something. I think I need to lie down.'

She grabbed his arm at the elbow. 'Come on, dear, up you get, up you get. I think we'd better get you outside into the fresh air. That seems best. You'll be wide awake and ready to get on with your day before you know it.'

The DS struggled to his feet, utilising the arm of the chair to assist himself. 'I'm sorry, I don't know what the hell's wrong with me.'

She gently guided him towards the stairs, one small unsteady step at a time. 'No need to apologise again, dear. I can see that you're feeling unwell. Come on, nearly there, a bit of fresh air will do you the world of good. That's it, a few more steps and we'll be there.'

Rankin stood swaying at the very top of the steep staircase, supporting himself by reaching out and placing the palms of his hands on opposite walls. His eyes slowly closed again as he stepped onto the first step.

'I'd rest for a minute, if I were you, dear. We don't want you losing your balance, do we?'

Just for a moment Rankin thought that he may have been drugged, but he dismissed the idea almost immediately. 'I think I need to sit down.'

That was the last thing she wanted. 'Oh, please don't do that, dear. I'd never get you up again. Just stand there for a moment longer and take deep breaths. I find that helps when I'm feeling queasy.'

The DS followed instructions like a lamb to the slaughter, breathing deeply, drawing the oxygen into his lungs and fighting the overwhelming desire to sleep. He'd never been so tired. He couldn't focus. He felt increasingly weak. What was wrong with him? What the hell was wrong with him?

As Rankin stood there, swaying slowly from left to right, right to left and back again, the old woman steadied herself, lifted her stick at an approximate ninety-degree angle, placed its black rubber tip at the very centre of his lower back, lent her weight forwards as far as she dared and pushed as hard as her ageing body allowed, sending Rankin tumbling head over heels to the bottom.

Margaret Goddard yelped in delight, and felt as excited as a puppy with a new toy, when Rankin's head cracked hard against the multicoloured olde English Victorian tiles at the base of the stairs.

She began making her way back into the lounge with a satisfied smile on her face. Her plan couldn't have worked better and she could clean the blood off the floor easily enough. Mark would be pleased. Why not enjoy another cup of celebratory coffee and relax until she saw him again later in the day? He wouldn't appreciate being disturbed prematurely, good news or not. Why did he spend so much time with that silly girl he seemed to like so much? What on earth did he do to fill the time?

She shook her head on approaching the kitchen. She'd said it before and she'd say it again: girls seemed to mature so much more quickly than boys with their very basic needs and unfortunate behaviour. Oh well, it was the way of the world and there was nothing she could do to change the fact, even if she wanted to. Would the foolish boy ever grow up?

Chapter 26

Rankin opened his blurry eyes briefly and looked up from
the hard cold floor before slowly closing them again, having
concluded that the weird clown looking down at him was the
product of a strange and confusing dream born of sleep. He
wasn't ready to get up quite yet. He'd never felt so very
tired. Why not relax and wait for Mary to wake him when it
was time to get up for work? He adjusted his position
slightly before drifting off again and reached out to pull an
imaginary quilt around his shoulders. 'Goodnight, love, see
you in the morning.'

Professor Goddard lifted his right foot high behind him
and kicked Rankin hard in the ribs, ten inches or so below
his armpit, but the detective didn't stir or move an inch.
'Was pushing him down the stairs really necessary, Mother?
It seems somewhat excessive, even for you.'

The old lady lowered herself onto the bottom step and
waved her stick in the air. What she wouldn't give for an
easy life. 'Right now I'm the only thing standing between
you and getting caught. You need to get rid of him. If he
wakes up before you make a decision and act on it, it's not
going to take him very long to start putting the pieces
together, now is it?'

The professor tore the mask from his face and threw it to
the floor, leaving a thin sheen of sweat on his face. 'What if
they come looking for him? They could already be on their

way here. What happens then, Mother? Can you answer that for me?'

She tapped the glass face of her watch repeatedly. 'You really need to calm down, Mark. Can you hear any sirens? Get rid of him, dispose of the body and hope no one knows he's here. Do it and do it quickly. There's nothing to gain by more anguished navel-gazing.'

Yes, that made sense. That was reasonable given the circumstances. It was time for action, not words. 'Where are his car keys?'

'How am I supposed to know the answer to that? Get your brain into gear, boy. Check his pockets!'

His pockets, yes, of course, where else? Professor Goddard knelt at Rankin's side, rolled him onto his back and began rooting through his pockets with frantic fingers, jacket first, followed by his trousers. He looked and looked again. Nothing, nothing! Where the hell were they?

He used all his strength and weight to push Rankin onto his side in the recovery position and checked the floor where he'd lain. Still no keys.

He rose to his feet and threw his arms in the air. 'Where the hell are they, Mother?'

'Check the car.'

The car... Yes, that made sense. They had to be in the car. He stepped over Rankin's body, opened the front door, which banged hard against the policeman's elbow, and sprinted towards the Mondeo. He tried one door, then another, then another, then another, but all were locked. He placed his forehead against the glass and peered through the driver's side window, but there were no keys in the ignition. He felt inclined to shriek and stamp and shout like a petulant child, but instead he focussed and ran back towards the front door. He jumped over Rankin's prone body as he approached the stairs. 'Out of the way, Mother. The police could arrive at any minute.'

She shook her head in frustration. 'Just calm down, Mark. His keys have to be here somewhere.'

Just shut up, Mother. Just shut your meddling mouth before I shut it for you. 'I've found them.'

'About time, now get that car out of sight.'

Professor Goddard left Rankin lying prostrate on the hall tiles whilst he opened both main garage doors wide and reversed the Mondeo inside. He closed them urgently from inside before exiting through the side door and shutting that as well.

Rankin didn't stir as the professor clutched him by the ankles, swivelled his legs so that they were facing the front door and dragged him towards the garage, one laborious step at a time. It took him almost ten minutes to reach his destination of choice and the second they were both safely inside, he slumped exhausted to the grey concrete floor alongside his victim's sleeping body. He lay there panting hard, drawing the air into his lungs and listening for any sound of approaching police cars which thankfully didn't come into being. All was silent. All was peaceful. There was no need to panic. Fate, he told himself, was on his side.

Once sufficiently rested, Professor Goddard opened the car's passenger's side front door, lifted Rankin into a sitting

293

position by his arms, placed his own arms around the detective's body with his hands linked tightly behind his back and manhandled him into the fully retracted seat. He stood there panting hard, catching his breath, resisting the primitive and instinctive urge to hit out and sink his teeth into the side of Rankin's exposed neck, reasoning that a considered thought-out and planned approach would best facilitate his ongoing relationship with Venus Six. That had to come first. As tempting as it was to cut and to gouge and to stab and to bite, he had to make Rankin's death look as if it were self-inflicted. It was the sensible approach and would bring its own rewards. There was a strange and magnetic beauty in misleading the authorities; a triumph of his genius over their mediocrity. If the police thought they'd catch him, they were wrong.

The professor lifted Rankin's legs into the car and left the door wide open whilst he searched for a hosepipe and a roll of parcel tape. Where was the hosepipe? Where the hell was it? Ah, yes, yes, he last saw it in a pile against the wall, behind the lawn mower.

He pushed the petrol mower to one side, untangled the hosepipe, dragged it towards the car, placed one end close to the exhaust pipe and left it there whilst retrieving a barely used roll of tape from a nearby toolbox. Everything was going his way. He was in control. A man on top of his game.

Professor Goddard sat on the floor at the rear of the Ford, placed the tape on top of the black plastic-covered bumper for convenience, tugged the PVC hosepipe in an upwards direction and threaded the first six inches or more into the exhaust pipe, before unrolling about four feet of tape and rapidly securing the arrangement in place. He stood slowly and admired his work for a second or two, before winding a further generous length of tape around the metal pipe just to be sure. Perfect, it couldn't be better.

Next, he wound down the car's front passenger door window an inch or two and placed the free end of the hosepipe through the resulting gap, before winding the window back up to apply sufficient pressure to secure the pipe in place. Finally, he placed the key in the ignition, started the engine on the third turn, pushed the door shut with a metallic clank and laughed loudly as Rankin slumped forwards and hunched over the dashboard. Goodbye, Sergeant inconsequent, it was good to know you, however briefly.

As the professor strolled casually back in the direction of the house a few minutes later with his mind focussed on other things, the ambling 1600cc engine was filling both the car and the garage with varying amounts of toxic fumes.

DS Rankin was breathing shallowly, but it was enough to draw the life-threatening carbon monoxide into his lungs, from where it entered his bloodstream, mixed with haemoglobin and prevented the essential distribution of oxygen around his body. Within a short time his cells and tissue began to fail and die. By the time the professor closed his front door, Clive Rankin was dead.

Professor Goddard spent several hours entertaining himself in Emma's company before eating a light supper and heading to bed just after ten. He set his alarm for 3:00 A.M. and settled down for a few hours' sleep without bothering to get undressed. It had been a long and stressful day and as he closed his eyes he told himself he needed the rest. There were still important things to achieve. Things that mattered. Things he had to get right.

He was awoken by the shrill tone of his alarm clock as intended, threw back his quilt and leapt from bed with an enthusiasm born of the desire to carry out what he considered an inspired and outstanding plan worthy of his superior intellect. By 3:15 A.M. he'd made a quick bathroom visit to empty his bladder, drunk two cups of strong milky coffee in the ground-floor kitchen and was back outside the garage, pleased to hear that the engine was still running, just as he'd left it. He threw open the main doors to their widest possible angle to allow the choking clouds of exhaust fumes to escape into the darkness of the night. After waiting for around thirty seconds he pressed a woollen jumper tightly over his mouth and nose, ran into the garage, opened the car door and switched off the engine. In a matter of seconds he was back outside with his eyes stinging and his head spinning. He staggered twenty feet or so back in the direction of the house, cursing his light-headiness, and threw up on an area of long overgrown grass before slumping to the ground.

The Professor spat the remaining acidic vomit from his mouth and breathed deeply, sucking in the oxygen and savouring the sweet, fresh and unpolluted air flooding his lungs. What a shame the pleb detective was unconscious

296

when breathing in the poisonous gas; what a shame he was blissfully unaware of his impending death. It would have been both informative and amusing to watch the process as the Nazis had, through a viewing window. Maybe in future it was worth flooding Venus' room with the appropriate fumes. It was certainly worth considering, if he could address the practical difficulties the process would inevitably entail.

He rose to his feet on unsteady legs, abandoned his ruminations and refocussed on the present. Come on Mark, time was getting on. Get on with it man, get on with it.

The professor re-entered the garage, disconnected the hosepipe from the exhaust pipe, rolled it up and threw it in the boot along with the roll of remaining tape. He climbed into the driver's seat and pushed Rankin's gradually stiffening corpse back in the seat next to him, securing it in place with the Ford's seat belt. Once satisfied with his efforts he restarted the engine, reversed out of the garage, performed a proficient three point turn in the yard and began driving through Trinity Fields in the direction of the main road. Everything was going just as he'd planned. He was a man in control of destiny.

It only took him about twenty-five minutes or so to drive the relatively short distance along the traffic-free county road to Llansteffan, his destination of choice. He steered cautiously through the picturesque West Wales village dominated by its impressive thirteenth-century castle, keen to avoid bringing any unwanted attention to the Mondeo.

He approached an unlit, narrow, single track no-through road leading from just below Castle Hill to the estuary beach with its view of Ferryside across the fast-flowing water, and parked at its halfway point, which was in almost total darkness due to the numerous overhanging trees.

He switched off the engine, exited the vehicle and reattached the hosepipe to the exhaust pipe as he had in the garage only hours earlier, utilising a small handheld torch to facilitate the process.

As he stood outside the car, leaning over the driver's seat with the intention of restarting the engine, he noticed the white corner of a paper poking out from Rankin's pocket. The professor considered ignoring it at first, but changed his mind instinctively and reached over to take the folded papers in his hand. He unfolded them and realised they were statement forms. With the aid of the car's internal light he read the details and stiffened as he digested the contents. There was nothing for it but to hope for the best and to finish what he was there to do. Maybe the pleb policeman hadn't shared the statement with other officers. Maybe that's why they were in his pocket. Perhaps fate had smiled on him again and he'd found them just in time.

He punched the windscreen hard with a clenched fist and felt a little better. Time to start the engine, close the door and get out of there. It was going to be a long walk home. Maybe sticking to the fields as far as possible wouldn't be such a bad idea. Yes, that made sense. If he got a move on he'd still be home before dawn.

Chapter 27

Professor Goddard checked for any potential witnesses before hurrying into Trinity Fields at 4:22 A.M. He hurried up the deserted road, took a bunch of keys from a trouser pocket and approached the house cautiously, surprised to see that the lights were on in the first-floor flat despite the early hour. He hurried around the entire circumference of the building, careful to stay in the shadows whenever possible, and finally deciding it was safe to go in about ten minutes later. There was no sign of a panda car. No flashing blue lights. No sign of uniform intruders invading his secret world. If his mother was up, it wasn't because of the police.

The professor opened the front door, stood in the hall and called up the stairs, 'Can you hear me, Mother? Did you wait up?'

All was silent as he strained his ears for any sign of life.

He shouted again, louder this time, insisting on being heard, but he still didn't receive a response.

He began climbing the stairs two steps at a time, all the time calling for his mother like a lost child desperately in need of succour.

When he entered the lounge and saw his mother slumped and cold in her favourite chair, he felt instantly sure that she was dead, long before checking her scrawny neck for a pulse.

She was just lying there, her grey head tilted back with unblinking eyes staring at the ceiling, her mouth dry and wide open, her false teeth in her aproned lap, and a spilt cup of weak tea and an angina spray on the multicoloured carpet at her feet.

The professor briefly considered attempting to resuscitate her, as he had others both close to and soon after death, but he knew in both his heart and from real life experience that it was far too late to have any chance of success. She was cold, she was stiffening… she was gone. Now he was alone in the world and would have to get used to his new reality. Maybe, in time, if she passed her final test, Venus Six would fill the gap, but they were big shoes to fill. Either way, it was time to move things along. Time to provoke her into an informative response. Time to decide if he'd finally found his soulmate.

He knelt at his mother's feet, wiped a tear from his cheek and gently stroked her knee. 'Why did you leave me, Mother? Did I upset you in some way? Don't you love me any more? As hateful as you were, I always relied on you.'

He rose to his feet, switched off the light and approached the staircase. Why did all the women in his life ultimately let him down? Why did they always insist on disappointing? The bitches, the total bitches! 'Goodnight Mother, sleep well. I'll see you in the morning.'

Chapter 28

PC Jane Prichard paused immediately outside DI Gravel's office door with tears welling in her fast-reddening, green-blue eyes for half a minute or more, before finally building up sufficient resolve to knock. She raised her hand, lowered it again, and then raised it for a second time and knocked quickly, without giving herself sufficient time to change her mind.

'Come in.'

'Hello sir, I need a word.'

Grav looked up from his paperwork, taken aback by the obvious look of sorrow on her pallid face. 'What's the matter, love? Is that husband of yours being a prick again?'

She just stood there in silence searching for words that wouldn't come.

The DI stood, approached her and put a supportive arm around one of her uniformed shoulders. 'Come on, Jane, take the weight off, girl, and tell your uncle Grav all about it.'

She sat as instructed and looked him in the eye, ignoring the desire to rush away. 'It's DS Rankin, sir.'

He shook his head incredulously. 'Clive? What the hell's he done now? I thought you two were good mates.'

'We were in training college together.'

He smiled in an attempt to raise her spirits. 'Yeah, I've heard the stories.'

Oh God, how was she going to tell him? They were so close. 'He hasn't done anything, sir, or at least not to me.'

What the hell was she trying to get at? There was something. There was definitely something. 'Look Jane, stop talking in bleeding riddles and tell me what the hell this is about. I've got a murder investigation to get on with.'

She averted her eyes and stared into the unseen distance. 'He's dead, sir.'

'What are you talking about?'

Just say it, Jane. Just tell him and be done with it. 'Sergeant Rankin… he was found dead this morning.'

Grav's mouth fell open as he floundered for a response. 'Clive's dead?'

'Yes, sir, a member of the public rang in after finding the DS's body in his car in Castle Lane, near the beach in Llansteffan.'

'What time was this?'

She checked her watch. 'I spoke to him about ten minutes ago.'

'So what makes you think it's Clive? His Nissan's in the car park. I saw it myself on the way in.'

'The man who rang in gave me the car's index number. It's the CID Mondeo signed out by the DS yesterday.'

'Okay, so it may not be Clive in the car. Someone else might have used it after he finished with it. I can't think of one single reason why he'd be in Llansteffan at this time. He's due to be in Cardiff nick later this morning.'

'Mr Larkin described the DS perfectly. I think his Primera must have been in the car park all night. I really think it's him, sir.'

Grav felt physically sick as an alternative version of events became less viable. 'Has anyone called an ambulance?'

She nodded. 'It's on its way, sir.'

The DI picked up his car keys from his desktop and headed for the door without another word.

She walked after him as he rushed down the corridor and tapped him on the shoulder. 'There's something I haven't told you, sir.'

He stopped at the entrance to the lift. 'What?'

'It looks like suicide.'

He stared at her incredulously, unable or unwilling to relate her statement to the man he knew so well. 'So, why do you say that?'

This wasn't going to be easy to either hear or say. 'There was a hosepipe running from the exhaust and into the vehicle. The engine was still running when Mr Larkin found him. It doesn't seem there's any room for doubt.'

It made no sense. He was happy. He had a baby on the way. 'Now look, Jane, I've got no idea what this is all about, but there is no fucking way Clive Rankin killed himself.'

Grav drove a lot faster than was sensible, twice reaching ninety in a sixty and almost leaving the road on one particularly tight corner. He arrived in Castle Lane just a minute or two after the ambulance, switched off the engine and exited his car as the first of two paramedics were

303

opening the Mondeo's driver's door and reaching across to where Rankin was slumped in the passenger seat.

Grav approached the car and attempted to peer through the emission-stained windscreen without significant success. All he could see was a silhouette of a man. A man who looked much as his friend did. 'Is he dead?'

The paramedic glanced towards the inspector, who was now squinting over his shoulder, before returning his attention to his long since deceased patient. 'Who's asking?'

The DI took his warrant card from his pocket and held it in plain view as the middle-aged, heavily tattooed man stood and faced him. 'DI Gravel, local police.'

'Oh yeah, he's dead. Whoever he was, he meant it. This wasn't a cry for help.'

Grav gently pushed the paramedic aside and placed his head through the open door. It was Rankin. Oh God, it was Rankin. The whole world had gone fucking mad. 'He's a mate of mine.'

'Sorry to hear that. You've got my sympathies.'

'I'm guessing there's no note.'

'Not that I've seen.'

The DI climbed into the driver's seat and checked Rankin's pockets and the glove box, finding nothing of interest.

The younger of the two paramedics appeared next to his workmate and spoke for the first time, 'Anything?'

'Fuck all.'

'Do you want us to take him now? Time's getting on and families with kids will be walking past here at some point.'

'This wasn't suicide.'

The two paramedics looked at each other in the eye and the older and senior of the two spoke up, verbalising what they were both thinking. 'Look, I understand he was a mate of yours, but it looks like he killed himself to me. These things happen. We see it all too often.'

'I've been in this job a long time. I know it happens, but it didn't happen here! There's no note, he's sitting in the passenger seat with the car parked tightly against a high earth bank. He'd have had to set it all up, get into the car via the driver's door and then climb over the gear stick into the passenger seat. And why put his seat belt on? It makes no sense. Why would you do that? Someone has tried to make this look like a suicide. I'm treating this as a crime scene.'

Chapter 29

Grav sat staring at the Rankins' modest but comfortable three-bedroom terrace house for almost ten minutes without leaving his car. How was he supposed to tell Mary Rankin something he knew would break her heart?

He took the last but one cigar from a packet of five, lit the tip on the second attempt and sucked at it hungrily, drawing the toxic fumes deep into his lungs, as he had many times before at times of stress. He sat there for another five minutes, listening to a favourite Catatonia CD and mentally rehearsing various equally unsatisfactory opening sentences. In the end he opened his window a few inches, threw the three-quarters-smoked cigar into the gutter and decided to speak from the heart. Whatever his choice of words, they'd hit her like a steam train. There was no softening this blow. It was time to man up and get it done.

The DI noticed that his hand was shaking more than usual as he raised it to ring the bell, which didn't surprise him in the slightest. He was about to deliver the most distressing information of Mary's life. Whatever he said, however he put it, it wasn't going to go well. Just get it done Grav. Just tell her and get it over with.

'Hello Grav, I haven't seen you for a while. If you're looking for Clive, I haven't seen him since yesterday morning. I think you work him too hard sometimes.'

'Can I come in, love?'

'Oh God, what's happened?'

He gently guided her in the direction of the lounge. 'Come on, Mary, I think it's best if you sit down before we talk.'

She was already weeping by the time she fell into her chair and clung on to the arms as if for life itself. 'What's happened, Grav? Has Clive been in an accident or something?'

Just say it Grav. Just say it. 'I'm so sorry, Mary, he was found dead this morning.'

She just sat there quietly humming a song they'd both loved in happier times.

'Did you hear me, love?'

'Yes, Grav, I heard you… What happened?'

If only he could soften the blow. Suicide hit loved ones harder than almost anything else. 'He was found in a car with a hosepipe running from the exhaust pipe, but…'

'You're saying my Clive killed himself?'

He shook his head and moved to the very edge of his seat. 'No, I'm not saying that, love. There are things that don't fit. I really don't think that's what's happened.'

'I don't suppose the selfish sod left me a letter?'

'I don't think he killed himself, Mary. I think someone's murdered him and tried to make it look like suicide.'

She took a paper tissue from a box on the small hardwood nest of tables next to her and blew her nose noisily. 'He was suffering from depression.'

Grav frowned. 'Clive? I've never known a more cheerful bloke in my life.'

'I lost the baby.'

307

He reached out and squeezed her hand. 'I'm so sorry, Mary, I had no idea.'

She pulled her hand away. 'Why would you? You only saw the act.'

'But why didn't he say something?'

'He couldn't accept it. He was still talking as if nothing happened until recently. He even went out and bought a cot two days after the doctor told him I'd miscarried. There was no reasoning with him. I'd never seen him like that before.'

'I wish he'd said something. Maybe I could have helped.'

'He went from denial to despondency almost overnight. The GP gave him some antidepressants a few days back after I insisted he call at the surgery, but he refused to take them.'

Grav began to question his earlier conclusions for the first time. Maybe he'd interpreted the facts to suit himself? Perhaps the pressure became too much. People sometimes behaved unpredictably and did things which seemed hugely out of character when under great personal stress. 'So, you think he may have killed himself? Is that really what you're saying?'

She lowered her eyes and focussed on the floor. 'Yes, Grav, I do. I begged him to take the tablets. I pleaded with him time and time again, but he wouldn't listen. I've been waiting for it to happen.'

Chapter 30

Emma recognised the feel and shape of the cast-iron radiator before she even opened her eyes, but was surprised to find that she wasn't shackled to it as she'd been on the previous occasion.

She opened one eye, then the other, and saw that rather than being in virtual darkness or dazzlingly white light as she'd expected, the room was lit by a single sixty-watt bulb which bathed it in a depressing yellow hue. There was a normality to it, with the stark exception of the various items of technical equipment and the masked clown slowly approaching her, not in the familiar business suit this time, but in casual navy slacks and a thin black woollen polo-necked jumper which clung to his body. She stared at him, feeling a combination of fear and loathing and pictured the human face behind the mask.

'Well, hello again, Venus. Good to have you back, my lovely. It's just the two of us now. Mother passed on some time ago. She's in the freezer.'

Mother? What the…? Had she been there all along? 'I'm sorry to hear that, master. I hope she didn't suffer.'

He laughed and shook his head. 'No, even I have to draw the line somewhere. She had a weak heart. I think recent events became too much for her.'

He was insane, completely insane, but at least she wasn't shackled this time. Just bide your time Emma, and wait for an opportunity, any opportunity. She forced a barely credible smile. 'I'm glad to hear it, master.'

He took a single step forwards and ran his hand through her blonde hair, causing her to twist and squirm. 'I think that's quite enough pointless chit-chat for one day, Venus. You must be wondering why I've allowed you out of your room for a second time.'

Did she really want to know the answer? Maybe the bastard was beginning to trust her. Just play the game Emma. Just play the game. 'Tell me more, master.'

'I thought I saw you glancing at the newly installed flatscreen television and rather impressive digital video disc player a second or two ago.'

What response was he looking for? The bastard was obviously pleased with himself. What best to say? 'It all looks very expensive, master.'

He nodded. 'I'm glad you like it, Venus. It's state-of-the-art equipment, the very latest in technical innovation. Somewhat pricey, as you so correctly surmised, but well worth the sacrifice. I have a rather interesting film to share with you. It's a montage of some of my favourite moments spent with previous guests. All five girls feature in one way or another. It's quite graphic in places, I'm afraid, even by my standards. I hope that's not too much of a problem. Your response will determine if you live or die. Look away from the screen even once and I'll know you're not the one for me. Shall we make a start?'

Oh God, no, please no. Just stare at the screen and think nice thoughts. That's all she could do, just think nice thoughts. 'Yes, master, I'm ready.'

For the next hour or more she sat in horrified silence and watched and listened to one dehumanising abomination after another, as he focussed on her and only on her from a seat just six feet away. She hated every single second and inwardly wept for the terrified girls subjected to such unspeakable horrors, but she didn't look away.

'You did surprisingly well, my lovely. I'm beginning to think you may share my unusual tastes in entertainment, despite my earlier doubts. Let's get you back in the room to allow me time to think.'

This was her chance. It may be her only chance. Once back in the room there was no escape. 'I'd like to know more about you, master. Tell me how it all started. Tell me how you developed your methods. I want to know everything.'

He felt his penis engorge with blood as he lowered himself to the floor and sat opposite her at touching distance with crossed legs. 'You really want to know?'

'Yes, master.'

'Then I shall tell you… I was twelve when I first developed an interest in death and suffering. I was walking in the wood just behind the house one morning, when I found a local tabby cat trapped in a poacher's snare. It was in the process of gnawing one of its paws off in an attempt to free itself. It seemed oblivious to my presence as I watched it writhing in agony for about twenty minutes, and I loved every glorious moment. I smashed its head in with a large stone in the end,

311

not because I wanted to end its suffering, but because I needed to witness the results. It was the greatest moment of my young life and there was no going back. I took various opportunities as they arose after that, but I soon realised that I needed to be more organised if I were to satisfy my cravings. I experimented with white rats at first, devising varying methods of torture and execution.'

He chuckled to himself as the memories flooded back. 'They were provided by my misguided parents, who paid little attention and chose to interpret what they knew of my activities as an admirable interest in the physical sciences. My fool teachers took the same view. I think my father actually thought I'd eventually become a doctor in his image and waste my time providing medical care to the Luddite masses. In reality, knowing him as well as I did, I've concluded we weren't much different… Shall I continue? Are you interested in how my story continues? Are you finding my presentation interesting?'

Emma didn't move an inch or utter a sound. She just sat there in despondent silence with her head hanging towards the floor and occasionally looking up to feign interest. What could one say in light of such evil?

He poked her hard in the chest. 'Are you listening, my lovely? Shall I continue?'

'Yes, master, please do.'

'As I said, I devised increasingly fascinating methods of torture and execution: burning, poisoning, starvation, dehydration, suffocation. I indulged them all. That kept my interest for a time, but in reality I knew from the very beginning that animals were never going to be enough to satisfy my needs. I fantasised about killing women from the age of fifteen. Always slim, always young and always blonde, just like you. I pictured myself indulging my desires to the maximum, and then, when I was just nineteen years of age, I finally acted on my fantasies for the first glorious time. I poisoned a girlfriend at college. Slowly, gradually, cautiously, and I watched her deteriorate little by little over a period of months whilst feigning concern, until I eventually fed her a lethal cocktail of paracetamol and alcohol. And, do you know, the inept fools at the hospital didn't suspect a damn thing. They put her death down to stress-induced suicide. How very stupid! I'd never laughed so much in my entire life.'

He began slowly rubbing his groin and continued, 'Watching her draw her last desperate breath was splendrous, marvellous, the greatest time of my young life, and I had to do it again. I yearned to do it again. I was desperate to do it again. I fantasised and made those fantasies reality… I killed once a year on average after that, utilising poison in the main, although I sometimes hunted in the dark neglected streets of various northern cities, striking from behind when the opportunity arose.'

Keep him talking. Just keep the bastard talking. 'What happened next, master?'

'I first began developing this place about six years ago and it's proved a revelation. I can take my time and indulge my inclinations without fear of interference. That's a massive advantage. I'm hoping that when I next secure a guest, we can entertain her together.'

She focussed on his swollen groin, considered her options and reached out to touch him, before quickly withdrawing her hand. 'Would you like sex, master? I can tell you're aroused. I could lie very still and hold my breath for you.'

He thought for a few seconds, dismissing the idea initially, but then changing his mind. It would be a significant departure from the norm. A small sacrifice to mark the beginning of their partnership. 'But, you're not wearing the shoes.'

'I could fetch them, master. They're in the bathroom, next to the sink.'

He nodded. 'Don't keep me waiting, Venus. There are limits to my patience.'

She attempted to stand with the support of the wall, but her legs collapsed at the ankles and she fell heavily, banging her head against the floor and lying still.

He kicked her violently in the base of her back with the point of his shoe. 'Crawl, Venus, crawl and be quick about it.'

Now's your chance Emma, now's your chance. It was now or never, do or die. She raised herself onto all fours and crawled slowly towards the door, but she stumbled and lay motionless on the carpet again awaiting the next assault, which came a second later.

'Are you trying to annoy me, Venus? And just when you were doing so well.'

She clutched her bruised and aching abdomen and looked up at him. 'Would you fetch the shoes please, master? Just this once! I don't want to disappoint you.'

He considered raising his foot and stamping down on her, but his desire for sex overrode his impulse for violence and he hurried towards the steel door.

Emma raised herself onto all fours again and crept forwards, ignoring her pain and increasing her pace as he entered the room. Come on Emma, you can do it, keep going, keep going.

'Where the hell are they, bitch? They're not in the bathroom!'

Almost there Emma, almost there! 'I'm sorry, master, they must be in the cupboard.'

As he opened the cupboard and peered in, she raised herself onto her knees and threw herself at the steel door, using all her strength and weight to slam it shut. Bang! She'd done it, she really had done it and her world was a safer place.

Emma crawled towards the nearest monitor, reached up and pulled herself briefly to her feet before slumping onto the countertop and supporting herself. She turned on the monitor, adjusted the volume and flicked a switch to her right. She watched as the man in the mask shielded his eyes as she had so many times before. She tapped the microphone on the shelf in front of her to confirm it was on and spoke into it with a newfound confidence she hadn't felt since her arrival. 'Hello my lovely, welcome to your new home. Now would be a good time to take off the mask. I know exactly who you are and you don't frighten me any more.'

He was snarling now like a ferocious beast. 'Open the door. Open the door, you manipulative bitch. I'll tear your fucking face off!'

'Oh, I don't think so, Professor. You're in there and I'm out here. There's no way out of there. You saw to that. I feel sure you'll find your new accommodation comfortable.' And with that she switched off the monitor and returned the room to darkness.

It took Emma almost an hour to crawl from the house, across the yard and down the hard and abrasive single-track tarmacadam road to the main road. By the time she left Trinity Fields and crept along the overgrown grass verge for another five hundred yards or more, both her hands and knees were stripped of flesh and bleeding profusely. She was in physical agony, but had never felt so elated in her life. She was free, the world was brighter and more beautiful than she had ever appreciated, and it was good to be alive.

Emma left the verge and stumbled exhausted onto the pavement at 6:32 A.M. on Thursday, 11 June. Within ten minutes she was lying in the back of a good Samaritan's comfortable Saab family car on the way to Caerystwyth Hospital, dressed only in skimpy black underwear and a grey polyester V-neck jumper provided by the driver. She looked up and out of the window at the sky and smiled. Being alive had never felt better.

Chapter 31

Emma's parents were already sitting at her bedside in the acute admissions ward when DI Gravel walked into the room later that morning. Both Mr and Mrs Jones stood as Grav strode stiffly towards the bed, the mother lifting a finger to her lips and holding it there as her daughter slept next to her.

'I'm going to have to talk to her. This is too important to wait.'

Mrs Jones stepped towards him, back to her combative best, Emma's escape having been infinitely more effective than any medicine the doctors could offer. 'She needs to sleep, Inspector. Look at the state she's in. The poor girl's absolutely exhausted.'

The DI looked at the girl, taken aback by her sunken eyes, misshapen nose and emaciated face. 'You do want me to catch the man who took her, don't you?'

'Well, of course I do, but surely you can speak to her later in the day when she's had time to rest. What difference is an hour or two going to make?'

Emma suddenly opened her bright blue eyes and waved a hand in the air. 'It's okay, Mum, I'm already awake.'

'Go back to sleep, cariad, I'm sure Inspector Gravel won't mind waiting.'

Emma sat upright and rearranged her pillows before reclining against them. 'It's all right, Mum, I'd like to speak to him now. There are things I need to say. Why don't you and Dad go to the canteen for a coffee and let me talk to the inspector by myself? It would be easier that way.'

Mrs Jones approached the bed and squeezed her daughter's arm. 'If you're sure, cariad?'

Emma nodded her eager confirmation. 'Yes, Mum, I'm sure. I really need to do this.'

The DI stood aside to allow them to leave, gratified by Emma's cooperation and her obvious desire to help. 'Good to have you back with us, love. I've been looking for you.'

He held out a hand but withdrew it quickly when he noticed the bloody bandages. 'Detective Inspector Gravel, but please call me Grav. I've got a few questions, if you're feeling up to it?'

'I want the bastard caught. What do you need to know?'

'I'm going to take a few notes, okay? We can get a full statement down on paper later in the day.'

'Yes, I understand.'

'Can you describe the man who kidnapped you?'

She shook her head discontentedly. 'He always wore a clown's mask. I couldn't even see his eyes.'

'So you never saw his face?'

'Not even once.'

Grav hid his disappointment and smiled thinly. 'Can you tell me anything about his description? Anything at all?'

'I saw his hands. He was white and about five ten or five eleven.'

'Fat, thin, average build?'

'Average, eleven or twelve stone.'

'Anything else?'

'He had a strong Eastern European accent.'

That knocked a few suspects off the list. 'You're sure?'

'Yes, certain!'

'So where were you held, love?'

She raised a bandaged hand to her face and spoke through her tears, 'I woke up alone in a windowless room. He fed me through a hatch and spoke to me via speakers installed in the ceiling. That's as much as I know.'

Grav looked puzzled. 'So, how did you escape?'

'He let me go.'

Really? That was unexpected. 'So, you must be able to tell me the location of this room.'

'He blindfolded me, led me from the room and pushed me into the back of some sort of van, before dumping me at the side of the road after about an hour's journey. I pulled the blindfold off just in time to see a large white van driving away.'

Okay, that was progress of sorts. 'I don't suppose you saw the number plate?'

'I'm sorry, no.'

'Any idea of the make?'

'No.'

'Do you think you'd recognise the type of vehicle if I showed you some pictures?'

'I could give it a try, but probably not. I just glanced at it for a fraction of a second and hurried away to hide in the grass.'

'Okay, just to reiterate, you've got no idea who your abductor was or where you were imprisoned. Take some time to think, love. Any clues could help us identify one or both of them.'

Emma wiped away her tears and frowned. 'I'm sorry, Inspector, I haven't got the slightest clue.'

A note to the reader

Thank you for reading Portraits of the Dead. I'm always interested to know what readers think of my books, and I'd be grateful if you'd leave a review on Amazon.

Also by John Nicholl

White is the coldest colour

The Mailer family are oblivious to the terrible danger that enters their lives when seven-year-old Anthony is referred to the child guidance service by the family GP following the breakdown of his parents' marriage. Fifty-eight-year-old Dr David Galbraith, a sadistic predatory paedophile employed as a consultant child psychiatrist, has already murdered one child in the soundproofed cellar below the South Wales Georgian townhouse he shares with his wife and two young daughters. Anthony becomes Galbraith's latest obsession, and he will stop at nothing to make his grotesque fantasies reality.

Available on Amazon in ebook, paperback and audiobook formats.

When evil calls your name

When twenty-nine year old Cynthia Galbraith struggles to come to terms with her traumatic past and the realities of prison life, a prison counsellor persuades her to write a personal journal exploring the events that led to a life sentence for murder. Although unconvinced at first, Cynthia finally decides she has all the time in the world and very little, if anything, to lose. She begins writing and holds back nothing: sharing the thoughts she hadn't dare vocalise, the things that keep her awake at night and haunt her waking hours. Even the darkest secrets can't stay hidden forever…

Available on Amazon in ebook, paperback and audiobook formats.

CPSIA information can be obtained
at www.ICGtesting.com
Printed in the USA
LVOW08s1728240317
528395LV00002B/228/P